# LANCE'S FOLLIES

GARRET D. ONDERDONK III

**Lance's Follies**
Copyright © 2024 by Garret D. Onderdonk III

ISBN: 979-8895310007(hc)
ISBN: 978-1639459988(sc)
ISBN: 978-1639459995(e)

Writers' Branding
(877) 608-6550
www.writersbranding.com
media@writersbranding.com

*Thanks, Jill*

# Contents

# 1
## American Girl

On the way home from a political rally, Lance dropped by a local beer bar he frequented often. They sold beer to drink at the bar and whiskey, but the whiskey was to go, not drink there. Lance was returning from a political meeting for a candidate he supported for city council. On this rare occasion, Lance was dressed up in a suit and tie. He heard the bar door open. She was an American girl. Walking by, the five-foot-two blond had dark blue eyes the color of bluebonnets, piercing yet soulless; large California breasts and spandex-covered ass; double man-made eyelashes top and bottom; six-inch-high heels; and plenty of makeup. She still had that fresh, young vigorous look. She was carrying a purse large enough to fit the *Titanic* inside. Hair pulled tightly into a ponytail, no roots showing. Freshly manicured nails, no jewelry on hands or feet. Her two ears were perfectly symmetrical; each had a shiny diamond (cubic zirconium?) post the size of a 1956 Buick headlight. As she walked by, he saw her smile. A wild garden of fragrance ever so slight titillated his olfactory senses; she smelled like spring. Between those fire-engine red puffy lips, she showed perfect teeth. She was attractive and hot; her T-shirt was bright red with an emblazoned Wonder Woman.

*Maybe this is the one*, thought Lance. Just as he bit into his jalapeno-jellied doughnut and the heat touched his tongue, she sat down at the bar next to him. She ordered a beer and bought a bottle of Jack Daniel's to go, stuffing it in that large purse. He noticed the look and suggested they go to a club where they could order real drinks. At that new club, they were sitting and talking. Lance ordered a second round and paid the cocktail waitress. He then looked her in the eye and said, "Let's go to your place and drink that bottle of Jack."

She responded, "Do you think you can make me with two drinks?"

With a smile, Lance queried, "How many drinks does it take?"

She laughed, got up, took his hand, and said, "Let's go."

When they arrived at her house a block from the bar, Lance sat on the couch. Two whiskey glasses and the Jack appeared along with two glasses of water. Lance presented a toast. "Life is short. Make the most of it."

She went off to the bedroom. She came back to the living room, spread out a large quilt or comforter and two pillows. "I don't want to wrinkle my clothes," she stated as she removed everything but her bra and panties.

As she lay down, Lance, never one to overlook opportunity, stated, "Don't want to wrinkle my suit," and he removed it. Yes, his erection was hard enough to put his suit on a hanger and support it with his penis. Lance, in only his boxer shorts, laid down next to her. She feigned sleep. Lance slid his erection now dripping with lubricant between her legs. She moaned yet acted like she was asleep. Lance slid down her hip-hugger panties and found a willing sexual participant. They both pumped and moved in unison amazingly reaching a rather quick orgasm. Great sex. She never said a word. Lance slid her panties back up, covered her, and got dressed and left. He never did get her name. It was just another lucky roll of the dice? Another day in Vegas? Smiling, Lance climbed into his Corvette and went home. He had lived in Vegas long enough to be aware that anything could happen and often did.

## 2
# The Beginning

*1946*

Lance was born innocent in upstate New York, on the hot humid day of August 16 in the summer of 1946. The night was amazingly clear. The half-moon cast shadows, and the mosquitoes took the night off. A French nurse, Aimee, married to an American GI named Ted gave birth to their second child. When he was born, the attending nurses gathered around and giggled while they cleaned him up and presented him to his mother. As soon as Aimee saw him, she became aware of the cause of the giggling. At birth he had a *gros pénis* or already prominent member, his Murasaki katana. The improbabilities of genetic mathematics gave this newborn almost a third leg; it was purple and prodigious. He entered the world with a boner. She named him Lancelot. She knew Lancelot was the bravest of knights and uniquely perfect, thus selecting his name. This newborn's life continuum had begun. His tabula rasa was the blank slate on which his future and its effect on others was set in motion. Lance was additionally blessed by having a nurse for a mother. From the time he started solid food, he learned to eat healthy forming strong bones and constitution. Except for childhood diseases, he rarely got sick. In America, Aimee knew this child had the potential to grow up and become anything. Lance was astrologically a Leo. Not just another of the seventy-six million baby boomers. This is his story. He would grow up to be wanted and wanted. His sexual gift would bring pleasure to many. Aimee told her beautiful baby boy, "You will eventually overcome life's temptations, which will be many, and become a good father and model citizen."

When Lance was born, his parents and family had a sense of optimism for their firstborn son, someone new and special. Yes, Lance was all that and more. Lance would make the world a better place. White Plains, a small country town in upstate New York thirty miles from the big city, had a new addition to its census. His dad, one of the Greatest Generation, had returned home from the war and was making up for lost time by fathering his second child, a son. His mother, Aimee, held him tightly as his grandfather Fredrick drove them home and introduced him to his sister, Stephanie, who was barely eleven months older. Two sets of diapers to change. The birds on the eighty-acre estate all seemed to be singing welcome Lance. With two young children, his mother, Aimee, spent Lance's early years at home. As a newly minted American citizen, she ensured that both of her children learned to speak French at home. Amazing how France, a country smaller than Texas, thinks it rules the world. Aimee was a practicing Catholic, and his dad, Ted, not so much on religion after his war experiences.

His grandparents Fredric and Liesel Werner immigrated to the US from Germany in 1900. Grandfather Fredric bought eighty acres in the White Plains area of New York State. He owned and published a newspaper, was a gifted writer and talented public speaker. His grandmother, Liesel, was a schoolteacher—algebra, trigonometry, and Latin. Lance's father, Ted, was an only child born in 1920 in White Plains, New York. His parents insisted he speak German at home, study, and get grades good enough to get into a respected university.

Call it destiny or timing, but Lance's father, Ted, graduated from college in December 1941. As a member of ROTC, he began his military career by immediately entering the Office of Strategic Services (OSS). William Joseph "Wild Bill" Donovan, soldier, lawyer and diplomat, and a family friend, was the head of the OSS. He had known Ted most of his life and was thrilled to bring him with his German-speaking mastery aboard. As a member of the OSS, Ted was sworn to secrecy and rarely, if ever, talked about the war.

The only positive brought about by the war was when Ted was injured, a beautiful, intelligent nurse brought him back to health. She spoke French and German. He spoke English and German. That is how

4

they communicated at first, in German. He fell in love with Aimee and married her in Paris in 1945. They returned to White Plains with their daughter as soon as his health allowed.

# 3

# Home, White Plains

Lance's family was not Rockefeller rich but certainly in good financial shape. Their land in New York was at the time undeveloped, mostly woods and small rolling hills. A rambling brook meandered through the property and into a lake by the dairy that bordered on one side of their land. His grandfather taught him how to fish and hunt. Lance and his dog, a German shepherd named Solo, spent many a Saturday fishing the stream. They were inseparable.

Lance started life with a huge advantage—he was adorable. Everyone talked to him. Little girls ran up and hugged him. As a toddler, Lance questioned everything to the point of driving his parents crazy. Many a day was spent at Grandma's house. She was retired, and his mother, Aimee, had returned to nursing.

Lance, at age three, found a bobby pin. He crawled under his grandmother's grand piano and stuck it into the electrical outlet. It shocked him, burned his hand, and blew the fuse. He never did it again. Buried deep in his brain, it was his first memory. Was his mischievous personality already on display?

"Lance, Lance, quit playing with your PP," hollered Aimee. "It's not a toy!"

Stephanie and her brother, Lance, got along well and rarely quarreled. Ladies stopped and looked at him at the supermarket. Little girls smiled as he walked by. He was surrounded by a very loving and extensive family. On occasions when Aimee was working and Grandma had obligations, four-year-old Lance spent the day at a children's day care. Owned by a friend of the family, Lance loved spending the day there as there was usually four to ten other kids to play with. It had a large fenced yard with an incline that sloped from the back fence to the rear of the house. It had swings, slides, and a seesaw. The owner's older son had built a soapbox gravity racer, basically a board with a seat, four wheels, and a rope to steer it. No brakes. When the older kids weren't looking, Lance dragged it to the top of the hill, sat on it, and off it sped. At four Lance was unable to safely steer it. The good news, it stopped when it hit the back concrete porch. The bad news, so did Lance when his forehead hit the corner of the same porch. Yes, blood gushing everywhere. Bandages slowed it down some. Lance's mother correctly triaged her son and got him to the family doctor. Twenty-four double stitches just below the hairline. No skull fracture and no discernible mental damage. His dad, Ted, bragged about how hardheaded he was. Slowly over the years the X-shaped scar disappeared. Lance no longer went to day care. Was he already an adrenaline junkie? Perhaps a recalcitrant child. Another new rule. His family began to wonder, did trouble find Lance, or did Lance find trouble? Would he outgrow his childish curiosity and become a responsible and respected adult? Or would his growing self-pride eventually derail him? Lance, at age four, did not believe rules covered him.

# 4
# Elementary School

His August birthday allowed Lance to start kindergarten in 1951. On the first day of school, Lance, unnoticed, snuck out of the school's front door and walked home. Their house was approximately a two-mile walk. A spanking and lecture ensued. "Lance, there are rules—there must be rules." Mother Aimee informed him his sister, Stephanie, was in charge. The next day under severe admonishments and a handful of threats, Lance began kindergarten again. This time he stayed. He now found a new attraction kissing two of the girls, Patti and Sharon, in the cloakroom. This was fun for Lance until the two girls told their mothers, and Lance was again learning about acceptable social norms. Another talking to with both his mom and dad followed. He was sure disappointed he could not just go and kiss pretty girls. He accepted the rule. Rules, rules, rules—so many. Lance learned in kindergarten you couldn't just walk up and kiss any girl. This would not be the last time Lance got in trouble because of girls. "Lance, you are not allowed to kiss the girls in school. Lance, you can't leave school. You must come home with your sister." Lance grudgingly did as he was told, but he did not like following orders.

Lance grew up in a small town, attended an elementary school where everyone knew everyone and their business. Several of the teachers belonged to a bridge club with his grandmother, Liesel, having known her from her days as a teacher. She was kept apprised of how the grandchildren were fairing in school. The butcher's daughter, the barber's son, a small but broad group representing the townsfolk's children, were well represented. Lance's sister, Stephanie, preceded him in each of the six grades. She was perfect. Stephanie never missed a day of school. She always followed the rules as she was trained by their mother. She was well behaved and polite to a fault. Lance, on the other hand, was not particularly interested in school. He answered all the questions, got good grades, but frustrated the teachers. He looked out the windows and daydreamed. He would rather be playing at recess with the other kids.

At about the age of five, Lance was awakened by a noise. He looked out his bedroom window on the second floor. Beneath the full moon, on the white snow-covered ground, a wolf stood staring up at him. Lance was so scared he woke his mom and told her. His parents both looked out the window, but of course it was gone. "Lance, you have just had a bad dream. Go back to sleep," implored his mother. He did. When morning arrived, his dad went out and found footprints in the snow. His grandfather came and checked it out. He had hunted wolves in Germany and was an expert. The wolf tracks in the snow proved Lance was correct. Many a night Lance looked out his window but never again saw the lone wolf. The howl of the lone wolf, an omen? Was young Lance the only one to hear it?

By the time first grade rolled around, Lance was catching on. He did what he was told when watched and just sort of melded in with the rest of the class. If it was fun, there probably was a rule against it. The innocence of youth with its blatant honesty was slowly slipping away as Lance mastered language skills. Working with his sister, he was usually way ahead of the class. Because of his family's standings, he was invited to all the right birthday parties. Things were relatively quiet and easygoing for Lance. At home he did chores keeping his room neat and washing or drying the dishes with Stephanie.

Visiting their grandparents, Stephanie asked her grandfather to buy her a new lunch box.

"What kind do you want, honey?" asked Grandpa.

She answered, "The heaviest one you can find, Grandpa."

Armed with her new metal lunch box and thermos, Stephanie walked home from school. The fifth grader that had bullied her on the way home previously had his face and head introduced to her lunch box. He required stitches. When his mother complained to Stephanie's parents, her father, Ted, suggested that perhaps her son should not bully little girls. To Lance's knowledge, he never did again.

His mother had him taught to swim at the YMCA because they lived by a lake. In the spring, Lance and his friends would sneak into the neighboring dairy lake as soon as the ice melted and go skinny dipping. An unexpected skill found in third grade, Lance was tested and put into music class. He got a clarinet, and besides having fun and playing with his dog after school, he now had to practice clarinet for an hour. By junior high, he was dripping with musical talent first chair and by high school in the marching band. Early on Lance demonstrated impressive mental acuity in all areas he pursued.

School started in fourth grade Lance's ninth year. Over the summer, the school had remodeled and painted the cafeteria. This brought about a not-so-happy moment in Lance's educational portion of his life. It all seemed so innocent to him. He had that youthful energy banging around the room not unlike a pinball. The first day back at school lunch included chocolate pudding. Lance stuck the end of his straw wrapper in the pudding, pointed upward, and blew. This launched the paper wrapper, and it stuck to the ceiling. Not a big deal? It wasn't until the rest of the kids in lunchroom crowd joined in. Laughing, dipping, and blowing, and soon the lunchroom ceiling was covered with chocolate and hanging straw wrappers. The freshly painted ceiling now was a mottled chocolate color with tiny stalactites of straw wrappers dispersed intermittently. This forced the closing of the lunchroom for cleaning and repainting and caused mayhem for all. This was not his original intention. His sister did not join in but did report Lance's actions to Mom as soon as they got home from school. Their property was relatively wild, and when his mom said, "Go out in the yard and get a switch," he knew what was coming. Lance did as he was told. He did not like following orders. He grew up when the belief was spare the rod and spoil the child. Both his mom and dad made sure he was not spoiled. Lance took his whippings in a stoic manner. Truly Lance marched to his own drummer.

At ten, Lance's best friend in fifth grade was Herb. He lived about a mile up the road. Both got together often and practiced playing the clarinet, each sure he was the next Benny Goodman. While riding their bikes to school one morning, Lance turned to talk to Herb. He lost direction and ran his right hand between the bike handlebar and a concrete wall. This ripped open the skin and flesh on three fingers on his right hand. Lance wrapped it in a handkerchief (his grandmother insisted he carry one).

Lance walked into class with Herb. He pulled off the handkerchief and said to his homeroom teacher, "Look, Mrs. Damiano." She, all of four feet tall, passed out cold. Lance rewrapped his hand, ran to the office, and got the school nurse. Smelling salts brought Mrs. Damiano around. Lance was sent to the doctor to get patched up.

At this juncture in life, Lance discovered a new passion, reading anything and everything. Often, he stayed up all night with a flashlight reading under the covers. All the fifth graders were taken on a field trip to the library, learning how to find books and check them out. Lance was often a visitor reading bunches of books. Lance read his textbooks from cover to cover as soon as they were issued. Books, newspapers advertisements, adventures, mysteries, greeting cards, history, anything but math. The family home included a well-stocked library, and this skill was encouraged as both Mom and Dad were avid readers. At this period of life, Lance developed a strong imagination loving to make up stories of his own. His inner self was developing. As a young boy, he was enriching his deep emotional thoughts.

A typical childhood, is there such a thing? Lance belonged to Cub Scouts, Boy Scouts and loved hunting and fishing and baseball. They had two acres of lawn. His dad taught him to drive the tractor at the age of nine, so cutting the lawn was one of his chores in summer. Lance raised blue-ribbon award-winning tomatoes. The secret, his chickens' manure. He and sister, Stephanie, belonged to 4H and raised chickens, tomatoes, and one stubborn horse named Sandy. The property had a five-acre lake stocked with fish. Lance spent many an afternoon in the rowboat fishing with Grandpa.

Everything did not always go well for Lance. One day his Cub Scout troop met at Lance's house. All dressed up in his Cub Scout uniform the plan was for Lance to take his fellow scouts for a horseback ride as he led the horse, Sandy. Big shot Lance was showing off. With the first two Cub Scouts, this went well. The third scout was on the horse with Lance leading him by the reins. Sandy the horse had enough and took his left front hoof and planted it on Lance's foot. It hurt, and Lance was howling in pain. He screamed at and hit the horse, but stubborn Sandy was not impressed. Lance was now in tears. As soon as Aimee saw the problem, she headed out shrieking and hitting the horse with her broomstick. The horse relented and moved; Lance's foot was blue, bruised, and swollen. His pride was sabotaged. In later years, he would remember this as one of his life's most embarrassing moments.

As kids in the summertime, they would sleep outdoors in their pup tents. His sister, Stephanie, his best friend Benny, and the neighbor's daughter Suzanne all enjoyed the summer evenings including fires, hot dogs, and roasting marshmallows. Often they went skinny-dipping in the lake. Summers were wonderful. One night at the campfire, Stephanie told of her first memory. At five years old, when Grandma Lisle was backing her Cadillac out of the driveway, Stephanie opened the back door. The big old oak tree ripped it completely off the car, and it crashed into the driveway. She told of how Grandma cried, and Lance laughed.

Lance was eleven, Suzanne was thirteen, and he had a crush on her. A continuum shift occurred. Suzy, over the summer, suddenly matured; she grew large, lovely breasts, had her menstrual moment, and her mother ended the camping out. Sister Stephanie soon followed suit, and the coed camping days were over.

Lance's dad worked hard, put in long hours, but always made sure the family had weekend getaways and a vacation each summer. He was also a member of the volunteer fire department. The station was located about two miles from the house standing right next door to a small grocery store and gasoline station. Every fall the volunteer fire department took one Saturday and held a fundraising carnival. The store next door had a sale going on three dozen eggs for one dollar. Perhaps Lance was wired for mischief. Lance bought three boxes, a dozen eggs each. He got two friends and directed them. As the sun was setting, he had each one take a corner and chunk the eggs into the crowd. Even though the store owner was a family friend, when asked, he never ratted out Lance as the buyer of the eggs. Lance was using his charisma getting others to follow his lead. Lance never experienced remorse or regrets. Lance, by sixth grade, had learned to accurately forge his mother's signature, a useful skill he would use to his advantage often in the future.

# 5

# Junior High

Lance was developing and encountering a powerful set of changes. Going into the seventh grade, his body was undergoing growth spurts. He had his first wet dream. He was sexually awakening, and now emotional adolescence passion took over his thinking. Lance now would stand at his upstairs bedroom with the light out and look at his neighbor's wife, a hot-looking Italian woman, and her superhot fourteen-year-old daughter. They hung around in their kitchen in their nightclothes and underwear. Often, he stroked his member imagining. His libido was awakening, and hormones were running amuck. Gym classes were required, and Lance had to have a special jockstrap and cup made big enough to fit his huge private parts. Lance, of course, was acutely aware of his great gift of being well-endowed. He began a debate with himself: *How will this wonderful apparition influence my life? Can and how will I use it to my advantage? And when?*

For several years Lance and his sister went to summer camp for two weeks, fishing, swimming, boating, masturbating, canoe racing, and an awkward last night dance social. Lance was one of the lucky boys. His sister had taught him to dance, and with his music education, he had that cool swing. By the end of summer, Lance and his camp buddies had mastered masturbation. Lance now had a new hobby. In bed, in the closet alone in the woods, he abused his member. One day while in the woods standing near a grove of white birch trees, he had to pee. Lance was amazed when he pulled it out how quickly the cool air and breeze made his penis get hard. He visited the birch trees often.

At the end of summer back in school, Lance had found a fellow miscreant, a source to supply him with exploding matches to sell. They looked like normal matches, but seconds after the match lit, it exploded. Showing them off in algebra class came another "I dare you" moment. The kid sitting next to him said, "Light one." When the teacher was occupied writing a problem on the blackboard, he of course lit one. Bang, he shook it out and tossed it in the desk. Large problem, the desk was full of old *New York Times* newspapers. Not only did the match not go out, flames and smoke were now shooting out of Lance's desk. The teacher waddled down the aisle, dumped the papers on the floor, and began stomping on them. A student up front pulled the fire alarm, and the school was evacuated. The fire department and assistant principal had a talk with Lance. This was one incident he could not deny or talk his way out of. He received three days' suspension. The frosty relationship he had with his algebra teacher, Mrs. Thompson, deteriorated. Fortunately, it was right at the end of the school year. This incident dropped his algebra grade from an A to a C.

The sexual revolution began on June 23, 1960. The birth control pill was available for purchase in the United States for contraceptive purposes. This major sociological event separated sex from procreation. Now women had control over their bodies. At fourteen years old, Lance had no clue that this new social phenomenon would sweep the nation providing him with many shared pleasurable moments. Lance was unaware of this societal change; it went unnoticed and whispering by in his youth.

When he returned home from camp in August a week before his fourteenth birthday, he was still a virgin. To his parents' surprise, when they picked him up, his right leg was in a cast. While playing baseball at camp, Lance had beaten out the throw to first base. Good news. The bad news, he broke a bone in his foot while rumbling over first base. The cast and a pair of crutches slowed down the rest of summer.

Lance was already imagining what kind of car he would get as his learner's permit would be available next year at fifteen. His father insisted both of his children learn to pay their own way. If they wanted a car, they would have to work and buy one. An important principle that stuck with Lance. Stephanie worked part-time as a checker in the local grocery. Lance, once his leg healed, got odd jobs, delivered the paper, cut grass in the summer, and shoveled drives and walks in the winter. The money went into a savings account. The deal his dad made was, if they paid their insurance, cash up front for the first year, he would cosign a note on a car. Unlike the other kids at school, his dad would not give his kids a car; they had to earn it.

Lance's dad had a workout room in the basement, and Lance learned bodybuilding routines for a lifetime habit of weightlifting and working out. He had figured out the best way to reach sexual peak was to constantly maintain physical health. His dad taught Lance both exercise and additionally some self-defense moves he had learned in OSS.

$6$

# Summer Awakening

August 1960, on Lance's fourteenth birthday, he was hired to cut the lawn of one of the homes of his father's contractor. Little did he know he was about to go through a rite of passage. This house had about two acres of lawn and took several hours of hot, hard work to mow. Due to the heat, Lance was working without a shirt and in cutoff jeans. Mrs. Jenkins, the contractor's wife, made some cool lemonade. She brought it out wearing a string bikini. Now she chose to lay on a lounge chair to work on her tan. She was just turning twenty-five and had a very athletic body. She removed her top straps to expose her back to the sun. She noticed Lance had cut the lawn in the same spot close to her continuously. She was forward-thinking and had been on the pill for a couple of months. Lance unknowingly was about to become a hitchhiker in the upcoming sexual revolution. Suddenly in a spontaneous moment, she hollered, "Hey, Lance, would you please rub some suntan lotion on my back?" He stumbled over; she poured some lotion into his hands. He nervously started to massage her back with lotion. Moaning softly, she turned overexposing her breasts. He immediately had a boner and was embarrassed. Lance was so well-endowed that the head of his erection was hanging out below the bottom of his cutoff jeans. She had been sexually active before her marriage but had never seen such a large member on a man, certainly not on a boy. She became so excited she reached up and touched the head of his penis, and Lance had an explosive reaction covering her perfectly manicured hand. She was not going to miss this opportunity to not only seduce a boy virgin but to have sex with such a well-built boy-man. "Lance, you have the largest cock I have ever seen." Quickly grabbing Lance by the hand, she took him inside to her bedroom. Removing his cutoff jeans, she washed his private parts with a washcloth and warm water. Her eyes glazed over as this immediately brought him to full arousal. She sensually took hold of his manhood with one hand and removed the bottom of her bathing suit with the other hand. Now they were both naked, admiring each other's body. She had him lie back on the bed. She placed her lips over his penis taking as much of it as she could in her mouth. She gently guided his hand to her woman parts and showed him how to massage her clit. They both climaxed in unison. Looking at the clock, she realized time was running out. Her husband would soon be home. She had Lance hurriedly get dressed and sent him on his way, wishing him a happy birthday. She paid him in cash and swore him to secrecy.

Lance had unwittingly been drafted into the sexual revolution through a doorway of no return. Lance went home still technically a virgin, masturbated in the shower, his mind recalling the sheer overwhelming excitement of this afternoon's occurrence. His brain now began to have its focal point on sex and the next exciting adventure. Wow, an adult woman was excited about his manhood size. Lance knew he was well-endowed. This was the first time that it was acknowledged and brought excitement to a woman. Lance now was figuring on how to use this advantage of his to get more sex. Lance's first sexual encounter or adventure was like a ripple on a lake spreading outward in all directions causing effect in the people's lives he will interface with.

He celebrated his birthday at home with his parents, sister, and grandparents. His father gave him a German Luger pistol he had taken from an SS field officer. He promised they would go out shooting in the morning. The cake, ice cream, and presents were a pleasant cap to an unusual and wonderful day. Lance was happy and confused. Should he feel good? Guilty? He felt sexual secrets were just that, natural moments between two people and not to be shared or blamed. As that day ran through his mind, Lance masturbated admiring his special large cock as he drifted off to sleep. Lance was now awakened to future possibilities.

Lance's grandmother took the two grandkids to church every Sunday until Lance was ten and Sister Stephanie was eleven. Grandma felt this was an important time in a child's life and development when lessons in morality would be learned. She stopped when she could not or would not answer Lance's questions. Lance had learned early that people lie, shade, or distort their real feelings to fit into social norms. Lance and Stephanie would continue attending church occasionally until they were fourteen and fifteen.

At a church picnic at a local lake and park one splendid summer Saturday, Lance noticed Tammy, a developing blond, had dark black pubic hairs curling out both sides of her swimsuit crotch. He fantasized about her. Stephanie decided to attend the preacher's two-week school and join the church. Once he knew Tammy was in the communion class, Lance jumped at the chance and signed up. From a sexual standpoint, he was still a naive fourteen-year-old and as lost as a dung beetle on a starless night. Lance did not put together a true blond would probably not have jet-black pubic hair; he was simply enthralled at the vision. Although they attended the same church training, fate never brought Lance and Tammy together.

Lance asked the preacher a simple question, "Instead of communion and joining church at that young age, why they did not allow a person to grow up and at that time make their own educated decision on religious belief?" Lance finished the class. This question of course was never answered, producing more seeds of doubt. Lance and Stephanie joined the church. The preacher and his mom were so proud. They both thought he would grow up and be a preacher. Lance knew better. He quit attending church and would put religion behind. Believe in the tooth fairy. Should I? Is he for real? As a child, he of course had questioned Santa. What kind of parent would tell their young child to sit on the lap of a strange gray-haired old man with a beard and cap? Lance, even as a child, never felt lonely. He had enough in his head to keep him company.

The awakening with Mrs. Jenkins had changed his life. His goals now were to get sex as often as possible.

Lance's father, Ted, was a builder, not of homes but of complete subdivisions. Houses for all the soldiers to buy with their GI loans. Miniature cities of new baby boomer families getting started. Selecting his best contractors, he built their family home on a five-acre parcel Lance's granddad had deeded over to them. It was situated on the east side of the lake with a sloping lawn that led to the dock. The kids never had to go far to swim, row a boat or canoe and, in the winter, ice-skate. As teenagers, they were sought after for all the fun things that they could do at their place.

On July 4, after the parade, a big party and celebration took place at the dock always with lots of fireworks. They loved to throw cherry bombs and ash cans into the water and watch the explosion. Their parents always felt it was best to have the parties at their house to keep their eyes on Stephanie and especially Lance. Lance hid and saved a cherry bomb. At school he lit it and dropped it down the toilet. When the explosion set off the sewer gases, a four-foot hole was blown in the side of the school. Fortunately, no one was injured. At this point, the school busted Lance and suspended him again, this time for a week. In school, if anything went awry, Lance was one of the first and the usual suspects. If Lance didn't do it, he was either involved or knew who did it.

Junior high graduation, Lance dated a fellow band member Melody. She was at that sweet moment from sixteen to twenty-six. She played the flute. Her mother was a serious violin player with the New York Philharmonic. It was a tender date, a practice of learning social rituals. The tuxedo, prom dress, and corsage. Silly pictures soon forgotten. A good night kiss, an embarrassing bump of braces. During this school year, Lance had made an agreement with his mother. After school for one year, he took piano lessons as agreed. The night of the junior high dance, he excused himself to his date, Melody, left the gymnasium dance, and walked to the auditorium. Lance strolled on to the stage, sat at the piano and played the "Merry Widow Waltz" from memory perfectly, bowed, and left the stage. Mental debate over, he had fulfilled his agreement to his mother and never played the piano again. Lance had already had the argument in his head. He was not going to change into something his mother or anyone else thought he should be. Now it was on to high school and getting sex. Period.

He soon learned that high school society was laid out in cliques. Freshman girls would not date freshman boys. Dating a lettered football player was success. Lance did not care about these shallow-minded people. Lance liked everyone until they proved to him he shouldn't. He did not want to play football yet got to go to every game in the marching band. Lance was never a bully, nor was he bullied; he was too strong, quick, and by this stage in life, intimidating. He never looked down on the "unwelcome class." Perhaps, however, Lance himself was an immoral child?

Lance's social acquaintances are spreading like a Venn diagram. While visiting an Italian school friend, his family invited Lance to stay for dinner—wonderful food, wonderful company. Oh, yes, as per tradition, everyone at the table was served a glass of wine. This was Lance's first alcoholic drink. He loved it! A wonderful feeling swept through his body. Opening of another sense he was previously unaware of? The start of a lifetime addiction? Another pleasure receptor awakened. Encore, please.

Lance took a course in modern playwrights. The drama teacher, Mr. P., liked Lance. He encouraged Lance to become a member of the stage crew. Now Lance had access to areas backstage areas unknown to most of the student body. One day the janitor was drunk and passed out behind the stage. Lance borrowed his key ring. One of his construction buddies got copies of the school master key made for him. Upstairs backstage was the storage room for props and scenery. This included a couch, lamps, and other furnishing. One of the school's main air-conditioning ducts passed through this room with an access door and a coil that was kept at forty degrees. From his German heritage, Lance knew a perfect temperature to keep beer at, and so he did. Lance literally had his own apartment at school that could only be opened with a master key.

No big change, Lance went to class and did the minimum on his schoolwork and got A's and B's. A new tradition began on March 17 that would carry on for three years. Lance forged a note, a perfect signature allegedly from his mother, stating he would miss school. Lance was learning the art of truth-shading. A little bit of misrepresentation? Lance and Jake caught a bus to New York City for the St. Patrick's Day parade. They had a great time mixing with the local New York City crazies, telling stories made up on the spot. This was another secret between Lance and Jake for three years. Both knew how to keep a secret.

Lance was a dependable and star performer. Once elected president of the stage crew, he loved the work, building the props, performing stage magic to follow the script, and running the lighting from the booth. Working with the rest of the crew, they designed lighting and sets to match the scenes, ran through dress rehearsals, and finally the production. The school put on two plays a year. Additionally, an appearance of dignitaries or stars who worked with Lance to set up their needs and preferences. With his fellow thespians, he loved hanging around with the creative crowd. Lance now had a goal; this was what he wanted to do in the future. Is not all the world a stage? *Eventually, Broadway will be calling*, thought Lance. In his mind, Lance now has a future goal.

# 7

# Summer Vacation

Lance, in his fifteenth year, knows he will get his driver's permit. He had the money in the bank. Lance was now working full-time for his dad over the summer. His job was to drive through the subdivision and spot problems. He also performed minor home warranty for the various subdivisions. He was driving a motor scooter, a birthday gift from his dad. This required no driver's license. A work order to check a leak at a dishwasher, Lance showed up with his tools. Lance was now rapidly approaching his sexual peak. While lying on the floor, he noticed the lady of the house. The master bedroom door was open at an angle next to the kitchen where Lance was working. There stood a very sexy woman in her mid-twenties that had that just graduated from college look. She was dressing, admiring herself in front of a full-length mirror with the bedroom door wide open, showing off, wearing bright red lace panties and putting on her matching bra while shifting her glance between the mirror and Lance. Lance stood up with eyes the size of saucers taking in the show and awkwardly mumbled, "Excuse me, I found the problem." She realized he was now at arm's length staring at her and quite aroused. She placed her left arm on his shoulder; her right hand grabbed his crotch. When she grasped the size of his erection, she unzipped his jeans which dropped and wrapped around his ankles. She pulled his member out, and she led him to the edge of the bed. "Lance, you are so huge. I know we are going to enjoy this." Now they both were shedding clothes in unison and tumbled to onto the bed. When Lance told her it was his first time, she had an overwhelming orgasm. She lovingly guided him as they spent the rest of the afternoon enjoying each other and this precious moment. Lance filled out the work order stating no one was home. Lance knew how to keep a secret. Years later when Little Sue asked Lance to teach her, he was reminded of this treasured learning moment of his own. For the second time, Lance was complimented on not only his large penis but the fact he always got it up. Even this early Lance was becoming aware he had been born with a unique gift and wondering what doors it would open and who he would be able to bring shared pleasure to. Lance was no longer a virgin. He had sex with an experienced older woman. He liked it very much. She liked it very much. Lance had found a new magic in life. Never again would he look back and wonder. Now he looked forward to his next sexual experience. Lance enjoyed the serendipity of new adventures just thrown before him. His well-trained mind led to many new sexual adventures. He was never good at following rules or doing the expected.

According to Shakespeare,

> We at the height are ready to decline.
> There is a tide in the affairs of men.
> Which, taken at the flood, leads on to fortune;
> Omitted, all the voyage of their life
> Is bound in shallows and in miseries.
> On such a full sea are we now afloat,
> And we must take the current when it serves,
> Or lose our ventures.

Lance's tide put him afloat on the sea of the new sexual revolution. For the first time, the pill allowed women to follow their sexual desires with freedom. This was a moment when the stars were aligned. Lance was hitting his sexual stride just in time to ride it for the entire sexual revolution period. In the popular culture at the time, it was the Age of Aquarius, the new age movement in the 1960s and 1970s. He had just run into one of the many women who had listened to their mothers and married for all the right reasons—a home, a husband, and security. How upset they were that the pill had come along giving them sexual freedom and somehow feeling they had missed the boat. Now they wanted a taste of that sexual experimentation they felt they had missed. Lance was just thrilled after losing his virginity on such a wonderful afternoon. Little did he know the lady of the house had just discovered that her husband was cheating on her, and she had used Lance for her charming revenge! It was a lovely gift they shared.

*8*

# Janice

Lance the sophomore quickly learned that every young boy needs a sister. Stephanie was now driving and had girlfriends her age with cars. Yes, Lance's sister was still miss good girl. Lance was now having girls interested in him. A girl named Janice befriended his sister, Stephanie, and kept getting herself invited over. They had to go on a double date. Was she cute? Yes. Was she hot? Sixteen, blond hair, five feet, two inches tall with blue eyes that were as deep and enticing as Crater Lake. Her skin was alabaster white and perfect. She wore her mother's perfume and pleasantly rewarded the olfactory glands. She could have dated any boy in school but wanted Lance. On the first date, they held hands and kissed in the back seat of Stephanie's Mustang Convertible. Drive-in movies were the perfect place to go on a date. Lance was anxiously awaiting more.

Lance's grandfather told him about a 1957 Chevrolet that was going up on police auction. Apparently, the car was used in a robbery, and the police gave chase. While attempting to escape, the crooks blew the engine, left the doors open, and attempted to get away on foot. Lance went with his father and purchased the car at auction. He immediately had it towed to the auto shop at school. He was the now proud owner of a beautiful 1957 Chevy Bel Air convertible. He bought a crate engine 327/340 HP from Chevrolet and added a set of headers and glass packs. Lance would start his junior year with one of the hottest cars in school. The car was jet black, and Lance kept it shining and spotless.

Lance, as a sophomore, he would soon discover Janice was interested in more than the movie. On their next date, they went to the drive-in in Janice's car. Friday night, Lance could not tell you on Monday what movie they had gone to see. The car was parked, speaker hooked in the driver's window. Janice slid next to Lance. He raised his arm over her shoulders. Janice rested her head on his chest. "Be sure to get some buttered popcorn" ad played across the screen. She pressed against him; he could feel her heartbeat. In a mutual move, their lips met. She smelled wonderful, again teasing his olfactory receptors like a flower garden in spring. Janice raised her head and kissed Lance with vigor. He responded, and she forced open his mouth with her tongue. Now his taste buds were reeling in awe with her zestfully sweetness. Lance felt control slipping away. *Who was this girl, why did she pick me?* thought Lance. He quietly went with the flow.

"Lance, I really, really like you and was so looking forward to our getting together," said Janice in a husky voice. "I must warn you. I am an old-fashioned girl and intend on remaining a virgin until my wedding night. I will, however, help you with your boy needs." She then unbuttoned her blouse, slid his hand on her breast.

Of course, Lance was dumbfounded and followed her lead. She took both her hands and unzipped his jeans. She proceeded to perform oral sex until Lance lost it. She calmly cleaned up the residue and asked him to go to the concession stand and get her a Coke and some popcorn. They sat and shared small talk during intermission. The movie began again, and she once again placed her head in his lap and, as she said, took care of his needs. Lance drove her home, kissed her good night. Janice said, "This was a great night. I hope you enjoyed it as much as I did. I know that my reputation is safe with you, and we can see each other real soon."

Lance gave her a protective hug, said, "It was great, Janice. See you in school on Monday, and I know how to keep a secret." This was the beginning of a great on-and-off relationship that changed them both on their way to becoming adults. Lance had a girlfriend. As a friend of Stephanie and daughter of an old respected family, she was welcomed into the mix. Lance loved to have her around. She was hot, intelligent, funny, and a good fit with his zany personality. Other boys were envious and asked for details. Lance always answered she was a nice, respectable girl—period. For the first time, he had a girl his age to be with and show off. They dated the rest of the school year. Lance kept making moves on her, but she held her ground.

One night he brought her home. At the door she announced she had lost a contact. Lance, ever quick on the draw, said, "Jan, it is probably in your clothes. Don't move." He proceeded to remove her shoes. Not there. Next her blouse. Not there. Her slacks he slid off slowly. Not there. He slowly pulled down her panties. Not there; however, a perfect triangle of blond hair almost invisible was there. Not black, so noted. Last article of clothing, her bra. There was the missing contact in the cup for the left breast. Lance finally had her where he wanted her, standing in the living room naked. She put the contact in her eye, and Lance quickly pulled her to him telling her how beautiful she was. Her body was at prime in high school perfect. He kissed and fondled her breasts while sliding his hand down to her woman parts. He caressed and fondled her tenderly as he had learned earlier in his life. He sat on the edge of the couch pulling her to him. Her turn for some oral sex and Lance was glad to provide it. By now Lance had discovered another talent that would come to use often. His tongue was so long he could touch his nose with it. Lance put her down on the couch, continuing his efforts to arouse her. Now he had his face in her crotch drawing her clit into his mouth and his tongue working magic. "Stop! stop!" she announced. "I really want and need you, and you can do anything you want, just don't put it in me." They lay together as young lovers. He slid his organ between her legs. She closed her legs and began writhing and moving up and down, his big cock bouncing against her clit, her viselike grip pushing up and back. They both achieved orgasm and the sexual relief she needed. They had moved on to a new phase. Everything went except insertion and her virginity. She was good with it, as was Lance, of course. On the drive home, Lance found himself humming "Après de ma blonde," a silly song he had learned from his mom.

# 9
# Junior with Car

As a junior with his own car, Lance now had the freedom to roam. His sister introduced him to a little, tiny Jewish girl, Sheila. She attended school in a different town, and they had a few mutual acquaintances. She called him one Saturday and invited him over; her parents were gone for the weekend. Lance seized upon the opportunity. They had gone on a fishing date previously at his lake and had some passionate kisses, but nothing else was possible. He arrived at her house. She took him to her bedroom and showed him her bed was round. Lance quickly fell back on the bed, asking, "How do you know where to put your head?" She reached out with her right arm, but before she could get a word out, Lance had pulled her into his arms, a kiss, tongues pushing into one mouth and then the other, raging teen hormones driving both. She surprised Lance by grabbing his belt, unbuckling and unzipping him. Of course, Lance's member was as hard as a diamond. She gasped at the enormous circumcised shaft and immediately went down on him. Lance lovingly placed his hand over the top of that pretty black head of hair thinking he had died and gone to heaven. Hands rapidly moving flung away any additional clothing. She was small, perhaps ninety pounds, with an olive complexion and dark black curly hair and black eyes, dark and enticing. Lance was amazed by her tiny girl-like breasts the size of avocados. Her nipples were the size of peas but as hard as granite. Now naked she slid over him presenting his mouth with her beautiful vagina covered in a large mat of black curly hair long enough to braid yet tasting like sweet honey. She was a sexual tiger. After multiple orgasms, they took a break and then showered. She told him that for some reason she could not get enough sex and longed for it constantly. Lance could certainly identify with that. The two of them spent the entire weekend working that problem. To a fly observing on the wall, you would think the two of them had invented sex. Unfortunately, her family was extremely religious and would not approve of her dating outside of the faith.

Both then and in future meetings, she trained Lance in another useful skill. Although he was too young to appreciate massages and their sexual connotation, he slowly mastered this ability. Her mom was a physical therapist and had trained Sheila on therapeutic back massages. Her mother left her college texts at home, and sweet little Sheila had learned and practiced with Lance on sexual arousal massages. She loved it as part of her foreplay and trained Lance in the rudimentary motions. Lance, ever the quick learner, added this to his sexual skills using muscles, nerves, back, and feet to bring a body to its maximum sexual plateau. Their occasional future meetings in secret were still wonderful learning experiences. They both relieved their muscles, nerves, and sexual tensions. Sheila was amazed that Lance seemed to have a giant perpetual hard-on. He was always stiff and ready, and she loved that. Lance went home and slept for almost twenty-four hours.

*La vie est belle.* Life is good.

# *10*
# Beach House

Janice's parents had a beach house in New Jersey on the Atlantic Ocean. She had the week of March 20 off for spring break. With her mom's permission, she and Lance spent a week at their beach house. No cars allowed; you parked your car in a parking lot and walked through a gate into this small private community. Her mother dropped them off for a week by themselves. What a wonderful week in Lance's life. They slept late, put on their swimming attire, and walked to the beach. She was now just turning seventeen and head spinning hot. She loved to show off walking around in her bikini knowing what effect she had on passing men of all ages. Home in the afternoon, they showered together and shared all the secrets of their bodies only holding back on penetration. They were extremely comfortable with their budding relationship. Two kids in love comfortable in a "not you, not me, but us" meeting of the minds.

Lance's life in his eyes was well filled out. He attended school with kids he has known his whole life. Some he liked; some he didn't. He was a realist. He knew which girls put out, which ones didn't, and which ones were ready to move to the first list, often with his help. Girls talk. Had Lance lived in ancient civilizations that sacrificed virgins, he would have saved many a young maiden's life.

He became quite skilled in both auto and in-home construction repair. For the last year he had worked as an apprentice with a master electrician. He was a junior in high school, a member of the debate team, and becoming a skilled speaker like his grandfather. He was first chair clarinet in the school band. His sister was a senior. Lance, at this moment, had the GPA and many offers to attend premier universities due to his family's position and his class standings. He had a hot car, hot girlfriend, and others waiting in the wings. He was on the right track to attaining success both in college and becoming an adult.

One of Stephanie's senior friends, Amanda, had been dating the same boy for three years. He was popular, school council president senior, and on his way to a prominent university. Both were members of the upper crust clique. They broke up three weeks before the senior prom. As a friend of Sister Stephanie, Lance was asked if he would be kind enough to be her date for the prom. Of course, the opportunity for a junior boy to take an attractive senior girl to the prom. Lance rented a tuxedo, bought a corsage, and even hired a limo. They danced, had their pictures taken, and had a great time. Lance had also brought a bottle of wine from his grandparents' cellar. They shared the wine and really had a wonderful memorable night. Yes, he held her close. Yes, the slow dancing was wonderful, and some sweet kisses took place. She began and ended the night still a virgin. They had the rest of summer to date and enjoy. Lance had an aura about him. He did not wear any cologne but gave off natural pheromones that worked their own kind of magic. Several dates with hot and heavy petting took place. Lance felt she was coming around. On a hot Tuesday in July, she and Lance were swimming in the pool at her house. Both of her parents were at work, and she, being an only child, meant the two of them were on their own. Some kissing, some hugging with both in bathing suits. He of course did not hold back or hide his male excitement. There was heavy breathing as he slid the top of her suit down and began to fondle and kiss both lovely small firm breasts. Lance reached to touch her vagina and wow. The flap opened and exposed her beautiful pubic area covered with hair that looked to Lance like flaming red corn silk. This was his first redhead, and he was in love. Slowly he lifted her suit over her head, and he sat on the lounge chair. Amanda was standing in the sunlight naked and covered herself with her arms. This was the first time she was unclothed in front of a boy and felt a little vulnerable. Her slim white body flushed to a reddish hue. Lance understood her uneasiness, slowly pulling her closer and telling her how lovely and sensuous she was. Lance kissed her belly button while putting his arms around her white belly with no hint of a tan or a freckle. He grabbed her butt cheeks and drew her body closer. He knew exactly what she needed. As Lance drew his lips to her body, his tongue reached out to the center of her excitement. He once again tasted heaven. She had her first oral sex orgasm, and Lance caught her as her knees gave out. Her magnificent corn silk was drenched. Amanda was lying on the lounge, smiling and grabbing her suit. "Lance, that was wonderful, and I know it will be our secret, but I can go no further. I am sorry to leave you in that state, but as you know, I am leaving for college in six weeks and do not want to complicate my life." Lance, ever the gentleman, kissed her goodbye and left. They never crossed paths again, but she left Lance with a lifetime affinity for redheads.

Lance had plenty of girlfriends and had established a reputation for being well-endowed and known for his love of going down on pussy and ability to bring a girl to satisfaction. He had one year left in high school and pretty much had it made. He had an altered driver's license stating he was eighteen, drinking age. He had a hot car, an assortment of mostly rowdy friends in several schools. No, he was not one of the in crowd, had no desire to be. He was good-looking enough to turn girls' heads but certainly not a pretty boy. He was Apollo to the girls and women, intelligent, and able to speak with ease to kids and adults. Lance was never a bully. He never looked down on any person. He had a hot car that consistently turned in good times at the drag races, lived in a perfect home with the lake and woods. As far as his schoolwork went, he passed with A and B averages without effort. This fall he would look at where he wanted to go to college. The only thing he knew for sure was he wanted to go into stage and/or movie production and, oh yes, have as much sex as he could.

That summer Angie, or Angel, as he called her, fell from heaven. She was working at an upscale supermarket babysitting kids while their moms were shopping. As soon as he saw her, he was in love. He got her number, called her up, and set up a date. She agreed to a double date with friends. It went great; they had a fun time. For the next six weeks, she was his life. He was dancing on air. This seventeen-year-old had it made, a new unique experience. Lance was overwhelmingly in love. The world was wonderful. He was writing poetry, walking above the ground.

# 11
# Vegas

Lance's mom and dad took a little vacation. They brought home a surprise of earthshaking significance. They had bought ten acres in a place called Las Vegas. "Dad, why did you do that?" Lance asked.

His father, who was the boss of his household, announced, "We are selling everything here and moving. We will be moving over your Christmas break in school."

And the work began. Everything was packed or sold, including the beautiful house on the lake. Lance was, of course, devastated. At the time Lance, being a minor, had little choice but to follow orders and assist, wondering, *Why, what could have happened to cause this breach?*

Lance was happy living in upstate New York. When he awoke, the view of the sun rising over the lake was fabulous. Little hues of gold bled through the gentle rippling waves. The willow trees cast dark shadows in corners. Grass and sometimes wild blackberries grew wildly along the shores. In the fall, there were more aesthetic rewards for the eyes as the leaves turned various shades of red, yellow, purple, black, orange, pink, magenta, blue, and brown. Now the leaves would fall, the lake would freeze, and it was ice-skating and hockey time. Four seasons each with its own type of natural beauty and fun. And for the first time, Lance was in love.

Lance, the seventeen-year-old senior, did not have the expected Christmas filled with cookies, friends, and sex. Instead, Lance had to say goodbye to all, pack his stuff, and move, not allowed to graduate with the senior class, the very people he had grown up with his entire life. He would have to finish the last half of his senior year in a school where he literally knew no one. The first real love of his life, Angel, broke up with him on hearing the news. *What have I done to deserve this?* thought Lance.

Stoically, he followed orders, moving away from everyone he knew, friends he had gone to school with since kindergarten. Forced to leave the only life he had recognized in the middle of his senior year. His sister, on the other hand, had already graduated, had a "go along to get along" personality, and just went with the flow.

# 12
# The Move

The large items Lance and his dad loaded on a boxcar. And now the caravan, Lance drove a truck and pulled a trailer. Mom and sis drove their cars. Dad drove another truck. Four days' drive all day, stop for gas, rent a motel, and try to sleep.

A new phenomenon driving into the sun, it was difficult to see. Without trees and clouds, the sun's rays were blinding. Lance did not own a pair of sunglasses. Slowly the grass and trees disappeared. Signs appeared: "Last gas for three hundred miles."

Major culture shock.

"We are here," announced Lance's father. They pulled in front of the rental home. While building a home in Las Vegas, his family had rented a house to live in. From an ideal setting, living in a house on a lake in a forest to a tiny rental house in a desert subdivision. It was January in Las Vegas. What grass there was had turned brown. There were more places that had no grass, just sand and scrub brush or cactus. When he looked out his bedroom window, he saw a tiny backyard, cinderblock fence, and the neighbors' houses. No trees in sight. When the wind blew, which was most of the time, dust found its way into all cracks and crevices. The smell of dust permeated everything inside the house and outside. No matter where you went, it smelled like dust. Surrounded by stark brown mountains and foothills looking like welts from a whipping, the mountains turned from green to brown looking like baked bread. Brown grass, brown mountains blazingly blinding bright sun in clear blue cloudless skies. People who lived there were not aware of this smell, just like people in Hershey, PA, couldn't smell chocolate, nor could the residents of Luling, Texas, smell oil. Wildlife in Vegas was on the strip.

Halfway through his high school senior year, Lance suddenly was attending a school in the desert knowing not a soul. His transcript had enough credits to graduate. The exception of Nevada history. He signed up for bogus classes to fill out the last semester. In New York, his friends called him Lucky Lance. At this moment, he certainly did not feel that way. Lance thought that he was well rounded and had seen most everything important: Niagara Falls, the Holland Tunnel and the Empire State Building, Statue of Liberty, and Horn & Hardart automatic restaurants. Lance had even dedicated a plaque at a historic house and lunch with dignitaries on an aircraft carrier. No chance of that happening here. He was totally taken aback by the appearance of slot machines everywhere, in grocery stores, drugstores, bars, the bus station, casinos, of course, a warren of slots in the airport attempting to wring the last coins from tourists.

## 13

# New School

Goodbye to the old world, welcome to the new. When Lance had his last day at his old high school in New York, the assistant principal came up to Lance, shook his hand, and said, "This is the happiest day of my life. You are leaving."

In Vegas, Lance's mom, Aimée, told Lance, "This is a new day and a new school. Wear your sports jacket, be polite, and make a good first impression." Lance thought why not. He got dressed up wearing his sport coat and a tie. He met with the school's assistant principal, reached out, and shook hands. He in turn looked Lanced over, saw the church key in his pocket, and stated loudly, "I will be keeping my eyes on you. We do not need troublemakers."

On a positive note, the school drama department was happy to see him and put him to work on designing a light bar for a theater in the round. He immediately hit it off with that new thespian group, and relationships started budding. On Sunday, a new friend, Andy, picked up Lance, and they took the forty-minute drive to Mount Charleston. It was cold enough for snow, and they loaded Andy's trunk with it. Four cars showed up at school early Monday morning loaded with snow. In the parking lot, the snowball fight was on. Great fun. Fortunately, Lance was comfortable in his own skin. He was smart, good-looking, and as many stated, had the gift of gab. At this point in life, any goals he had previously shifted. He never would understand nor forgive his parents for forcing him to move in the middle of his senior year. Yes, he adapted, as is the nature of a survivor, but now his only real thought was to get through the school year, graduate, and move out on to his own the day he turned eighteen and legally could. Little did he anticipate the next mountain that would be thrown his way.

# 14
# Dead

Tuesday afternoon in March 19, 1964, Lance left school at the end of the day. Lance was walking with David to his car. A group of kids were playing golf on the school lawn. David picked up a club, a nine iron, and took a mighty swing. He lost his balance and struck Lance with the club in the left temple. Lights out, unconscious blood gushing out of his head. The next thing Lance remembered he was riding in the back of an ambulance to the hospital. He was in and out of consciousness. His mother was talking to the emergency room doctor who explained to her how Lance's skull had been crushed like an eggshell, and his only chance was to have the pieces removed from his brain at the main hospital. Two days later Lance regained consciousness. The doctor and his mother were there. The doctor told his mother and Lance that he had died on the operating table. All normal respiration had ceased.

The doctor held up a mirror. First look into the mirror was a horror show frightening. Lance saw that the left side of his head was purplish blue with a concave hole in his head and stitches running in a semicircle from his ear to his forehead. Lance's left eye was bloodshot with every vein showing in a fire-engine red color. His throat felt as raw as fresh roadkill. No one would fall in love with a person who had a face the color of ham.

Would he be next Halloween's scary mask? Would little children run away in fear? He had the appearance of cruel ogre. Lance figured he would never get a date again. Comforting words from doctors and family were less than convincing. Two weeks of hospital food that was marginally better than airline food and he was sent home to stay in bed and slowly recover. His mother put her nursing skills to work and pushed him with physical therapy. Slowly his body recovered muscle mass. His hair grew and covered the scar. The bruising and bloodshot eye recovered. The repaired jaw muscle gained strength. Because Lance's jaw muscle was cut, in the beginning of recovery, Lance could not open his mouth wide enough to eat a hot dog and bun. Yes, he would always have a hole in the head, but he was alive and functioning, at least physically.

The one class he needed to graduate he completed at home. Lance tested out, and his high school diploma was mailed to him. More salt in the wound, no senior prom, and he did not get to attend graduation ceremonies with two-thousand-plus seniors he did not know. Major life changes, one of the most important rites of passage ceremonies. Thirteen years of school and no cap and gown. Lance graduated from high school with a diploma received in the mail.

Lance, while slowly recovering, had an epiphany. He had died at age seventeen by accident or chance. Even at death's door, Lance had a hard-on. The best he could do in whatever amount of life was left, short or long, was to have as much fun as possible before he died again. Now Lance decided to live his life having fun. That meant sex to Lance. Lance did not wish to grow old regretting opportunities missed instead of great memories. Lance decided not to spend his life being bound to uniformity.

# 15
# Life after Death

Living in the desert with a black convertible with a black top and no air-conditioning, it was 112 degrees and dusty outside. The wind which blew often did not show up by observing the rustling of the tree leaves; instead, little dust devils danced across the sands. Lance was out of high school but still seventeen. Now Lance was forming his identity, actively choosing to live a life with no regrets.

Lance's first job out of high school was a parts chaser at an imported car dealership. Lance knew little about imports. He tried to buy a Jaguar once in New York, but his father said, "No, you will buy American cars—period." The car dealership Lance worked at specialized in fast imported sports cars. Lance drove a Studebaker pickup to go pick up parts. Lance had the opportunity to drive Jaguars, Lotus Elan, Hillman, Aston Martin, Alfa Romeo, Morris Minor, and Austin-Healey 3000, which he fell in love with. His first experience with sports cars had begun. When not running parts or riding with customers, Lance worked in the mechanical shop. Here he was able to hone his mechanical skills at the shop working with the mechanics. Amazing, you could disconnect the speedometer cable with the car on a rack hook up an electric drill and run the odometer back to zero! More truth-shading in the real world.

One assignment, Lance was sent with a customer to test-drive his car after a tune-up. At the end of Fremont Street just hitting Boulder Highway, the customers said, "This thing was crapping out at one hundred miles per hour." Pedal to the floor, Lance had his first experience traveling at one-hundred-plus miles an hour, not on a drag strip but a public highway. The customer was happy, and Lance survived. The business soon sold, and Lance moved on. He had gained a respect for sports cars, not people.

# 16

# Not in Kansas

Lance's mother felt sorry for him and took him to Lake Mead fishing. It was 112° Fahrenheit and no shade trees anywhere. Lance, at this point, gave up fishing. Stoic in the face of all that had come down on him, Lance waited with smothering patience. From this point forward, Lance felt perhaps he was different from the herd and probably would never comfortably conform or fit in. Why was he here in the desert? Lance found another part-time job working the graveyard shift pumping gas at a discount gas station. He began to understand that Vegas was unusual. Customers would come in and desperately need a tank of gas to get back to Los Angeles. They would sell their car radio, spare tire, fur coats, and some even offered their wife's services. His friend's fathers were pit bosses and their mothers show girls who danced around topless wearing petite elaborate costumes and permanent smiles or were cocktail waitresses, change girls, or keno runners. This was an adult playground town, and there was little for teenagers to do.

Yes, Lance and his buddies would cruise Fremont Street looking for girls, parties, or drag races. Everyone met at the Blue Onion, a hamburger drive in at one end of Freemont. There they told lies, met girlfriends, showed off, and tuned their cars for drag racing. Life was slowly shifting to normalcy of fitting in for Lance. He and Andy started jamming at work. The graveyard shift at the gas station was often dead for hours. They practiced, wrote some songs, and had a great time.

Two buddies took Lance for a mystery ride to visit a ranch. Of course, he was thinking, *Why would we want to do that?* Imagine his surprise when they arrived at Sally's Ranch, a legal brothel. This was a treat for Lance they had kicked in and paid for. They rang the front bell and were escorted into a parlor. A group of fine-looking, scantily clad ladies showed off. In their heels standing in a lineup, they all looked desirable and hot. "Just pick one," said Andy, and Lance did. Misty (Lance was sure this was not her real name) led him off to a small private boudoir with a chair, a hook for clothes, a nightstand, and a single bed. On the nightstand was a jar of Vaseline and a box of Kleenex. Lance was amazed by the lack of feeling demonstrated by Misty. "Take off your clothes and hang them on the hook." When Lance turned around, she was out of her see-through top that accentuated her ample breasts, had dropped her panties, and lay back on the bed. She took her index finger, snagged some Vaseline, and lubricated herself. Put Lance in a room with a hot naked lady and he was ready. The two of them went through the motions until Lance came. Her parting words, "Because of your large size, when you get married, be gentle with your wife." For the first time, Lance had sex yet felt it was anticlimactic. Yes, he had achieved physical climax, but something was lacking. He of course did not admit it but joined in the rowdy-boy braggadocio on the sixty-mile trip home. Yes, prostitution is legal in some counties in Nevada and practiced in most.

Andy started dating Jane with the stinky feet. She was from Los Angeles and lived with her mom, Audrey, who was only thirty-four. Jane worked as a change girl and, after eight hours on her feet, came home and removed her shoes. The smell would drive you from the room. Jane took off her shoes, and everyone said, "Please don't," and they were forced to leave the room. To Andy, it did not matter; they were in love. Andy turned eighteen and moved in. Jane's mom was fine with that arrangement. When Lance was not working, he hung around Andy and was often at Audrey's house.

August 16, 1964, Lance turned eighteen. He, as planned from a legal standpoint, moved out of his parents' house at one minute into that day. Audrey had an extra bedroom and welcomed him. Lance was now finally on his own. He certainly had no strong bond with his parents. He never understood why they had forced him to leave a perfect, almost ideal life in New York and move in the middle of his senior year to the desert. He had died, recovered physically, but not mentally. He knew you could die at any moment; he had. Lance was still a naive eighteen-year-old.

Lance had saved the money for college and started at the University of Nevada, Las Vegas, in September. He was on a roll, on the dean's list and even won a part in the fall play. What could go wrong? Lance took his saved the money for school and had Audrey put it in her bank account. When he registered for college, he paid with a check she gave him. Six weeks later, a call from the office of the registrar stated his tuition check had bounced and he had three days to pay in cash. Audrey had excuses, and Lance had no money. He was forced to drop out. Long term, he now no longer had interest in college, bettering himself, or becoming societal model citizen.

His goals now were simple—sex, drugs, and rock and roll. This did not separate him from many kids at the time. At eighteen, Lance had already seen his dreams slip away. Having read Epicurus, Lance believed that utilitarians had correctly identified good with pleasure. He now merely began to follow that utilitarian philosophy, rather hedonistic in his outlook. Spend your time acting in a way that maximizes pleasure or good. Lance, at that point in life, believed there were two motivators in life: pleasure and pain. Sex brought pleasure; rules brought pain.

# *17*

# **Homesick**

Homesick, Lance sold his car, bought a plane ticket, and flew back to New York. His grandparents were thrilled to have him back. He immediately got hold of old friends who were not away in college. He bought a 1961 Chevy Impala. He replaced the engine with a 369-horsepowered 409-cubic-inch block adding glass packs and dual exhausts. This car had air-conditioning. A lesson learned. One of his old girlfriends Angel was beside herself when he called. He began dating her again and even took her home to meet his grandparents. Love? Maybe. Everything was in place for a happily ever after. One night while he and Angel were playing in the poolroom at his grandparents' house, Lance had a moment of doubt. In his mind, things were going too fast. He told Angel they needed to cool it for a while. Angel told him flat out, "Lance, the next time you call, I will be married." Lance thought, *Yeah, right*. About two weeks later, having second thoughts, Lance called Angel. She did not come to the phone; her mother did the announcing. "Angel was moving out and getting married that weekend."

*C'est la vie*, thought Lance.

Lance got hooked up with an electrical contractor he had known and went to work as an electrical apprentice. Once again Lance felt his life was on track. He had a decent job with a future, a hot car, and friends he had grown up with. A broken heart that was healing. He started running with Ken again, an old friend from high school. The drinking age was eighteen, not twenty-one like Vegas, allowing Lance to go barhopping.

Lance had an infectious personality. One night they met three sisters. Lance grabbed on to the older one, a nurse named Jennifer. On their second date, they went in her car, a 1961 Ford Galaxie convertible fire-engine red. The car was lowered and had a continental kit. Her car was hot. She was dressed in a red leather miniskirt with sexy black crochet panties that were readily visible as her skirt pulled up from sitting on the car seat. She was sexy and hot. It was winter and had snowed with about four inches lying on the ground. Lance was driving. They got a six-pack and found a remote spot. When they parked, Lance opened the driver's side door and laid the beer cans one by one in the snow to keep them cold. Eyes locked in on each other, lips pressing together, tongues teaching each other. She, as a nurse, had come prepared handing Lance a condom. She gasped when she saw the erection and rolled the condom over Lance's member. She had slid up her skirt and out of her panties. They were both breathing hard and steamed up the windows making mad, passionate car sex. A wonderful shared moment. Timing in life is everything. She climbed off, and Lance tossed the used condom out the driver's side window. She slid back into her clothes, feeling good, satiated. Abruptly a flashlight was shining in the driver's side window, attached to a cop's arm. Lance rolled down the window. The cop lectured him about having beer cans out in the snow. While shining his flashlight on the beer, there laid the freshly used condom steaming in the cold air. It was still hot; the snow and the air were cold. The condom was causing its own little weather. Lance picked up the beer, and they went back to the bar so Lance could get his car. Life was getting good. This hot romance lasted about five weeks. Lance and Jennifer would meet at different clubs, dance, drink, and have a good time. Lance was amazed how often a woman hesitant to have sex the first time became a willing and often the instigator from there on out. Their last night, Lance slipped off to the restroom and was pulled aside by the bartender. He warned him that Jennifer was married to a real bad dude, and he had been in earlier looking for her and her sisters. If he was wise, he would become scarce. Lance was only in it for the sex and fun. He said, "Au revoir, Jen, your husband is looking for you." This moment occurred on a Sunday night. Lance went home as he had to work on Monday.

When Lance got home, his grandmother handed him a newspaper obituary she had cut out. The column told the story how his ex-girlfriend, Angel, had died in childbirth. She had died in a navy hospital; her new husband was a sailor. Lance thanked his grandmother and never said another word or mentioned her again. Lance was barely eighteen and becoming anesthetized to life. He had died; his first love had died. Lance handled it like an eighteen-year-old. He called his buddy, Ken. They went out and got drunk. After all, this was New York, and the drinking age was eighteen. The next morning included a hangover and slow recovery. Ever the trooper, the next day Lance still put in a full day of hard work.

# 18

# Janice

Lance stopped by A&P to get a six-pack and ran into Janice, a fortuitous event. "Lance, when did you get back, and why did you not call me?"

Lance told her how lovely she looked and pulled her close and held and squeezed her. "Janice, I did not know how you felt about us and did not want to interfere in your life."

"You are not getting off that easy. You know how much I care for you," she replied. "Are you staying at your grandparents? When can we meet? My mom is in Europe for two weeks. Why don't you come on by? Please, please Friday evening."

Lance got off work, went home, and showered. He filled his car with gas and bought a bottle of wine. Janice was home alone waiting. She met him at the door wearing a pink baby doll nightgown with ruffles. The material was sheer enough that you could read a newspaper through it. Two glasses of wine, two sips, and they were all over each other. She took his hand leading him to her room. The ceiling was white with reflective stars scattered about; the walls were a very subtle pink. Her bed was covered with a flowered comforter, bright yellow sunflower with green leaves. Looked like a lovely garden. Two scented candles, one on each nightstand, emitted a wonderful earthy odor. In the middle of the bed was a blue beach towel. Janice took control. She had dreamed about this moment for years. As she led Lance into her lair, every nerve in her body was at its apex. With one hand, she was drawing Lance to the bed. He was offering no resistance of course. He started to rip off his clothes. She gently and lovingly said, "No, Lance, let me." She started at his top button slowly and seductively opening one button at a time with a warm juicy kiss at each level she had exposed. Shirt on the floor, she sat on the edge of the bed and unbuckled his belt. Starting at the top, Janice unbuttoned his jeans. As the fourth button released its hold, Lance's jeans slid down over his ankles. Jan was ready; she slid down his boxer shorts. She bestowed upon his member that was at full attention a warm wet kiss. She opened her nightstand drawer. Out came a Trojan which Lance skillfully rolled over his erection. "Lance, I was so afraid when you moved away that this moment would not be ours. I love you and want you inside of me." Remembering their previous times together, Lance did not hurry. Slowly he removed her nightgown, kissing and sucking her lovely breasts. She lay back and raised her butt while he slid off her sexy lace, silk panties. He began kissing her toes and worked his way up to her pubes. Now he began with a kiss on her moist pussy lips pushing with his tongue. It was as though time had stood still. They were already comfortable with each other's bodies and needs, and now they spent the weekend satisfying them. She was now a senior in high school and graduating in six weeks. She was thrilled he would be there to attend her graduation. Lance's presence was of course expected.

A simple phone call changed all of that. Jake called Lance. "How would you like to go to LA?" Jake had signed an agreement to transport a brand-new 1965 Chevelle SS 396/375HP convertible across country from New York to Los Angeles. All expenses paid and two weeks to get to LA. "I need a second driver. One of us sleeps while the other drives. We will not stop except for gas and food until we get to LA. Lance, we have two weeks before we have to turn the car in, and we will take the old Route 66 all the way. I have an uncle who lives in Downey, and we can stay with him." Lance gave everyone a week's notice, closed out his checking account, and signed his car over to his grandparents to sell. After all, he had missed his own graduation.

Jake picked him up at the front gate, and off they were spinning rubber and smoking tires. The goal was to reach California as soon as possible. Any sightseeing was serendipitous. Lance took the wheel in Chicago and drove the next shift. Lance had driven cross-country before and seen much of the scenery. At 2:30 a.m., Lance was sleeping in the back seat. Lance jerked awake by flashing red lights and the siren's metallic wailing. "Well, shit," hollered Jake. The Winslow, Arizona, cop looked over the paperwork and saw they were legally driving the car. He told us there was a $50 fine, and they had to follow him to the judge's house and pay in cash. Fine paid, Jake and Lance were on their way, both sure that the cop and judge split the money. Years later when the Eagles had the hit "Take It Easy" with the line "standing on a corner in Winslow, Arizona," Lance flashed back to that night. Thirty-six hours driving and they were at the house of Jake's uncle in Downey, California, that left twelve days to party. They chased girls, raced other teenagers, and had a ball. The company that hired Jake finally found him and took back the car. This was probably a good thing as the transmission was starting to slip. Jake bought an old 1955 Chevy Bel Air coupe to drive back home. He had the car one day and blew the engine. Lance's mechanical skills came into play again. They bought a used engine from a wrecking yard and had it delivered. Using the tools of Jake's uncle and driveway, they got the car up and running.

Sometime that night Jake went through Lance's wallet and stole all his cash. When Lance woke up, he was broken and stuck in Downey, California. Lance spent that day cleaning up the mess from the engine change. Jake's uncle lent Lance bus fare, and Lance was off to Vegas where he still had friends. Lance never saw or heard from Jake again. In Jake's opinion, he was not worth his mother's or any other woman's tears. As soon as he found a job, he repaid Jake's uncle; it was the right thing to do.

July 1965, nineteen-year-old Lance called his best buddy, Andy, in Vegas. "Surprise, I'm back." After a couple of months hanging around in Vegas, he discovered everyone was married, engaged, or away at college. The legal age for drinking and gambling was twenty-one. Lance decided he wanted to travel and see the world before he settled down. He was too young to settle down. That concept was an anathema to him. He stopped by the Navy recruiter and with his mom's help, got all the needed paperwork in order. After the Downey fiasco, Lance wondered, how many times did you do things right and they turned out all wrong?

# *19*
# Navy Boot Camp

Off to Los Angeles for a physical and tests. He was given his orders and placed on a bus, reporting to boot camp in San Diego, November 19, 1965. One day in boot camp, the Navy showed a movie presentation about the submarine service. Lance thought, *That's for me.* Even though his dad and granddad with their military experience said do not volunteer for anything, he did. Additional testing both physical, pressure, and psychological testing and he was accepted. Orders were being cut for sub school. Boot camp was easy. Lance was not only physically but also mentally well-endowed. Lots of double time, wash all your uniforms on concrete tables in front of the barracks. Easy, Lance's mother sent him powdered bleach in his mail. His whites were pass-inspection perfect.

With his musical background, he was placed in the drum and bugle corps. He played bugle, base and tenor drums and, yes, even the glockenspiel. While others learned knots, he traveled around to march in parades. Still the show-off. Boot camp graduation and everyone in his barracks had orders cut and left. Lance had planned on going to New Orleans for Mardi Gras. Alas, upon completing boot camp, Lance alone had no orders, remaining at boot camp for two weeks standing duty while awaiting orders. Nothing ever in Lance's life ever seemed to follow norms. Good news, Lance finally got orders for submarine school. Bad news, the Navy decided to save money and have a second school in San Francisco. New home for Lance was a small two-story barrack left over from World War II. More good news, it was only one block from the enlisted men's club. No time left for leave before school started, Lance checked in and was all by himself. Two days later a second student, Walter, from Detroit arrived. It would be just the two of them for several weeks.

These two future sub school students Lance and Walter's first job was to help clean up and prepare the barracks for school. Liberty was canceled the first weekend. Lance and Walter had to stay on base and paint the wooden fire escape. Working all weekend, they finished Sunday night. Monday morning at 0800, a civilian construction crew showed up and tore it down. They replaced it with a metal fire escape. Lesson learned, for the next four years, Lance never took anything he was told by the Navy seriously. The two of them would turn on all the eight showers full hot and used it for a steam room.

Walter was an only child fresh out of high school and boot camp. When he washed his first load of clothes, he put in the clothes, poured in the bleach, and at some point, later started the washer. His civilian clothes all came out with white, colorless bleach spots. Not yet trained, his next brilliant move was taking his new canvas running shoes and letting them soak in pure bleach overnight. When he washed them the next day, the only thing that survived was the rubber soles and the little metal ringlets. When Walter offered to wash Lance's clothes, a quick and emphatic no was Lance's reply. The other six sailors arrived, and sub school started. Lance of course came in first in his class.

## 20
# Sub Sailor

His orders were to his first boat undergoing dry dock repairs at Vallejo. Lance, with orders in hand and seabag, took a bus to Mare Island Naval *Shipyard* twenty-five miles northeast of San Francisco in *Vallejo, California*. He reported aboard as a NUB (nearly useless body). As he stepped down the ladder into the forward torpedo room, the first-class torpedo man said, "How would you like to join the torpedo gang? You will get a ninety-six-hour liberty." Wow, four days off. Lance was now a striker in the torpedo gang. Another snap decision that altered his life. He had joined the Navy for ET to get electronics training.

Being in the shipyards was like a day job. Sub in dry dock civilian crews worked on the boat during the day. No watches. At night Lance and the crew discovered that the fire extinguishers spread everywhere throughout the boat for construction would cool down a six-pack of beer rapidly. This occurred often. A notice was put out to the crew: "Cease and desist using extinguishers for cooling beer." Living in the barracks was a dream job. Lots of paint chipping and other mundane tasks. No masks or personal protection worn while scraping lead-based paint and asbestos insulation. Who knew?

The boat's home base was in San Diego, and Lance was invited to join three other crew members on the weekend ride. Ninety-six hours off. Three of them were married and were on the way to see their wives. Lance was still of the belief that if the Navy wanted you to have a wife, she would have been issued. Married sailors always had excuses for a chit to get off. Halfway down the state of California, the driver, Mark, got into a heated argument with Kevin riding shotgun. Brusquely pulling the car over, they both got out and began throwing punches at each other.

Lance remained in the back seat just observing. Several punches and hurt feelings and they were underway again as though nothing out of the ordinary had happened. New kid on the block, Lance was not sure if it had or not. This would turn out to be his first but certainly not his best long liberty. Little did he realize these three would be his shipmates for the next two years. He spent the weekend drinking and talking and visiting with his newfound shipmates. Nursing a well-earned hangover, he slept on the ride back. Unknown to Lance, he was on his way to becoming a functioning alcoholic.

Flood the dry dock. No leaks, time to get underway for sea tests. Lance the NUB was underway for the first time in his life. The boat was rocking back and forth, up and down. When would it stop? Lance's first time on a submarine and he was seasick. Major problem, they were still in San Francisco Bay. Fortunately, when they got to sea in the Pacific, they submerged, and Lance's system settled down. From that point until he was discharged riding some very rough seas in the Northern Atlantic and Pacific, he never got sick again. No matter how drunk and hungover from liberty, he developed his sea legs and was good to go. Lance was not an old salt but a real sailor. He would spend the better part of the next four years at sea, but there was nothing like the first time underway. Sea trials successful, they sailed to home port.

US Navy submarine base Ballast Point, San Diego, the boat was tied up to the pier. Lance became friends with the torpedo members on the submarine tender. First order of business, loading war shot torpedoes every operation was a new skill and training. Many times, in the next four years, he would be involved in loading, firing, and recovering torpedoes. Living in the barracks while in port kept Lance away from downtown San Diego for the moment. Lance needed a car. Having enough leave built up, he took a week off and went to Vegas where he still had contacts. A week in Vegas he found a cherry 1966 Bel Air V-8 two-door coupe with chrome reverse wheels and four speed close ratio transmission. He bought it from a dealer who was going out of business, and it was the last car he had left. The price was right; the car was cool. Lance bought insurance and was on his way back to San Diego.

He had been lucky by starting out by getting a boat in the yard. He was able to complete all his system drawings for qualifying by actually seeing them uncovered. At home in San Diego, he qualified as topside watch. Crazy rule. He carried two clips of ammo for the 45-topside pistol in the belt. None in the weapon. Lance knew this was nuts, so he always carried the weapon locked and loaded. Working in the torpedo gang, he made it to seaman rank. His boss, a first class, hollered at him often to get a knife and stop borrowing his. Final warning, he told Lance on Friday. "If you show up on Monday without a knife, your liberty will be canceled." No problem. Lance and some fellow sailors went to Tijuana, Mexico. Lance bought a nifty eight-inch switchblade. On Monday, when his first class called him on it, Lance popped open the switchblade. His boss was not happy with it, but it did qualify as a knife. A few choice sailor words passed from his lips, but Lance was immune to this navy talk by now. He knew enough not to carry the knife off base.

Opportunities often strike in life; decisions are made, and one lives with the consequences of the path they chose. Lance had at that time been the top scorer in his Navy entry exams. The executive officer pulled Lance aside and told him he was qualified to attend prep school for the Naval Academy. "Lance, you have two weeks to decide."

"I don't need two weeks or two minutes," replied Lance. "I will fulfill my enlistment, my obligation I signed on for. I do not wish to have a career in the Navy." At this point in life, all Lance wanted to do was have fun. This meant getting drunk and having sex. He did not want to spend his life living where someone else decided he should, moving him at a minute's notice and not being around for his kids when they did come along. Lance had enough faith in himself to say no. Years later he thought, *I passed up a chance for a free education at one of the premier educational institutions in the world. Perhaps turning down this opportunity was not the best of my decisions.*

# 21
# **A Virgin on the Beach**

A virgin on the beach. Lance, now nineteen years old, went to visit his aunt. She had remarried well and had a beautiful house on the beach in a well-known California town a short drive from San Diego. While swimming and surfing that day, Lance noticed a family with an alluring teenage daughter. She was a dazzling California girl. Blond hair, blue-green eyes, and at the cross point of girl-to-woman body. Lance of course could not help but notice her eyeing him. He did not respond to her sly looks as she was young with her parents, and he was a guest. It was a fun day at the beach, sun, swimming, and barbecue. Add in a few beers. Lance was in his boxer shorts and lying in bed that night when he heard a scratching at his door around midnight. Lance got up and opened the door. This nubile temptress waltzed in past Lance, pulled him up to her, and kissed him while guiding his hand to her firm young breasts. She was wearing a transparent peignoir showing all her tempting treasures. Due to the small size of the room, they fell upon the bed. Lance reached down between her legs and touched her Venus mound of hair soft and caressable. Like Sisyphus, Lance pushed this young lady up and from him. It certainly was not for lack of desire on his part. Lance figured she was probably fifteen. She was so innocent, and he felt it would be a crime both literally and figuratively for proceeding any further. She deserved to find the right young man to share this once-in-a-lifetime-and-then-it-is-gone experience. He quickly dressed, put his arm around her, and escorted the young temptress to her parents' beach house. Lance now slapped his right hand against his head and said, "Thanks, brain."

Lance was moving up in the navy world. He now qualified in subs earning his dolphins. He made third class petty officer. He got together with two other single buddies, Jeff and Tom. They rented a house on the beach, an old white stucco one-bedroom, one-bath with a living room and kitchen house. Cheap and furnished of course. Working three different duty sections, only two of them were off at any given time. One of them slept on the bed or on the couch. For party decorations, Lance went to the x-ray technician on the tender, trading a box of sticky buns (jelly doughnuts) for an x-ray of Lance giving the finger. He put it on a lighted glass. For parties, a lit-up middle finger skeleton flipping the bird.

A creaky old house with double hung windows, everything three young sailors need. A place to keep booze and beer cold. A place to shower, pee, and sleep. A bed and a couch to make love or sleep on, preferably the first. Let the parties begin. Every payday they pooled their money, went to Tijuana, and stocked up on booze. By the end of the month, they were broke and drinking cheap wine by the gallon. Two other boat sailors rented an apartment in a four-apartment complex three blocks away on the beach. A short walk even for a drunken sailor. One night Tom came crawling up to the front window and knocked on it. Lance slid the window up, and Tom crawled in. Worried, Lance queried him, "Tom, why are you crawling?"

"I forgot how to walk," he responded.

Lance helped his drunken shipmate to bed to sleep it off.

Wine socials were common occurrence. A pint of vanilla ice cream placed in a glass Pyrex bowl. Fill the bowel with a high-class red burgundy, $1.49 a gallon, with a screw on top. Voilà, a wine float—eat, drink, and have fun. The girls went to them. Lance was now on fire. Since the age of fourteen, he took more orders from the head of his penis than the head on his shoulders. Sometimes in the background these hot, smoldering embers suddenly burst into a full-blown conflagration. Lance was coming in to his own. Getting drunk and getting laid became second nature to him.

Young girls and sailors, who would have guessed. Two girls, Shannon and Denise, moved to San Diego from Washington State. They rented an apartment on the beach next to two of the boat sailors. Soon they were part of the posse, a growing collection of drinking, partying, and enjoying being young group. One night they had a wine social. Six of them grabbed their glass Pyrex bowls, and soon all were mellow. This night the conversation turned to pierced ears. "Simple," said the girls. We have done our own," they bragged.

By now, copious wine consumption had taken place. Shannon said, "Lance, let me pierce your left ear."

"Will it hurt?" asked Lance.

"No, Lance, we will freeze it with an ice cube and then pierce it with a needle."

"Okay, let's do it," replied Lance with gusto.

Denise proceeded to hold an ice cube to the back of his left ear lobe. Shannon showed up with a sail needle. Lance was sure it was sixteen-gauge thickness. Shannon opened her blouse popping out her large and firm tits and told Lance hold on to these two beauties. While his attention was drawn to her boobs, the needle went through. Due to either lust or wine, Lance never felt a thing. Attached to the needle was a string with knots in it. Denise tied the string ends together forming a circle. She sterilized it with alcohol. "Lance, you must pull the string back and forth through the hole for it to remain open and make this successful."

It was not long before Denise was puking in the bathtub, Lance was puking in the toilet, and Shannon was puking in the sink. A good time was had by all, maybe. Lance awoke having slept on the floor next to the couch. Yes, his left ear hurt. The six survivors went out for a hearty breakfast of pancakes, eggs, and bacon. After all, their stomachs had been emptied the night before; it's good to be young.

"Happy Sunday, Lance. We are going to remove the string and put in an earring. You must keep it in and turn it often so the hole does not close and heal."

Now it hurt so bad Lance would have confessed to any crime. Shannon took manicure scissors, cut the string, and pulled it. Lance screamed in pain. Denise now put a metal post stud earring through the hole and the clip on the back. "Lance, even though it is painful, you must keep this in your ear." Lance went home to his rental house, looked in the mirror. Looking good, thought Lance, admiring his new earring. Lance spent the rest of the day drinking Bloody Marys.

Lance was currently in torpedo school, and typical of surface fleet sailors, they were pretty chicken shit. Lance had the first gate watch, and as soon as the duty officer saw him, he told him to remove the earring. Apparently, they did not want everyone coming through the front gate to see him in dress uniform with the earring. Lance stated, "I can't remove it. It is infected." Lance was immediately sent to sick bay. It was massively infected. Red and swollen, the earlobe was three times its normal size. The corpsmen cut the earring and removed it. He cleaned up the earlobe, treated it for infection, and bandaged it. The school sent a report to Lance's sub. His weapons officer sat down with Lance and delivered the required ass-chewing. Fortunately, by this time, Lance had more ass than he had teeth.

It was Lance's boats turn to be the visiting ship. This wonderful public relations duty meant the subs crew had to cover or lock up all top-secret equipment. Field day everything to white glove clean and shipshape. Even though visitors were recommended wearing casual attire and no skirts, Lance often had the rewarding view of woman entering the submarine via the ten-foot vertical ladder in the forward torpedo room wearing a skirt often a rewarding view. His job as a torpedo man was to guide civilian guests down the ladder entering the forward torpedo room. As the member of the ship's company in charge at the scene, Lance explained his role and answered questions. An interesting variety of people showed up curious about subs. Some were so large they had difficulty navigating the ladder and the watertight doors. Some got halfway down the ladder, panicked, and froze in place.

The boat was diesel electric still in service from World War II. There were two battery compartments, one forward and one aft. Part of the electrician's job was to perform maintenance including dropping down into the lead acid battery compartments. Due to these requirements, electricians were given a clothing allowance as their work uniforms were eaten up by acid.

The chief electrician was bullshitting with Lance in the forward torpedo room. A family including a wife, father, and young son came down the ladder. The brilliant eight-year-old son looked down on the chief's shoes. Their exposure to the battery acid had taken its toll. His shoes were crinkled and a strange multicolored brown. The stitching was giving way, and the shoe tops were curled up away from the soles. As typical of kids, the boy shouted out, "Hey, look at the funny shoes!" That was it. The chief had a new moniker. From that day forward, he was called Chief Funny Shoes.

## 22
# Desert Flowers

One special weekend, a married sailor's wife from Utah set up a blind date for Lance and Tom with two BYU students down visiting for the weekend. Lance, having lived in Vegas, was familiar with Mormon girls. They did not smoke, did not drink. All other sins were negotiable. The four of them jumped in Tom's car and went to Tijuana. They toured the bars entering several. They saw Juicy Lucy's performance, the strippers, prostitutes, and floor shows. They both had a few alcoholic drinks. Back to the house, Tom took his date into the bedroom, and Lance and date sat on the couch. Lance's date Rebecca's nipples were taught, piercing her silk V-necked top. With heartbeat fluttering and a crimson red blush, she announced, "Lance, after I graduate, I might grow up and rule the world, but in college, I am a Mormon virgin." Lance laid her back on the couch placing his hand under her skirt feeling her panties. They were soaked. She was more than ready. Lance yanked her plain white cotton panties crotch aside and began sucking on her clit. She was becoming overwhelmed as he slide his tongue in and out of her pussy lips. Thrashing, moving, shaking, suddenly pushing forward, she stiffened, and the shuddering stopped as she screamed, "I love it!"

Now Lance and Rebecca were momentarily silent and heard from the bedroom her friend gasping, "Oh god, Tom, oh god, yes, fuck me harder!"

A big smile covered Lance and Rebecca's faces. Lance said, "Now, let's get serious and make love." Both stood up and began undressing each other. Lance pulled her to him and gave her a big hug, at the same time unzipping her skirt in the back. She pulled his shirt over his upraised arms. Lance deftly removed her top exposing her firm young breasts and hard nipples looking straight up. Rebecca stepped out of her panties as Lance dropped his jeans. He was not in the habit of wearing skivvies, and his cock was hard and showing off.

Rebecca gasped, "I did not know it could be so big."

Lance promised it would not only fit but bring great pleasure. "I will lie down, and you can get on top and guide it in slowly, taking only as much of me as you feel comfortable with." Lance lay on the couch, and she cautiously took his big cock sliding it into her already dripping wet pussy. As she took in all of Lance, he began massaging her clit. Her turn to scream, and she did loud enough for the neighbors to hear. At 10:00 a.m. on Sunday, the four of them were all fucked out. Lance and Tom walked them to their car and said goodbye. She returned to San Diego the next weekend, but Lance had duty. He was sure she found another sailor. Lance's feelings on sex and love were simple. Lance did not mix the two of them early on and held love to a higher standard. He was ready, willing, and able to have sex anytime, anyplace, anywhere with love thoughts never crossing his mind.

Often young horny sailors went to Tijuana. Lance and his buddies were no different. No drinking age, many bars and shows and working girls aplenty. Lance and Larry went often. It seemed the drinking and dirty shows also turned on the woman. One unusual evening, six of them jumped in the car, three girls and three guys. The girls said, "How about us?" A night of drinking, dancing, and grab ass. While returning to the US at the San Ysidro border, they were waiting in line in the car. Normally the crossing guard asked each individual where you were from. US, all responded. Drive on back to San Diego. This was obvious and happened all evening. Not this time. Shannon, sitting in the back, became a smartass, piped up, and shouted, "Ensenada!"

The cop said, "Pull over there, and everyone out of the car."

All six had to go into the station and show proper identification. In the left corner sat a jail cell probably eight-by-twelve wide, and floor to ceiling, the bars were twenty feet high. Walking back to the car, Tom shouted out, "Hey, Lance, look at what I've got!" He had picked up a California cop's helmet and was bringing it to the car. When the duty cop standing there to inspect cars saw him, he ran and picked up Tom, lifting his feet off the ground. With Tom looking like a bobblehead in one hand and the stolen helmet in the other, he tossed him into the cell and locked it. Our group went home one person short. Lance would never forget the look on Tom's face. The five of them were in the "holy shit, I don't know why he did that" state. He made one mighty angry cop strong enough to carry him off the ground in one hand, the helmet in the other, and slam his body into the cell. Not your normal Saturday night.

One Saturday night on the Tijuana trip with Jeff, they latched on to a hooker named Alejandra. They went to her room for drinking and three-way sex. The three of them hit it off and became friends. They were young and horny, and all enjoyed the experience, learning new tricks and ways to have fun. She drove a new Corvette and spent a weekend with Lance in Catalina. For a short period, the three of them had happy times. Life moved on, and so did the trio. Lance, a year and a half later, married. Silly, three people speaking two different languages while fucking, sucking, and laughing. A special moment in international relations. Imagine the surprise when Lance got a beautiful gold Christmas card from her at home. There was some explaining to the new wife.

# 23
# Northern Run

The sub headed north for practice war games with the Canadian navy. First stop Seattle for two days. Of course, it was raining. Then underway to the next stop, a small logging town in Washington. The boat tied up to the pier around noon. Lance and Larry walked to town. Halfway there the local shore patrol took them back to the sub. The shore patrol didn't like their rolled sailor hats. The duty officer told them to piss off and leave his crew alone. The crew was in town for the weekend. On the way back to town, they grabbed a bottle of Ripple wine at a convenience market. First stop, they hit the local bar in a hotel. It was Friday afternoon. The local crowd consisted of lumberjacks and their wives and girlfriends. They were less than pleased to have a sub crew show up and take over the bar. Some drinking and fighting ensued. Lance hooked up with a woman named Carol who lived in the hotel. They slipped upstairs to her room where they spent most of the weekend. She was ready and pleasantly surprised. Not only had she found a well-endowed young sailor but, after a week at sea, sexually ready to wear her out. Saturday morning Larry the radioman showed up with Carol's girlfriend dragging her husband along. Larry was trying to get her husband drunk enough to pass out so he could get her into bed. He was successful, halfway. Her husband got drunk and passed out. Problem was, so did Larry. Lance and his lady spent that Saturday ordering room service and sharing great sex. They said goodbye. She, well-satiated and worn-out. Lance was ready to move on.

Sunday night was all hands-on liberty at the bar with locals. The duty shore patrol took off his armband, billy club, and belt. In one swift motion, he laid them on the bar then punched the biggest logger that was in the bar. Pandemonium broke out. Lance wisely slipped out the back door and went to another club.

There Lance met and got to drinking and dancing with Peggy Sweet, a young attractive woman he sat next to at the bar. They danced, drank, and really enjoyed each other's company. She had two kids. Her husband was in the Coast Guard, and when push came to shove, she was not ready to cheat. Sitting in the back seat of her car, Lance, always the gentleman, gave her a big passionate kiss. He told her perhaps it was not meant to be, but thanks for sharing that wonderful evening. Lance went back and crashed on the boat. Lance was a gentleman at heart and always tried to speak with kind consideration.

With the operations with the Canadian navy over, the boat headed for home port San Diego. The fog was thick, eerie, and totally encompassing as they stopped in Monterey, California. Slowly the boat moved into the pier. After they tied up and liberty went down, Lance had belowdecks watch. He went up on deck to visit with the topside watch. While talking and complaining that they had wound up with duty, a sea lion quietly slid alongside the sub and suddenly bellowed out a most scary growling sound. They both jumped. After a while, they got used to it; the beaches and rocks were covered with sea lions.

At 0800 hours, the duty section was relieved. Lance, Jeff, and Tom now headed for town. They spent money like they were drunken sailors. Experienced at that, yes, they were. They were going from one bar to the next. Lance got carried away with the rum and started falling asleep at the bar. News flash, Lance was informed that it was against the city law to fall asleep at the bar, and the cops would arrest him for this major infraction. At closing time, they found an empty Greyhound bus, opened the door, and slept for about four hours. Tired, hungover, the three went to a restaurant for breakfast. Observing their disheveled appearance, one of the customers told them, "I am glad we are not at war today." When it came time to pay, they were told the stranger had generously taken care of their bill. Lance never forgot this thoughtfulness and, in the future, paid for other military members. Paying it forward is a good way to live your life.

## 24
# Northern Run Encore

Underway for another northern run, this time back into the straights of *Juan de Fuca*. This time the boat first blessed Canada by tying up in Vancouver. The minute the topside phone was hooked up, it started ringing. No shortage of Canadian girls looking for a date. Lance had duty that night. The next night into town they hit bar after bar, drinking and acting like sailors. Lance and Chief Funny Shoes walked into a bar full of British sailors. The chief hollered out, "The Queen sucks the Piccadilly Circus." Lance had no clue why he said that, but it seemed every limey sailor left their barstool and started swinging. Lance held his own with a few bruises. The chief got a black eye. The local cops were quick to separate the groups and sent Lance and the chief on their way. Lance went left, and the chief went right. Lance knew when to walk away. Lance was looking for romance, not refighting the American Revolution.

A small local bar drew Lance in. He loved talking to people. One person got to gabbing with him and offered to sell Lance a suit for only $20 American. Sounded like a hell of a deal to a sailor full of alcohol. Lance and the Canadian went to his apartment. A few more drinks and the suit appeared wrapped in dry cleaner's plastic cover. The exchange took place, twenty dollars American money for suit. The Canadian said good night, eased Lance out of the door without the suit. Lance knocked, beat on the door, and hollered to no avail. Lance went out to the street and found a beat cop. Even with Lance being drunk, the police officer took pity. He escorted Lance back to the apartment, retrieved the suit, and got Lance a ride back to the boat. Happy, happy Lance drifted off to sleep thrilled about his wonderful purchase. Morning came early. Most of the boat's crew were laughing. Hanging on Lance's rack in the forward torpedo room for everyone to see, and they did, was a zoot suit from the 1940s. Having duty, Lance stayed aboard the rest of the weekend. A week of playing war games with the Canadians again. Lance had risen to third class petty officer and knew his job well. When sober, he performed his job at the highest level. When ashore drinking, he partied at the highest level, and yes, he was the only one on board with a zoot suit.

Friday the boat sailed back up the straights of Juan de Fuca to the small Washington town again. The liberty section had rented the ballroom at the hotel for the weekend. Lance, Larry, and several others also rented hotel rooms, sure they would need them after the last visit. Lance began by calling up one of the girls, Denise, he had known from the apartment in San Diego. She was a friend, a platonic relationship. It was his duty to contact her and say, "Hello, how are you?" A short how-you-doing visit, and she left.

Lance showered, dressed, and went down to the hotel bar. Big time surprise, Peggy Sweet was there with a girlfriend named Wendy. Lance and Larry joined them at a table in the lounge. Peggy had read in the local paper of the sub's return visit to her small town. After several cocktails, Larry and Wendy had disappeared. Lance and Peggy took the elevator to their floor. As they exited the elevator, Peggy immediately said, "They are doing their own thing. Let's just go to your room." Now Peggy was more than ready. Kissing and hugging, Lance opened the door, guided her as she walked backward to the bed. Laying her down, he grabbed hold of her panties as she raised her butt to help them slip off. Lance had developed a weakness for married women. They tended to let their pubic hair grow wild. She was growing the national forest, and Lance buried his face in the glorious black hairy beauty. Peggy came as she had never before. Peggy said, "Now it's my turn to satisfy you." She took Lance's dick in her hand and started stroking. It rose to full size almost immediately. Peggy now took the head into her mouth. Lance now appreciated her long graceful fingers. She kept stroking with her hand matching her up-and-down motion with her mouth. Her other hand found Lance's scrotum and began massaging his balls. As Lance came, she slipped a finger up his butt massaging his prostrate. Lance now had an explosive orgasm. Peggy swallowed most of his cum with a little gagging. Lance was in a state of euphoria. Peggy laid back in Lance's arms and purred. One of the benefits of being at sea for a week left Lance sexually charged up. Peggy now whispered in his ear, "The oral sex was wonderful. Now I want you to fuck me with that great, big dick, and I am getting on top. I have dreamed and fantasized about this since we met." Several more hours of romance and she had to be home; her babysitter only worked until midnight. She dragged Lance home with her. Lance sat on the couch while she changed. Kids were asleep. She crawled up next to Lance moaning, "Once more, once more, please." She said, "Mmmn, mmmmm, making love to you is better and more addictive than chocolate." She was so hot she got a bucket of ice from the kitchen. Lance took the cubes and gleefully played with her body. Lance was ready and happy to oblige. She lay next to Lance on the couch and put his arm around her as he entered from behind. As they rapidly approached orgasm, the phone rang. She answered. It was her friend that got hooked up with Larry. Peggy told Wendy that her sex life was much more exciting now than with her husband. Lance was ready and happy to oblige.

With Sunday left and getting underway at 5:00 a.m. Monday to play war games with the Canadians was one last day of liberty. The liberty crew all got shitfaced. Larry and Lance crashed at someone's house. Both were lying down on the couches when a young lady came home. A few persuasive words from Lance and he joined her in bed. Hot wonderful sex ensued for hours. She said it was great and they should get on again in the morning. Of course, this resulted only a couple of hours' sleep and then panic making it back to the sub on time and getting underway. Before leaving, he kissed her forehead, and she became another fine memory.

As the sub left and sailed through the straights of Juan de Fuca *heading out to the Pacific Ocean, the* sub's right screw hit a half-hidden waterlogged tree. This bent the screw, and it had to be replaced. A submarine cannot run silent with a bent screw causing cavitations.

This forced a surprise visit to San Francisco to have divers replace it. Drinking until the bars closed, a large part of the liberty crew went on to drinking at an after-hours club. They were carrying a zero float, as sub sailors were prone to call it. One of the fine ladies was showing off how she had more tattoos than the chief of the boat. The tattoos covering her arms looked like a comic book. Larry was hitting on a black chick, Kinesha. Lance was watching and enjoying the self-indulgent game playing. She was hot enough to win a beauty contest. She invited both Larry and Lance to her apartment. They picked up two bottles of wine and walked to her apartment several blocks away. She set out three hand-spun crystal glasses filling them with red wine and excused herself. Ten minutes later she came out from her bedroom wearing a see-through nightgown and a thong, her face royal-looking, eyes like a cat. At five feet ten inches, she was one tall beautiful woman. Her skin was perfect, the color of chocolate milk, and perfect from head to toe no wrinkles and no blemishes. As the three settled down, she let it be known she was available for sex for a price.

Larry always had a pocket full of cash, and they quickly disappeared into her bedroom. Lance was sitting on the couch sipping his wine. Larry came out of her room with a grin from ear to ear lighting up his handsome Norwegian face. "Lance, now it's your turn."

"Larry, I'm broke, and I really don't like paying."

"Lance, I will lend you the money, and it is damn well worth it."

Cash in hand, Lance went into her room, set the money on the nightstand, paused, and took in her movie-star good looks. As Lance removed his clothes, it was her turn to gasp. Now she got to admire Lance's well-endowed member and perfect physique. She moaned sweetly as she took his member in her mouth and brought him to the edge of orgasm. She stopped and said turnabout was fair play. Lance gladly went down on her bringing his years of experience into play. She tasted sweeter than a DQ Blizzard. He now brought her to the edge of orgasm. They became entwined in lovemaking as she screamed with pleasure while digging in and scratching Lance's back. They laid back and caught their breath. "My mother is coming over this morning, so you two will have to get out of here." As Lance finished dressing, Kinesha stated the sex was as good as she had ever had, and she would not take money for a session as satisfying as that. She handed Lance his cash and kissed him goodbye.

As the duo headed back to the boat, Larry said, "Lance, what the hell happened in there?"

Lance merely smiled and repaid Larry his loan. The boat returned to home port in San Diego. Time for running weekly operations.

## 25
# Back to San Diego

Lynn's breasts entered the room, then her body followed. She had a centerfold body that didn't need airbrushing. Lance saw her and wept. *How do I get there?* thinking he would need something different for sure. Lance believed this would occur serendipitously. She, of course, was aware of the impression she made. Two mounds way up large and proud with protruding nipples that would fill a three-fourth-inch socket.

Once again life opened the opportunity. Lance had to remain in port for a week of training. The sub put out to sea for the week with her husband one of the subs electricians aboard. Maybe this blond, blue-eyed beauty with her pair of the most gorgeous and alluring breasts might need some company. Her breasts begged to Lance; he wondered how to get to this neighbor. Opportunity came as a message from Aphrodite. Lynn called Lance asking him to come over, bring a bottle of wine and some playing cards. He was at her house at 8:30 p.m. She had her kids in bed asleep. A deck of cards a bottle of wine and a game of strip poker began. Lance was of course cheating using sleight of hand card tricks he had learned in Vegas. Lance was down to his jeans and shoes; Lynn was down to her panties and bra. She lost the next card and was in the process of removing her bra. She reached back, unsnapped, and ah, heaven, as they fell freely into Lance's view. Feeling her good vibrations, they were everything Lance had imagined and more. Timing in life is everything, and this night was no different. It's not just about being in the right place at the wrong time but knowing what to do when you find yourself there. Just when the goal was within reach, at that exact moment, Lynn's husband, Clarence, walked through the front door. He had the face of a pit bull. What would you do?

There had been a fire on the sub, and the boat had returned to port for emergency repairs. Suddenly Lynn was now putting her bra back on. There were two glasses of wine, a deck of cards on the coffee table, and piles of clothes lying on the floor. Lance stood up, looked at Clarence, excused himself picking up his shirt and shoes, and left carrying them and walking out the front door. Never another word from Clarence. Lance never saw her again, but that beautiful sight was burned into his memory banks.

Larry went home to Minnesota on leave. He met, married, and came back to San Diego with a wife. By his own word, she was a player. One night Larry and the new Mrs. Debbie came by the house picking up Lance. The three of them split a gallon of wine and went to Jack in the Box to eat. Sitting in the parking lot, Debbie turned around smiling with a Cheshire grin and told Lance, "Let's take your pants off." Fearless Lance decided to go along to see what her game was. Placing his feet onto the front seat, she slid off his sandals. Lance undid his buckle and unbuttoned his jeans and wiggled his ass. Debbie grabbed his jeans at the leg bottoms and pulled removing his jeans. Larry and Debbie, sitting on the front seat, laughed while she was holding his pants. As mentioned, some drinking had been involved. She now threw his pants into the parking lot. Lance got out to retrieve his pants. Larry locked the doors and started to honk the horn, both laughing at Lance. Lance calmly picked up his pants, held them over his head, and danced around the car. As he got around to Debbie's side of the car, he pulled his hard-on out and stuck it in her face at her closed window. Debbie just gasped and could not get over the size of his member.

Larry unlocked the doors and hollered, "Let's get out of here." Lance, pants in hand, jumped in the back, pulled up his pants. Everyone was laughing, but none louder than Lance. He had used this opportunity knowing it would pay off. Once a woman had seen his monster-sized dick, it usually led to some real good sex.

Larry was in a different duty section than Lance. Debbie was easily bored and a restless spirit. She called Lance and said, "Larry has the duty this weekend, and I don't want to spend it alone." After the car-pants-down night, Debbie was now more than curious. Debbie informed Lance, "I saw your monster at my car window and got your message. This time I want to be alone with you while removing your pants and not be interrupted."

Lance bought two bottles of wine and grabbed a bottle of his scented body lotion. That night was as dark as a newly polished hearse as Lance drove to her apartment. Lance dressed in white shorts, no skivvies, a pullover shirt, and sandals. Debbie answered the door in a see-through teddy. The view was alluring. Debbie put the two bottles up. She had already poured two glasses; they were sitting on the coffee table. She now jumped onto Lance, one arm around his back, the other hand unzipping his shorts. They slid quickly to the floor. Walking backward, she dragged Lance to the couch. Debbie sat down. "I am glad you showed this to me. You're a big tease. How sure were you I would call you after seeing that imposing love muscle of yours?" She now grabbed Lance by the cock sticking the monstrous head into her mouth. With one hand, she stroked his shaft, the other hand massaging the boys. Slowly she fingered his asshole. Grabbing a finger full of Vaseline sitting on the end table, she slid a finger up Lance's ass teasing his prostrate. There was a steady coordination of motions, taking as much of Lance's erection as would fit in her dainty little mouth. Lance came in such a huge explosion he thought he would blow her head off or at least gag her. She took and swallowed every drop. "Lance." She smiled. "I wanted to get that out of the way. Now we have all weekend to play. You are not leaving my apartment until Sunday night."

Lance responded, "I am at your service, Debbie."

She dropped her teddy and took Lance's hands. "Let's take a shower."

Lance was astounded at how well-proportioned she looked. He took the shower head on a hose and put it on pulse. Soap on a rope, he washed every part of her body from her hair to her feet. When he had all her nerves tingling, he put the shower head on her clit. Debbie came almost immediately collapsing in his arms. Toweling each other off, they headed back to the living room, Lance already hard again and dripping. He bent Debbie over the couch and slid his big cock into her and did her doggie style. When he was finished, they took a seat, caught their breath, and ordered a pepperoni pizza. When the doorbell rang, Debbie said, "Watch this reaction. I love to do it." She opened the door totally naked, had the pizza delivery guy come in. Lance, still naked, stood up, handed him a ten, and said, "Keep the change." Both giggling like kids, they each consumed several pieces of pizza washing it down with lavish amounts of red wine. Full tummies they went to bed, cuddled up, and fell asleep. They had burned a lot of energy.

Lance awoke to the smell of scented candles, sweet intoxicating vanilla, one candle on each nightstand. Debbie handed him a bottle of scented massage oil. Lance knew what to do and proceeded to give her a total body massage from head to toe, front and back, until she was putty in his hands. When he rolled her over on her back, she had shaved her pubes. Lance loved the look. Freshly shaved when he went down on her, no stubble. Debbie grabbed Lance by the hair, pulled him up, grabbed his cock, and inserted it. She was ready. Suddenly she hollered stop. Debbie slid out from underneath, rolled Lance over, and mounted him sliding on top. Slowly she lowered herself taking in all of Lance. She began pumping using Lance's unbelievable size to work herself into a massive series of orgasms. Her whole body was jerking and shuddering. When they both had come, she collapsed and fell asleep on top of Lance.

Lance woke up Sunday morning to the smell of coffee, bacon, and eggs. "I think we will skip church," she joked. They watched the news. Debbie now handed Lance a tube of KY jelly. She got on all fours and said, "Lance, fuck me in the ass with that magnificent rod of pleasure." The fit was tight, but she took all of it as Lance unmercifully pounded away. First Debbie and then Lance had overwhelming orgasms. "Lance, it is Sunday, and I should go visit my husband. Thanks for the memorable weekend. I am satisfied, for now."

Lance slipped on his shorts and shirt and went home. After all, it was Sunday, day of rest.

# 26
# Meet Delilah

Lance dated a local girl from San Diego. Black hair, very average looking, would not have stood out in a crowd. She wore bright-colored clothes and had a friendly personality. They went to the beach, sat on the rocks watching the surf and a gorgeous sunset. Lance was always amazed at how the sound of the ocean seemed to recharge one's batteries. A fleeting moment of happiness. She possessed an honest value of self as many intelligent people do and was good company. What evolved, two people that ascertained they were not compatible without Myers-Briggs personality tests. They had a great meet and greet with enjoyable conversation. Two strong-minded Leos both needing to be in charge. Calling it an evening, both knew it would not happen again. Before Barbara left, she said, "Lance, I know the perfect girl for you," and gave him Delilah's phone number.

Saturday morning Lance dialed the number and introduced himself to Delilah. Barbara had told her, and she had been expecting his call. They set up a date for that evening. Little did Lance know he was about to meet his *Parthian arrow*. Getting her address, Lance agreed to pick her up that evening around four. Arriving on time, Lance rang the doorbell. A little tiny redhead answered the door. "I'm Delilah," she said.

Lance said, "Pleased to meet you." Here Lance has discovered a new redhead with a Barbie doll figure. She was wearing a simple floral dress that made her long fire-engine red hair sparkle. A sexy dress with the hem way above the knees, panty hose, and high-heel platform shoes. Lance took her hand, bowed kissing her hand, and said, "I am Lancelot, but my friends call me Lance." Did she blush? Lance could not tell due to her red hair and freckles, but she showed a smile indicating she liked it. "You look wonderful, but I guess Barbara didn't tell you. We are going to a beach party."

She poured Lance a glass of red wine and went into her bedroom to change. Moments later she reappeared dressed in jeans and a black blouse. Off to the party.

At his shipmate's apartment, he introduced her to all, his rowdy sailor friends and their assorted girlfriends, five couples, and two girls who lived down the street. They were sort of a little group, young singles drawn together. A night of drinking and dancing on the beach. A fire and some cheap wine. A good time was had by all.

Lance drove Delilah home, with a kiss good night on her porch and a date set up for next week when he got back from sea. Lance was thrilled with his newfound acquaintance. Wow, a nineteen-year-old redheaded beauty, hot, and fun to be with. The week at sea could not pass quick ' enough.

Lance swung by her house Saturday morning around eight. She lived with her dad, and he was gone for the weekend. She opened the door wearing a sheer white peignoir and smiled. Her bountiful breasts, 38 triple D, stood up firm yet bouncy points. Perhaps the smell of coffee overwhelmed the pheromones as Delilah poured each a cup. Delilah said, "Lance, sit, we must talk. We just met and don't really know each other. I graduated from high school last year. My boyfriend asked me to marry him at the prom. We drank a lot, rented a motel room, and I lost my virginity. We were in love. Monday morning on the way to work he was killed in a motorcycle accident. I can't promise you how, when, or if getting over it is possible. If you are interested, I am willing to share my life with you, not expecting any promises or future expectations. After Broderick's death, I'm into living for today. If I have a future, let it come. I am not looking for a serious long-term relationship."

Lance listened kindly without distracting her. He then told her about how he had died, and that somehow brought them closer together. Delilah stood up, all four feet ten inches, walked over to Lance, and put her arms around him giving him a big sweet kiss. Lance stood up, all six feet three inches, lifted her lovely ninety-five-pound body, and carried her to her bedroom. Delilah lifted her peignoir exposing her beautiful breasts.

Lance caressed each, tweaking the hard nipples and kissing and sucking on each. Delilah moaned as Lance removed his shirt. As his jeans and boxer shorts fell to the floor, Delilah cried out in panic. "Oh my god, it's way too huge." Lance sat her on the edge of the bed, dropped to his knees. As Lance kissed her knees one after the other, he slowly worked his lips and tongue along Delilah's freckle-covered legs, getting closer and closer to the promised land. Lace panties she must have worn just for him, and he was thrilled. Kissing and licking around the seam edge of her bright sunshine-yellow panties, as cute as they were, he artfully removed them in one swift well-practiced motion. Like a magician, they went from on to off. This was not his first rodeo. Her body now lay completely naked, and Lance was certainly not disappointed. She smelled so fresh if you were to close your eyes, you would have thought you were in a forest. It was as perfect as imagined, and the topper, her pubic hair was plentiful and perfectly matched the red coloring of the hair on her head, a true burning bush. Lance now slowly began touching her all over from her ears to her feet and everywhere in between. Kisses and licks with a probing tongue brought Delilah to climbing arousal. Although he was only twenty, he meticulously brought his lifetime of experience into play. Lance was not thinking with his brain at the moment, yet he realized and appreciated this moment taking place. Surely a gift from Venus. Lance had played musical instruments and knew the importance of practice. Slow and steady, they had the whole weekend.

The trap was set. A beautiful red mound of Venus and like a Venus flytrap, he was slowly being drawn in unaware of the danger ahead. Hearing her voice sounded like music. She emitted the most sensuous odor; close your eyes and you knew she was in the room. Much like an unsuspecting fly flitting around a Venus flytrap, Lance was young and foolish not recognizing the danger ahead. He did not recognize her siren call. She was to a pixel perfect. She even had a freckle shaped like a star just above her pubic hairline. Lance loved wine but was unfamiliar with Amontillado. For a trap to work, it must be unseen, unknown to the prey. Hide it, make it pretty, appealing, and smell good. All of that was in play. The air was thick with pheromones overwhelming their senses. All the two of them could do was follow Mother Nature's sublime orders.

Lance got up carefully and went to the bathroom. They were both naked. Delilah was sound asleep. Lance removed the covers, not awakening her. She had an aura of beauty radiating out. Lance sat down on her makeup chair. Looking at this angelic figure, he was so turned on he began stroking his member. Delilah awoke and shivered with delight. She had never seen a man masturbate before. Her hand went down to her private area and began stroking in unison with Lance. They both climaxed, smiled, cuddled up, and went back to sleep.

Over the weekend they played with their newly discovered sex toy, each other, and by Sunday, they had covered all areas—fellatio, cunnilingus, and sixty-nine, as turnabout is fair play. Sunday afternoon, back to the boat, getting underway Monday morning. Lance thought he was living a dream. He had found a beautiful girl who loved sex as much as him and matched his mammoth appetite. For the next three months, if Lance was off duty, he was with her. She kept him entertained and happy, and Lance was no longer on the prowl for sexual encounters. Every need she took care of, and some he had not even considered. Every weekend was like a honeymoon. He picked her up Friday night or Saturday morning, and they spent their time with their friends drinking, partying, or off in the bedroom or on the beach trying to wear out their sex organs. Delilah had a villainous side she kept well hidden by her sweet caring facade about everyone and everything. You truly don't know someone until you live with them. If you are on active duty in the military, you may not know your spouse because you do not live with her constantly unless you are on shore duty. And so it was with Lance and Delilah. Off to sea gone a week in port on most weekends.

Rapidly three months sped by. They did not fight over stupid things. Lance did not care how the toothpaste was removed from the tube or which direction the toilet paper was placed into the roller. He had been to too many countries where you had to carry your own. She did. A mutual decision was made. They went shopping for a wedding ring. Yes, Lance could see himself going home to her each night. Lance felt he had found his soul mate. One way in and no way out, she kept Lance returning, slowly controlling Lance mentally after sexually capturing him physically. Of course, Lance had doubts. He was getting all the sex he needed and then some. In this great age of enlightenment and great social freedom, why marriage, why monogamy? Having cuckolded many, Lance of course had doubts. Being a sailor, being gone to sea weeks, for months at a time increased his uncertainty. Yet at this time, society still expected people to get married before they were thirty. His parents were married; even his sister had gotten married. Lance and Delilah were a young couple caught in the pressure of the marriage trap. Lance was now looking for an exit strategy. They did buy the ring; they were engaged. Lance was now in a state of cognitive dissonance. He had given his word he would get married. Did she have cards she wasn't showing? Mentally he was sure he was not ready for that lifetime commitment. However, he had given his word, which was no small matter to him.

Underway on August 16, 1967, on the sub, Lance finally turned twenty-one. Woo-hoo. Now Lance could go to bars anywhere legally. On his birthday, the crew kept bringing him screwdrivers, powdered orange juice mixed with pure alcohol. He got lightheaded, drunk, puked, passed out in his rack, and missed his watch. His friend covered for him. The one big birthday he had looked forward to being happened while underway. No big party or celebration, gathering of friends, just drunk on the sub at sea. Underwhelming, to say the least. Life moved on, and nonchalantly, so did Lance.

## 27
# Get Away

He now had two new goals. One, to get transferred out of San Diego, save himself from the marriage trap. Two, go on a Mediterranean cruise. Lance volunteered for and signed the paperwork for a transfer to nuclear launch school in Dam Neck, Virginia. Lance's orders came in within ten days. *Goal number one achieved.* Some great goodbye sex and off to Virginia.

With fourteen days travel time, Lance called Janice at University of Tennessee. "Yes, wonderful," she giggled, "come pick me up." Lance packed his seabag and put on his civvies, got into his Oldsmobile, turned the keys, and headed for Tennessee. Driving straight through, he got there in thirty-eight hours. Janice drove from Knoxville to New York while Lance slept. First night they slept at her girlfriend's home, picking up where they had left off, great sex. This of course made Lance wonder. Here he had a gorgeous gal that turned heads wherever they went, a most pleasing personality, and he honestly could not think of a time she was cross with him or spoke disparagingly about anything. When she walked into the room, heads turned, and all eyes were on her. Why on earth was he engaged to another on the other side of the country?

With two days travel time remaining, they left New York and hit the road for Tennessee and then Virginia. *Bang, bang, bang.* The engine started knocking at the end of the Jersey Turnpike. Lucky Lance found a state technical school that taught automotive mechanics. They agreed to repair the car only charging for the parts. They found a blown piston skirt and agreed to repair it. Lance and Janice found a motel across the street. Nothing to do for two days but sex, sex, and more sex, occasionally taking a break for eating and sleeping. They were well practiced in the art of mutual satisfaction. Lance paid for the motel and $34.80 for the car parts. Janice decided to take a Greyhound to return to college. She did not want to ride the bus alone. Ever the gentleman, Lance bought a round-trip ticket for himself. On the bus heading through the Smoky Mountains, sunset arrived. Despite passing through some of the finest scenery in the world, Janice dragged Lance to the bus's backseat. It was roomy enough to stretch out, and they did. As they sat down, Janice pulled a blanket over the two of them. Everyone on the bus seemed to be sleeping. She kissed Lance and pulled his left hand under the covers. Imagine when he realized she had pulled down her panties and his hand landed on her hot, wet naked pussy. As Lance looked around at the sleeping passengers, she skillfully opened Lance's zipper, pulled out his prick, and started massaging. They matched each other stroke for stroke, her clit, his cock. Janice now whispered in his ear, "Fuck me, Lance, right here and right now. I need you." Keeping the blanket over the both of them, Lance laid down on top and easily slid in. They were both ready and came to mutual orgasm quickly. They sat up, cuddled up, and slept the rest of the way. Lance paid for her cab back to school, climbed on the bus, and took the lonely ride back to pick up his Oldsmobile.

Lance, still single, headed for Dam Neck, Virginia, and checked in at the gate. Three sides swamp and one side ocean, a perfect place not to be. Locating his assigned barracks and parking spot, he then immediately withdrew his volunteering for launch school. This threw the ball back in the Navy's court. Talk about a vacation, Lance had six weeks without a job, yet he still got paid. Square peg, round hole. Then it dawned on base navy personnel that Lance was getting a free ride. Here was Lance, a third-class petty officer qualified in submarines with no job. Due to the Vietnam War, there was a critical shortage of torpedomen qualified on subs. They were quite angry when he was called into the office.

Lance was handed a dream sheet. This was basically a form where you select five duty stations where you hope to be assigned to. Number one being most desirable, the one you really want. Dream assignment. Number five on the sheet being least desirable where you really do not want to go. Lance was catching on to the dysfunctional military bureaucracy. The staff at Dam Neck were less than pleased with him, and Lance astutely gambled by reversing the list and putting New London as number five as his last choice hoping that's where they, in anger, would send him. Within two hours, Lance had orders to a sub based in New London.

"Some days are diamond" (John Denver).

## *28*
# New London

Nine hundred miles to travel in four days. Lance knew he could do it in a less than a day. Seabag and civvies packed, he went back to New London. Lance stopped to visit his grandparents in New York for two days. On to the sub base in New London, Connecticut, checking in at the main gate, Lance was directed to report to his newly assigned sub. He climbed aboard, dropped his seabag into the forward torpedo room. He followed it down the ladder and was welcomed aboard having been expected as his orders had proceeded him. The first-class torpedoman asked if he would be interested in going on a Mediterranean cruise. The boat on the other side of the pier was scheduled to go to the Mediterranean. A third-class torpedoman aboard that boat was married and wanted to swap to stay home. Once again Lance was in the right place at the right time with the needed preparation. *Second goal met, woo-hoo.*

The Med trip was in April. Lance now went about becoming familiar with his new boat and crew including getting qualified for below-deck watch. Now began a routine of weekly deployments, usually training sub school officers. Underway Monday through Friday. Duty every three weeks. Lance used this time wisely reading classics and working out. The food was excellent, as was required in the sub service. In his locker at the barracks, he kept a jar of peanuts in case he came back drunk and starving. It was a short train ride to New York City. Occasionally Lance made that trip sitting in the club car drinking. Lance's life was quite simple now. Get to work in a clean uniform washed and ironed. Do your job professionally, study, and get promoted. When off the clock, get drunk and laid as often as possible. He was familiar with all the bars and restaurants catering to sub sailors in New London. The torpedo gang had six petty officer members and two strikers; all but one were single. Lance took the test and made second class sewing on the stripes with two years and five months of enlisting in the Navy. Party time. All the crew that made advancement rented a bar for the afternoon. Great quantities of booze were consumed.

Lance began running with a third-class torpedoman, Tim, who was as young and crazy as him. He also ran around with a second class who was even weirder; he was a lifer with money. He had inherited a Christmas tree farm, and each year he got a sizable check. One night the three of them were out drinking and partying. The second class was bitching about the car behind him with his bright lights on. Even with the snow and ice, it was distracting. At the next stop sign, Tim got out with a lug wrench, went to the car behind them, and knocked out the high-beam lights. At that moment, the police officer driving the car turned on his red lights. Backup arrived, and Lance's luck was still holding. The only one arrested was Tim for destroying public property.

## 29

# Springboard

The yearly springboard cruise included six weeks deployment to the Caribbean. Ports of call were Roosevelt Rhodes (Rosy), Ponce, San Juan, St. Thomas, and St. Croix. The boat arrived and was tied up to pier at Rosy 1400 Friday. Lance had duty. The crew's liberty section caught Publicos and went to get drunk and hopefully get laid. It was a sailor thing. Lance was getting quite good at it. Sitting at the end of the pier was an ordinary-looking soda machine and was thus ignored until 1800. Suddenly the crew broke out in an enthusiastic search for change all over the boat, searching every bunk bag. The machine was loaded with ice-cold beer. Success reached. The machine was soon emptied with the duty crew consuming every beer. A fun time was had by all. Saturday morning was spent loading exercise torpedoes and getting underway for practice exercises.

Final port on this operation was San Juan, Puerto Rico, 1600 hours tied up, and Lance and his cohorts headed ashore. Time for fun, spend all the money you have because you will be at sea until next payday. Being a sub sailor, you get underway knowing that the sea is always trying to kill you. Lance wounded up sitting in a bar drinking and bullshitting. A man walked in, and all the working girls jumped up, hollering, "El Toro, El Toro." He sat his butt on a stool next to Lance and said, "Howdy." He lived in America but owned a Kotex factory in Puerto Rico and visited there frequently on business. He loved talking and drinking. He was a writer, and they shared ideas in that area. He offered Lance some advice. "If you genuinely want to be a writer, do not get married." Lance, still young and foolish, did not heed those words of wisdom. Years later it clicked. El Toro left with several of the girls.

Moving on to another bar, Lance ran across other crew members and bar girls. Lance hooked up with one of the girls. They went upstairs and took care of business exchanging sex for money, a common transaction that had taken place in sea ports endlessly. When they returned to the bar, several shipmates asked, "How was it?"

In his loudest, drunken clown voice, Lance shouted for all to hear, "She was a lousy lay!"

Wow, big mistake. Out came her straight razor. With her first slash, Lance saw the reflection from the blade. Fear took over, adrenaline kicked in, and Lance moved out of range faster than a roadrunner. Lance was quickly learning the back streets while racing through old San Juan. Lance was an athlete and worked out every day. The additional adrenaline-induced fear speed allowed him to easily outrun her. When he was a safe distance away, he caught a cab back to the boat. The next night he went to the San Juan Hilton. He hit on a Canadian chick that night but no romance. It was a good run, met lots of friendly folks. Rum was eighty cents a bottle, and Lance hid two cases in the after-torpedo room tubes in front of an electronic torpedo. Good news, they did not go to war and waste the booze.

## 30
# Married

Even though Lance had gotten transferred across country, he, alas, was still engaged. Delilah sent love letters daily. She was even more enchanting on paper. So lovely. He took two weeks' leave and went back to San Diego. It seemed hundreds of women were involved in the wedding planning.

Surprise, she wanted to get married in a Catholic church. That meant they had to have lessons from a priest. In Lance's view, the priest had the puckered face of an old man whose dreams had failed. Some heated discussions took place as Lance enjoyed pushing his buttons. Finally, Lance went along to get along; after all, the church had been making rules for almost two thousand years. Lance of course knew the church had excommunicated Galileo and kept him under house arrest for the remainder of his life for proving the earth was not the center of the universe. Lance was a big fan of John Stewart Mills and Nietzsche. He understood the logic in Pascal's wager; however, formal religion was not his forte.

Even though Lance felt obligated and took the two weeks' leave, he went to San Diego to get married, but how close did he come? The preacher had Lance wait outside until called in to the altar. Had it not been a closed-in and fenced garden, Lance would have bolted, run for his freedom. Instead, he followed the wedding practice, said I do, and on to the wedding reception.

Somehow Lance had succumbed to the wedding madness that affected young people. Friends, new in-laws, and whomever the wedding planning women felt should have been invited were there. About half drunk, Lance and Delilah headed for Vegas where they met Lance's parents. Saying they were not impressed would be an understatement. The trip back to New London was the honeymoon. It was a wonderful time for getting to know each other. They rented their first apartment in Groton, Connecticut. Lance reported back to the boat. Tim, the third-class torpedoman, told Lance congratulations for recently making the rank of E-5. "After all, anyone can get married." Delilah had good qualities that showed as a girlfriend and fiancé. A veritable smorgasbord of bad qualities emerged after the nuptials. A husband and wife are strangers when they first marry, and they were no exception. Here was Lance plucked from the wild stream long before he was ready. She got a job, and they settled into married life. Did Lance now have his albatross?

# 31
# Mediterranean Cruise

Lance's sub now broke its normal routine for a Mediterranean cruise with the Sixth Fleet. This tour of duty took Lance's submarine away from home for four months. After a long and arduous trip of two weeks spent crossing the Atlantic, the boat tied up at Rota, Spain, sub base next to another visiting sub. The first visiting sub had already tied up to the dock. When Lance's sub arrived, it tied up outboard of that sub. With the two subs nestled together, this meant that for sailors from Lance's sub to get ashore, they had to first walk across the gangway or brow that went to the deck of Lance's sub to the deck of the other boat. Then they had to cross its deck to get to its brow from that sub's deck onto the pier. This was a normal docking situation. Crossing both decks and both brows, Lance went to the commissary. Lance bought a black acoustical guitar with dual electric pickups. With plenty of time at sea, Lance taught himself to play.

The base rules in Rota, Spain, were really simple. Visiting sub sailors were restricted to the base and had to remain in uniform. Lance and his new friend Jim broke that rule immediately. They borrowed civilian clothes from sub sailors stationed there and took a cab to town. Amazing things came as rewards. The first local bar had about a dozen stools. Four huge wooden wine barrels stuck through the back bar wall with wooden spigots. The price of a glass of wine was about five cents American. Mass consumption of the local vineyard's wines took place. Lance was now exposed to his first European squat toilet. He turned around facing away from the bar, and a woman was squatting and peeing. When she was done, Lance observed a small tiled-off area with a hole in the middle and two porcelain footprints. Timing is everything. The wine was filling his bladder. Lance stood over the hole and peed. Sweet relief.

Lance and Jim were now looking for another kind of relief. After two weeks at sea, they were horny. No problem; they were in a European naval town. They were directed to the red-light district. Lance picked an attractive-looking young lady. She obviously did not own a razor. The hair under her armpits was dark black and long enough to braid. Lance knew this because he had braided his sister's hair when she was young. Off to a tiny bedroom and she quickly was naked putting Lance's hand on her hot, moist clit. "Squeeze harder," she hollered. When she unbuttoned Lance's jeans, she gasped as she saw his third leg. She kissed it lovingly, drawing a vacuum on it. When Lance started dribbling pre cum, she fell back on the bed. She drew in all his giant member. Either she was an academy award actress, or she just really loved fucking him. A sweaty hug from this hooker and knowing they had Cinderella liberty and had to be back at the boat at midnight, the two made it back to the base.

They continued drinking on the base by heading to the Acey-Deucy Club, but not for long. Jim was a little skinny redheaded nineteen-year-old who probably weighed in at one hundred pounds. By this time, he was extremely intoxicated and trying to pick up a second-class petty officer's wife. A battle ensued, and both Lance and Jim were thrown out by the shore patrol. They changed back into their uniforms, keeping the civvies for future use. They caught the base shuttle back to their pier. It was a gray Navy suburban. Jim was sitting in the back seat with two other sailors. Lance was sitting on the right side of another sailor in the middle seat. Lance suddenly heard Jim screaming. He turned around to see him held by one sailor and beaten by the other sailor with his own shoe. Lance jumped into the battle to help his shipmate. The driver stopped and threw Lance and Jim out of the shuttle. Jim managed to get his shoe back on, and they walked the last couple of blocks to the boat.

Lance and Jim arrived at the pier. Now being the outboard sub became a major problem. From the pier, drunken Jim hollered out at the top of his lungs, "My buddy Lance and I can whip your entire crew." Like fire ants, the other sub's crew were across their brow and on the pier swinging. Lance had one hand tied up with the civilian clothes on a hanger slung over his shoulder when the first blow hit him in the face. Jim, the mouth that roared, caused a drunken brawl on the pier. Sailors from both subs joined in. Cooler heads finally prevailed. The parties were separated and went below to their bunks. The next morning as they got underway, Lance was in extreme pain due to a broken rib. Jim had a broken collarbone. Lance slowly got over the pain. The entire crew told him jokes, trying to get him to laugh as it was acutely painful.

Next stop: Thessalonica, Greece. As soon as liberty went down, Jim found Lance and said, "Let's hit the beach." Lance passed, still a little sore and a wee bit smarter. Three things occurred to Lance at liberty time in Thessalonica. Take cigarettes, they were better than money; toilet paper, it's hard to find; and stay away from Jim. At that time, toilet paper in Europe was rare. While Europeans do use toilet paper, toilets were not well stocked. Lance carried pocket-size tissue packs as apparently Mediterranean countries had wimpy plumbing. American cigarettes were more valuable than money. Even though he did not smoke, he stocked up stateside and bartered well with smokes both in Europe and Asia.

A day at the beach in Greece, a large group of the liberty crew jumped in a Greek military 6 × 6 cargo truck and off to the beaches. A beautiful white-sand beach and Mediterranean waves rolled in. Young boys were selling Michelob beer out of sacks filled with ice. A refreshment stand was selling local wine. Converted to Drachmas, it was about two cents for an eight-ounce glass. Needless to say, our truck driver was a member of the Greek army, and he never said no to a glass of wine. A very wonderful day was enjoyed soaking up sun on the beach and consuming many alcoholic drinks. When it became time to return one to the boat, one of the sailors had to take over the wheel as our assigned driver was too drunk to drive. Down the road, we sped. If there were speed limit signs, we were unaware of them. Pedal to the metal, the truck loaded with drunken sailors passed a Greek army convoy at high speed. As we blew past the general's lead car, two sailors were peeing over the back tailgate. A block before the base entry the assigned driver took over. The convoy had radioed ahead. As soon as we hit the base's gate, a party was ready for him, arresting him on the spot. His sober replacement drove the crew members back to the boat. Underway the next day were operations with the fleet.

Next port, Turkey. As the boat was preparing to tie up to the dock in Izmir, Turkey, a man with one leg jumped into the water and swam around the boat. As soon as the brow was placed ashore, he pulled himself up on the pier and was begging for money. Izmir is one of the oldest cities in the world. Lance was fascinated by the mix of old and new.

Before being allowed to go on liberty, the crew was mustered topside and informed that the laws were unusual there. If you take a cab and the cab has an accident, get out of there. The law says if you hadn't taken the cab, it would not have been there, and thus no accident would have taken place, so it is your fault.

Two blocks from the pier Lance discovered the agora or forum. This place in ancient times was used as both a political meeting place and shopping area. Great columns, porticos-colonnaded walkways for shoppers or listeners, stores with rounded arches and statues of Demeter and Poseidon made a great impact reminding Lance of the Roman times. These agora remains belonged to the Roman era built in AD 178 by Marcus Aurelius. It expanded again in Byzantine times. Today it is an important stop for tourists as one of the oldest markets in the world. Lance had a great time bartering for goodies. For two packs of cigarettes, he got a Turkish multicolored bathrobe. For four packs, a hookah. For twenty dollars cash, a five-carat alexandrite ring. As one of the oldest and largest markets in the world, it was like a huge garage sale. Lance loved to negotiate. He would later use these skills at auctions, car sales, job interviews, and of course, getting laid.

Monday morning Lance had to go to the US Air Force base to get pyrotechnics. The sub launched these flares to transmit information on maneuvering, colored smoke, a distress signal, or underwater countermeasures. They were like little torpedoes and had their own miniature launch tube in the after-torpedo room. Lance, as a second-class petty officer, was in charge of the after-torpedo room and responsible for the flares. Due to the unusual laws, the Navy had a Turkish driver pick Lance up in a blue half-ton Ford pickup. The driver introduced himself. "Hi, I am Mohamed, your driver." Off they went heading toward the base. Driving through the town of Izmir, the pickup hit a pedestrian walking across the street. Mohamed put on the parking brake, left the truck idling. He leaped out of the driver's side door leaving it open. Lance was now sitting on the front seat of a US Navy pickup idling in the middle of the street in Izmir, Turkey. The driver, Mohamed, and the pedestrian got into a major fistfight.

Fortunately for Lance, his driver quickly won the battle. Sliding back in the truck, Mohamed, with a big smirk showing all his teeth, wiped the blood off his face. Happily for Lance, the rest of the drive was uneventful. Flares were delivered to the boat, recorded, and stored in place. Lance was now ready for liberty.

Back on board, it was time for dinner. Mmm, lasagna. The cook made Lance not a plate but an entire platter for himself. Lance loved to eat but never gained a pound. He was often called the GDU, or garbage disposal unit, due to his enormous appetite. Back on the boat the word was spread about a place called the compound. Lance was told that by law, anyone that did not pay their bills or went bankrupt had the women in the house placed in the compound. They were required to provide sexual services for men until the debt was paid. Lance never did check this sea story out as he found the idea abhorrent.

Donald, the first-class quartermaster, asked Lance to go on liberty with him. First, they hit a club that featured belly dancers. The dancer was exceptionally talented and exotic. The beer came in a brown bottle, no label, was warm, and tasted gross. Lance suspected it might be camel piss. They left that club and found the Air Force club just in time for nickel hour. Every drink in the bar for a nickel for one hour. The Air Force guys ordered two beers. Lance and Don had the barkeep set up twenty shots of Jack Daniel's each. While enjoying that wonderful whiskey and looking out the window, they noticed a horse-drawn cart. A big flat wooden trailer with car wheels, the old nag that was pulling it suddenly just rolled over and died. Why or what caused this horse passing? Unknown! Within fifteen minutes, however, people had surrounded the dead horse and butchered it for the meat. After viewing this incident, Lance ate the rest of his meals in Turkey aboard the boat. A new and sudden admiration for health inspectors crossed his mind.

Another great bonus of docking in Izmir was its proximity to the ancient city of Ephesus. During the second century BC, Ephesus was the fourth largest city in the Eastern Roman Empire in what is today West Turkey. On a Navy-approved tour, a Toyota minivan showed up at the boat. A young lady, probably around twenty, was the tour guide. Driving the three miles, she was quite knowledgeable and an excellent tour guide. Speaking while driving historical facts were well filled in during the trip.

Lance got to see the House of Virgin Mary, the Church of Saint John, Temple of Artemis, and dating back to the first century CE, the Marble Road. This road made its way by the agora or open marketplace to the library, the second largest library in the Roman Empire.

What? A hidden brothel. On the Marble Road, within sight of the library, the guide pointed out a carving in the road; it was an ancient advertisement. Follow the road carvings to the brothel. It featured an image of a cross, a woman, a heart, a foot, a money purse, and a library, plus a hole dug into the rock. She interpreted the carving: "At the crossroads, on the left, you will find women whose love can be purchased. But only stop in if your foot is at least this big, young man, and you have enough coins to fill this hole."

Lance just smiled, thinking, the oldest profession. Also weird to Lance were the minarets scattered around the city learning that from these Islamic towers, five times each day there is a call to prayer. Lance asked the young girl guide, "Does everyone pray five times a day?"

She replied, "Only the old people," and they both shared a look, a knowing smile.

"Release number one line," and now underway to Palma de Mallorca, Europe's vacation playground. Lance had never seen so many hot topless young women. The four days spent there were like heaven. Had every port been as exciting as these five days, he would have stayed in the Navy. The local newspaper did a story on the visiting sub. Lance was the ship's photographer. They used Lance's photos in the story.

# 32
# Music?

Goal accomplished, Lance had gotten his Med cruise. All ahead full speed, the four-month Med cruise was over, set a heading for home port. Sub base Groton, Connecticut, tie up to the pier. Lance took a week's leave. Time to get reacquainted with Delilah.

Lance had an epiphany. *Lance, this is your chance to straighten out your life. You are married. Start acting like it.* Welcome-home sex, they tried to wear it out. Fantastic like a honeymoon all over again. Wow. Weekends were fun. Recovery with hugs and kissing time. Getting together with friends.

Buzz and his wife, Amelia, invited Lance and Delilah to dinner. Amelia played guitar and wanted to do a duet with Lance. Some fine home-cooked Italian food washed down with red wine and the conversation began to flow. Lance, as requested, brought his acoustic/electric guitar he had purchased in Rota, Spain. With his musical background he had with three months of practicing at sea, he was ready. His fingertips were hard and callused, and he had mastered some riffs, bar chords, and numerous folk and popular songs. After several glasses of wine came that moody, flushed feeling, and naturally the conversation turned to sex. Both wives had just spent the last four months at home as faithful marriage partners.

Buzz, in a moment of absolute non-brilliance, announced that he had fooled around with other women while in Europe while Lance had remained faithful. Lance was cool and verified this statement, remembering the English proverb "Children have not yet learned, and fools never did learn, that it is often advantageous to lie." Learning to forge your mother's signature in school or truth-shading, he was quite comfortable with the concept. Amelia handled the situation with class: "Buzz is my husband,

92

and I love him. We will work through this." With her next breath, she said, "Lance, you are getting really good on the guitar. I used to teach music and will gladly help you with lessons for free."

Lance gratefully thanked her and felt this was time to leave. She gave him the sly eye, and Lance walked away knowing. His wife, Delilah, on the way home, protecting her territory, said, "Guitar lessons, no way. She is trying to seduce you."

Monday, Delilah went to work at 9:00 a.m. Buzz, of course, was at work on the boat; he had used up all his leave on the cruise. Lance, home alone, had broken out his Murasaki katana and was daydreaming and masturbating. The front door to his one-bedroom apartment swung open, and there stood Amelia, guitar in hand and eyes as big as saucers. "Wow, Lance," she exclaimed, "your cock would make three of Buzz's."

"Amelia, we have four hours to play, and I am not talking about the guitar," said Lance, his hand still on his hard, wet dick. So much for his epiphany.

Amelia removed her blouse exposing her tits. Placing her blouse neatly over the back of a kitchen chair, she slid out of her white slacks folding them oh so perfectly crease on crease. What class. Amelia had let her black curly pubic hair grow wild, and it rolled out over both sides of her panties as she slipped them down. She smiled, walked over to Lance, and took as much of his manhood in her mouth as she could, holding his member with one hand and vigorously massaging his nuts with her other hand. Lance moaned with absolute pleasure as she swallowed most of his cum. "My turn," she exclaimed as she climbed over his face and pulled Lance up into her black hairy forest. Minutes later Amelia was panting, jerking, and screaming as she reached orgasm. Amelia now sat down next to Lance. "Lance, I was a virgin when I got married and truly believed Buzz would be my only lover. His amorous adventures on the Med cruise were selfish and hurtful. You have just started my mental recovery. Let's share a glass of wine and spend the afternoon fucking with that big dick of yours." They spent a dreamlike afternoon touching, teasing, and exploring each other's erogenous zones. At three forty-five, Amelia cleaned herself up in the bathroom, slid back into her perfectly unwrinkled clothes, and kissed Lance goodbye. They each moved on with their lives.

A week at sea and home for the weekend, a happy pattern began. Saturday and Sunday were parties and drinking mixed with plenty of sex. They both had voracious sexual appetites. Delilah was at the apartment or work during the week. This, of course, was based on trust. No phone calls or a drive-by while Lance was at sea at an undisclosed location. Lance was happy and looking forward to getting out and returning to civilian life. After all, they were just two kids trying to make their way in the world. Delilah, who was lacking in education, just finished high school. No salable skills. She had flunked out of Hanks's small engine and dental assistant college. Lance filed this knowledge for future what-ifs. Thanks to the Navy and the little time they spent together, life was having as much sex as possible while never really getting to know each other. Delilah had some magical, almost biblical, mystical power over him.

## 33

# Out of the Navy

Lance now cut the last link of his short timer's chain. He got out of the Navy while young and full of self-confidence. He was smart, good-looking, well-endowed, and had paid his patriotic dues. He loved to party, laugh, and talk. Lance was also aware that once you had served in the military, you are changed and will never be the same. Delilah, despite Lance's objections, insisted they move to San Diego.

In San Diego, Lance, with his bubbly personality, took a position as a new car salesman, training included. This gave him both income and a new car for a driver. One evening he was dragged out by Delilah to meet one of her old high school girlfriends. They went to meet her girlfriend, Diane, from high school and her husband, John. Introductions passed around. They sat by this huge ugly coffee table. This monstrosity was six feet long about three feet wide. It had multicolored paint pattern on top: red, yellow, blue, green, purple, and black. To Lance, it appeared as though someone had put four buckets of paint still in the cans on the center of the table and tossed a grenade into the middle. The colors exploded in a unique fashion not unlike Rorschach inkblot covering the entire top of the table.

After a second beer, her husband, John, asked, "Lance, what do you think of the coffee table?" This was his wife's "piece de resistance," the center of her living room and her family pride.

Lance responded frankly, as was his nature, "It's dog-assed ugly. I wouldn't have it in my bathroom."

John roared in laughter. Finally, someone that is honest. "I'm out of beer, Lance. Let's go get some." John and Lance left around nine and went barhopping. Drinking copious quantities of beer, Lance and John got blasted and somehow separated. John found Lance on the front seat of his Chevy with some Indian chick humping away. Lance finished, and home they went around 4:00 a.m.

As they walked through John's front door, his wife, Diane, all four-foot-six and eighty-five pounds, came running at her husband, John. She hit him under the chin; his back hit the wall. He folded and slid down the wall like Gumby, unconscious, out cold. Lance and his wife looked at each other. No words were spoken on the drive home. No, they were not invited back.

Backsliding, Lance was now becoming like Pavlov's dogs salivating at any new female prospect. After a fun day of selling cars, Lance stopped by a local bar he frequented on a regular basis. Two women were sitting there talking. Lance's first assessment, they were not barflies and looked out of place in that setting. The shorter lady glanced at Lance with that "I want to get laid" look. By now Lance was getting good at spotting that copulatory look. She was giving him the "I am interested" eye language. Women stared intently at potential mates for about two to three seconds; their pupils dilate. Lance, as a poker player, was adept at reading faces. This eye contact Lance correctly recognized. The look triggered the brain, stayed, and played or passed. Lance responded with a smile, bought the ladies another round. Lance knew the bartender and put it on his tab. He sat down at their table and introduced himself to Marcella and Connie. He raised his glass and proposed a toast he had heard at work. "Here's to lobster, tail, and beer, three of my favorite things." Marcella excused herself for a trip to the lady's room. Lance took this opportunity to tell Connie, "Let's meet and get a room at Hill Top Motel at ten in the morning tomorrow." She blushed, smiled, and gave Lance her phone number. Connie was thirty-one, married, and reasonably well-off financially.

The next morning, she called Lance, verified, and met him at the motel. When Lance showed up, she was sitting in her Mercedes coupe. She had already booked room 103 and handed Lance the key. "I have never done this before," said Connie as they stepped into the room. Closing the door, it was a typical cheap motel room, with a king size bed with a nightstand and lamp. Blackout curtains closed over the front window with the room air conditioner underneath. There was a television, a chair, and a mini desk loaded with coupons and maps for local attractions; a closet with six non-removable hangers; a Robert Woods seascape painting; a bathroom with sink, toilet and shower, six towels folded and stuffed into a stainless-steel rack, sample size shampoo, and soap. The only thing Lance was interested in was Connie. She stood five feet three inches, had average size breasts, and a good figure, just starting to show her age. Lance pulled her to him while kissing her and unzipping her dress. As it slid to the floor, Connie said, "I'm a little bit overweight," as she removed her girdle.

Lance smiled and told her how excited he was to be there with her. Lance kissed her, guiding her to the bed.

"Wow, you are so anxious," Connie said with a grin.

"Lie down, Connie, we are both going to enjoy this day," responded Lance.

She complied removing her bra. Lance was taken aback as she, like every woman he had known, lifted her butt so he could easily remove her plain white panties. Connie's eyes were closed, and she leaped in pleasant surprise as Lance went down on her. Now she saw Lance's love muscle and screeched, "It's so big." The first time was good for her, great for Lance. It seemed that each new lover, the first time was magical. She noticed his growing erection and said, "Wow, I am ready." She lay back naked, and Lance penetrated her, and both soon rocked to orgasm. A good fit. She was really needy, and Lance loved the sex. A quick shower and they got into an afternoon of sharing and satisfying each other's libido. She was proud to have a lover, and he loved filling the role and really enjoyed her company. After seven years of marriage, she had unsatisfied needs. The times they spent together were wonderful for both. Lance's job in sales gave him the freedom to use his time wisely. Lance rented the room two or three times a month, and they wore each other out. They filled the motel room in multiple orgasms. She and Lance loved the sex. One night she met Lance, he left his car, jumped into her Mercedes with a big ear-to-ear smile, and she drove him to a piece of land where she and her husband were going to build a house. Connie and her husband had bought this land overlooking the city lights. She loved the property and took Lance out to the site to show it off. Lance loved it; it was beautiful with a romantic view, a prime piece of land in the glowing moonlight overlooking the city, breathtaking. Connie was so excited she seemed to have electricity flowing through her nerves. Vividly she described the future house, how the porch would overlook the city. Lance immediately went down on her and brought her off. He was hot; she was hot. They got out of the car. Lance lifted her onto the hood of her Mercedes and once again, mutually enjoyable sex.

## 34

# Bartender

Lance as a civilian. He was great at his job as a torpedoman on subs. Not much demand for this skill set in the civilian world. The car dealership sold, so time to move on. Lance was at home in a bar. He was good in that arena. Lance's new goal struck him like a lightning bolt. He had enlisted in the Navy, served his four years honorably, and been in bars all over the world. Bartending to Lance seemed like a magic job. Stand behind the bar, get paid, free drinks, and still meet the chicks. Lance put on his confident face, walked in, and talked to the owner of a sailor bar downtown in San Diego. He told him he would be willing to work for free for one month as a test. If the owner felt it was a good fit, he would hire him. Lance was a natural in a bar on either side, having spent so much time on the customer side. Lance now had a job tending bar in a sailor topless joint. Once again, he successfully used his good looks, adaptable skill set, and the power of bullshit. Fortunately for Lance, he had the day shift. He opened at 10:00 a.m., did setups, and counted down the register. This was a slow shift. The occasional customer walked in from nine to eleven; the crowd grew larger until four when Lance's shift was over. The topless dancers numbering seven to twelve started showing up around four. Lance was surprised by how, generally speaking, they were flaky, petty, and extremely jealous. Lance showed the owner he was dependable of course, capable of tending a full bar plus listening to the same joke over and over and still laughing. Lance did such an excellent job the owner promoted him to the day bartender at his main bar. Lance was now in charge of a major bar with better pay, tips, and a barmaid who worked for him. He got the ideal shift, nine in the morning until four in the afternoon. Lance fell into bartending with gusto. He provided excellent service to each customer as though they were the only one there. He greeted each guest, seeing to their needs. All customers were served with respect. Lance's happy and upbeat personality kept the bar full and the owner happy with a full register. With the barmaid's help, the bar and tables were kept immaculate at all times during the shift.

A regular barfly Cindy came in around ten thirty. She walked up to Lance and said she had decided to quit wearing a bra. Did he think her tits looked good enough? Lance looked and responded, "Show me your tits." She pulled up her blouse, and Lance grabbed one in each hand, fondled them, held them up, and said, "These are fine, premium tits, Cindy. Display them proudly." She smiled and bought him a drink.

The barmaid named Leslie was married. Her husband was in the Navy and overseas on a nine-month Westpac deployment. Lance worked her every day trying to get into her knickers. He would give her a back rub, having her bend over the beer cooler. Lance stood behind her. As he rubbed her entire back, he leaned against her pressing his hard-on against her butt. She loved the back rub and the arousal, but that was as far as she ever allowed it to go. One New Year's Day in the afternoon, Leslie invited Lance to meet her and a girlfriend at a dance club after work. It was for a New Year's Eve party. Lance of course jumped at the chance. Lance went. He saw and met her friend. Some more drinking, dancing, and talking with her friend. Another woman, however, caught his eye. She gave him the look. Lance knew she was looking to get laid. At 12:10 a.m. in the New Year, she and Lance jumped into his car. On the way to her house, she slid next to him and placed Lance's right hand on her leg. Lance slid it up to her panties pulling them aside and playing with her lady parts. She in turn opened Lance's zipper, pulled out Mr. Wiggly, and began stroking it. Talk about them both being ready.

Major interruption catching them both by surprise. Red lights and siren. Quickly zipping up, Lance got out of his car and greeted the cop. "Is that your wife?" asked the police officer. Lance, without qualms, immediately lied to the cop and said yes. He now proceeded to put Lance through the drunk driving tests. No problem, Lance easily passed them all.

"How old are you?" Lance inquired.

"Twenty-one," the cop responded.

"Cool, you don't look a day over eighteen."

"I get that a lot," responded the cop.

Back in the car was a quiet two-block drive just below the speed limit to her house. Lance parked. She said, "Oh, too bad my daughter is home."

Lance pulled her to him kissing her while putting her hand back on his erection. They proceeded to make love on the front seat. Lance went home and slept until noon.

Lance was now catching on; in conversation, he quickly got sex out on the table. Lance was out meeting women looking to hook up with someone. He had developed or fine-tuned his spider sense. They were out to have sex. Lance sensed that. If not, he did not waste any time with them. Lance was out to have sex. He continuously improved his skills in that arena. Lance started the day opening the bar. By closing out his shift, he was ready to go out on the prowl. He had the looks and that certain je ne sais quoi about him that attracted ladies looking to get laid.

A fortuitous event, this evening he ran into his mother-in-law at one of his favorite hangouts. She had been drinking heavily. Sliding up to Lance, she asked for a ride home. Ever the gentleman, Lance helped her to the car and drove her home. He walked her to the door, took her keys, and let her in. She said, "Lance, sit down. I will pour us a glass of wine."

Lance sat down on the couch, watching her move. She did look like her daughter, sexy in her own right. Short like her daughter, barely five feet tall. Black shiny hair and captivating eyes. Juliet was wearing a bright yellow minidress that left little to the imagination. Setting two glasses of red wine on the table, it appeared to Lance that her miniskirt was sliding higher as she dropped her sexy ass next to Lance, her thigh touching his.

Raising glasses, she toasted, "Sex is only dirty if it's done right."

Lance's mind started racing. *Is she coming on to me? My mother-in-law?* A Caesar's wife moment. How would sex with her compare to her daughter?

"Lance," she moaned, "would you mind rubbing my back?"

Lance immediately put his trained, skilled massage hands to work. He had her lay on her stomach and started at her neck. Slowly working her muscles and flesh, he calmly unzipped her dress from shoulders to panties. Lance was sure she was ready. She sat up, and Lance took her left hand and placed it on his throbbing member.

Once she felt the size of Lance's member, she said, "I really shouldn't do this." In a matter of seconds, she dropped out of her dress, slid off her panties. She found and was lying naked on a terry cloth towel on the floor. Juliet drew Lance into her hot, wet vagina. Great sex it was.

Lance was amazed at the similarities between sex with her and sex with her daughter.

Several weeks later Lance answered her call to stop by. Juliet opened the door. It was a sunny perfect San Diego day. As Lance stepped in, Juliet put a finger over her lips. "Be quiet. The grandkids are here." Her son's two toddlers were asleep in the bedroom. The two- and four-year-old boys were sound asleep on her bed.

"Juliet, we can get together another time."

"No, no, no, Lance, I need you now. They will sleep at least another hour."

"What if one of them wakes up and comes walking into the living room?"

Juliet grabbed Lance by the right hand and dragged him into the hall closet. It was empty and spacious. Beating the rate that bumblebees flap their wings, they had their clothes off. Closet door closed, Juliet got in position. She bent forward, both hands on the floor, presenting her sweet center of pleasure. Lance did not hesitate. God, that woman made him hot. As he was happily pumping away and she was doing her throaty moaning, she reached around and started massaging his scrotum like milking a cow. Lance was now moving at full speed ahead, biting his lip to keep quiet too and fucking much. Lance grabbed hold of her hips pulling her up tight, lost control, and exploded.

"Well, that was quick," whined Juliet.

For this rare time, Lance was far ahead of his sex partner. Lance's reason was coming here to bring her to orgasm and happily satisfied. "Does the bathroom have a locking door?" he asked.

"Yes, it does."

They grabbed their pile of clothes and moved down the hallway. She locked the door verifying the room was secure. There was a clothes hook on the door. Handy. Towels were hanging on the right wall. A linen closet full of shelves was on the left. There was a sink on a faux wood vanity and a large mirrored medicine cabinet. Toilet white, seat down. At the end of the room stood the tub/shower with sliding glass doors and a handheld shower head with spray settings including massage on a five-foot hose. Oil of Olay moisturizers, lipstick, shampoo perfumes, and other feminine products covered any horizontal space. Here were two more than consenting adults both in a state of lust. Turning on and warming up the shower, Juliet had Lance step in first. Lance stepped back, and she handed him the shower hose placed on massage setting. Lance soaped her down with one hand and ran the shower head massager over her body with the other. Juliet sighed and moaned while leaning against the shower wall. Lance stood behind her and began going over her entire body. She had forgotten how stimulating a hot water message woke every outside nerve with hot blood flowing. Excitement grew as Lance went up and down from head to back to butt to feet and switched from neck to breasts to stomach over mound of Venus on down to feet in the front. Now Lance's Murasaki katana was hard and poking her here and there from behind. This was not Lance's first shower sex, and he knew natural lubricants get washed away, and chafing was possible. He owed Julie an orgasm; that was why she had called. He put the shower head back in its holder. With his trained hands, he started to massage her neck and back. "Step out," commanded Lance as he turned the water off. He put the seat cover down, sitting on the toilet. A tube of KY jelly sitting on sink, he covered his erection poking straight up in the air and pulled her onto him. Juliet backed up to Lance and hungrily slid his member in slowly taking all of it, moving slow, moving fast just sitting on Lance's lap enjoying the fulfillment, stroking again up and down in a steady pace. Lance took her left nipple and tweaked and caressed it. His right hand now went down to her swollen clit, and he began a steady sliding and then caressing it, keeping pace with her up-and-down motion. When two were so enjoined in dreamy sex, time disappeared. At some point, Julie picked up speed, shuddered; every muscle in her body tensed up, and she came in sweet relief. Lance followed coming again, filling her lovely vagina. Great sex. Quickly relaxing, Lance took a shower, dressed, and left before the kids awoke from heir nap. After all, if your mother-in-law was horny, what were you supposed to do?

Listen and learn.

Lance, as the day bartender, was aware of the owner owing back taxes to the IRS. He agreed to keep working under one condition. Every morning he would count out his pay for the day from the register and put it in his pocket before he started his shift. This proved to be a rather astute decision as one day Lance showed up for work and pocketed his pay. About one hour into his shift, the IRS showed up and locked up the bar. He went from there to the health club and worked out for two hours. His one belief was to keep his body and mind in shape. He knew sexual ability was driven by a good, strong, healthy body. Lance maintained his physical and mental health working out.

He noticed that in life, the picture was crooked. By this age, Lance believed the world was ninety percent snake oil bullshit. Lance had figured out that life ends whether you have regrets or not. Now out of work, never one to pass up opportunity, he made a good living using his mechanical skills, buying, fixing up, and selling cars while between jobs. He bought from sailors he met at bars going on nine-month Westpac cruises and sold them to sailors that just returned home.

## *35*

# **Narcissism**

When Lance had successes, Delilah dragged him down and belittled him. She doubled down with snide sarcastic comments. A constant barrage of insults, she constantly marinated him in self-shame. She had become a regular vortex of venom. Delilah had low self-esteem issues and tried to bring others down to her level. Life with Delilah was like being slowly eaten by inchworms. Little bites eventually destroy a leaf, the tree, and then a forest. She at times was as disorganized as an explosion in a fireworks factory and at others as organized as a flock of geese flying south for the winter. Lance had shared tables with sailors, killers, politicians, attorneys, used car salesmen, and prostitutes—all preferable to Delilah and her constant pummeling with attempts at thwarting his successes. Living with Delilah was much the same as a dull, slow grinding pain close to the brain, like an ear or toothache. He thought of one of his favorite John Stewart Mill quotes: "Pleasure and freedom from pain are the only things desirable as ends."

Lance bought a nice Ford coupe that would not run for pocket change. Fixed it up for dollars. Now he sold it for a large profit, all cash. All he got from her was a typical blast of shit when he got home. With her Jekyll-and-Hyde personality, he never felt comfortable. Now Lance finally decided to shuck the idea or concept of Delilah. *Enough*, thought his brain, *no more. That's it.*

Monday night Lance fired up his car and left, driving back to Las Vegas. Getting away from her was like escaping the devil. Lance now became selective of how he spent his time and who he spent it with. He thought how until this date he had lived his life with rules placed on him by society, school, the military, and a narcissistic wife. Tuesday morning

Lance hired an attorney in Las Vegas and filed for divorce. She had a picture of Abraham Lincoln on her attorney's office wall. Getting a divorce broke his heart, wounded his psyche deeply. Living alone had to be better than the constant verbal abuse. Lance was taking a step toward his freedom. Back in Vegas again, without the shrew, Lance began piecing his own life back together. Being single (divorced), never again will he hang around with negative losers. There were still some friends from school he knew. He called in some markers and went to work for the city.

## 36

# Divorced in Vegas

Lance was now facing consequences due to an action he had specifically taken. Now single, Lance would spend years as a person of the night often seeing the sunrise because he was still awake. The quiet and sneaky seduction of Sin City, Las Vegas, had begun. Twenty-four-seven drinking and partying. He was single living in Vegas where over half of the population was comprised of women. Life imparts its gifts in a random way. Sex, some get lots; others get very little or nothing. Lance often looked at others and thought, *There but for me go I*. Lance had been either drinking in or tending bar long enough to know which clubs were the best to pick up women. He was like truly in his element.

Lance parlayed his city job by acing the test for firefighter and attended the firefighting academy. Now he had a decent career. Lance now truly had it made. He traded in his pickup truck for a used Corvette. He had girls that would call him for sex, a "nooner," or to hook up with a girlfriend needing sex. Two separate times girlfriends that were having hysterectomies called, requested, and spent their last night as a woman in Lance's arms. Lance now had sex with regularity. Being a professional firefighter meant working twenty-four-hour shifts from eight in the morning until eight the next morning on duty. However, these shifts were spread out. One day on, one day off. One day on and two days off. One day on and four days off. By this stage of life, he was as adept at picking up women as a UPS driver is at managing a dolly full of packages. Lance ignored his circadian clock; after all, it's Vegas.

## 37
# Botticelli

A Botticelli or Michelangelo? Lance was proud of his sister, Stephanie. She had attended University of Nevada, Las Vegas, earning a degree in hotel management in three years. A long and stressful process. Having her babysitter watch her young daughter was crucial to her attaining her goals. Stephanie remarried. She and her husband held executive level positions, and they lived quite well. She had worked hard putting herself through college as a single parent. Her first husband, it turned out, was a lowlife, liar, and bigamist. After her daughter was born, she found out her husband was still married to his first wife whom he had never mentioned. Stephanie got a Vegas divorce, and he was out of their life.

With her degree in hotel management, Stephanie landed a great job at a Casino working in human resources as a player development specialist. She leveraged connections around town to score casino high rollers with not only the standard Vegas reward package of free rooms, booze, and meals but also VIP tables at the hot clubs and restaurants. Front-row show seats, prime tee times, and anything else that client desired. Her position was to bring in and keep the high rollers returning to her casino. Working with restaurant and nightclub owners and their staff around town, she created memorable experiences in Vegas. She was Lance's go-to for tickets, reservations, etc.

Lance was now the devil-may-care playboy having also gone through a bad marriage and resolved not to let that happen again. Wherever Lance lived, he taped his divorce certificate to the toilet seat. Every time he peed, it was there to remind him marriage was not for him.

Lance got a call from his sister. "Brother Lance, I need a favor. My girlfriend, Annette, is getting married and moving to Oregon. Her fiancée works evenings, and she wants to spend one night on the town in Vegas with someone 'different' before she gets married. The famous Las Vegas strip gourmet dinner and dancing, this will be her coming out once-in-a-lifetime chance to do it up in style before she gets married and moves to Oregon." Although he had never met her, Lance knew that Stephanie owed Annette big time. She babysat Stephanie's daughter allowing Steph to attend UNLV. "Lance, she is hot, intelligent, fun to be with, and doesn't take herself too seriously. I will set everything up," pleaded Stephanie, "five-star restaurant, complimentary room, and club reservations." Lance normally did not let himself get roped into blind dates but agreed; he owed his sister.

As she did for clients, Stephanie set up appointments at her hotel's beauty shop and spa: manicure, pedicure, and massage. Off to the hotel's shopping area where Steph and Annette picked out an appropriate cocktail dress. A floor-length black A-line sleeveless sexy long dress. The dress was covered in sequins, had a plunging sweetheart neckline, and a thigh-high slit. This dress looked great on Annette showing off her ample curves, the perfect daring yet glamorous dress. She had on shoes, black high heels. Stephanie lent her a gold clutch purse. Stephanie got an upscale room comped. Steph now went to work on Lance: hairstyle, shave, tailored suit, shirt and tie, and dress shoes. The topper, his manicure-pedicure. Lance went along grudgingly. This was Lance's first pedicure. He was amazed, discovering this brand-new way of meeting a woman. For this evening, Lance traded cars with his attorney friend, Kirk. He used Kirk's brand-new Cadillac Eldorado for their date, and Kirk drove Lance's Corvette.

At Stephanie's casino, Lance went to her office. When the door opened, Lance saw Annette for the first time. He was overwhelmed at her beauty. Truly a sexual goddess. She had perfect waist-length chestnut-colored hair. At five foot six, she stood tall and proud. She radiated health, and her teeth were all as perfectly white as fresh fallen snow. Her black split dress showed off flashes of her alluring legs, fitted to her body accentuating firm sensual curves. She had a small attractive aquiline nose and large dazzling blue-green eyes that looked into your soul. "*Enchanté*," said Lance as he dropped on one knee and kissed her hand.

At Stephanie's casino entrance, the valet opened the car door, and the two of them were off for dinner. The maître d' at one of the strips' premier dining establishments welcomed them. He led the lovely pair to their table. A Michelin five star chef prepared their tasting menu. The dining room had massive chandeliers, purple cushioned couch seating one, blue wall with paintings, and the rest of the walls off-white with gold trim. Another wall held a large mirror reflecting most of the room. Upon sitting, they were introduced to their sommelier in charge of wine pairing. Now began a fifteen-course tasting menu. The courses were organized into a trio of dishes. Starting with some small bites, a sorbet palate cleanser, and two baked treats; then cold, fresh vegetables, three soups, and a magnificent meat course; and closing, a trio of desserts. Wine poured in five ounces were paired, a new wine for every other course. The service ran around ten minutes between courses. This elaborate multicourse meal was a lifetime memorable experience. Lance and Annette had marvelous time of silly eating, drinking, and getting to know each other.

Next stop, one of Lance's favorite places to play: valet parking at the Flamingo, reserved seats at the Skyroom. Lance was known there, and they did not ID Annette. Stephanie had reserved the seats overlooking Caesars' Palace fountains. Annette was a beauty that Lance was glad to accompany and display. As they climbed the spiral staircase and walked to their table, men both young and old followed her with their eyes. Even the women stopped talking and looked on with admiration and jealousy.

She was a so spectacularly appealing, looked so good, that she was a showstopper. As they were escorted to their reserved table, all eyes were on them, and everyone stopped to check them out. Lance was thrilled, his ego beaming. Lance walked her to the dance floor noticing the envy of the men guests and the jealousy of the women. Lance knew he was privileged to have been given this opportunity. A beautiful perfectly built eighteen-year-old with Hollywood movie star appearance. He knew her goal was a night on the town and including a sexual fling before her wedding. "O frabjous day," said Lance under his breath! Once again, Lance was in the right place at the right time and taking advantage of opportunities.

Following an engaging evening of drinking and dancing, they now contacted the front desk. It was time for Lance to be the tutor. A bellman guided them to the top-floor room Stephanie had reserved, a high rollers' room with a heart-shaped spa. The bellhop opened the champagne, poured two glasses, and put the bottle on ice. Lance tipped the bellhop, threw the keys on the wet bar, and opened the curtain. They were on the top floor with a panoramic view of the strip.

As they looked out taking in the spectacular view, Annette leaned back against Lance. He took his talented hands massaging her neck and shoulders, and she began moaning. Lance slid down her zipper, and her dress fell softly onto the carpet. The heart-shaped tub was slowly bubbling with hot water. She turned around, and they shared a warm, sweet probing kiss. Lance was unclasping her bra while she unbuttoned his shirt. The air was permeated with the smell of their pheromones comingling. While Lance removed her bra, he began kissing her ears and neck. She unbuttoned his shirt, and it joined her dress on the floor. She had only had sex with her fiancé. This evening she came loaded with hormones and nervous anticipation. She was a human dynamo radiating out an invisible electric force field, a crackling energy charging them both to full capacity. Annette was also aware there was no danger here as she was safe with Stephanie's brother. "Are you going to turn off the lights?" she whispered.

"No," replied Lance, "I want to admire your wondrous beauty, all of it." Lance now reached behind her grabbing her buttocks and pulling her tightly to him. They both shuddered in anticipation. Placing his open palmed hands on her hips, Lance slid her black lace panties down.

With nervously shaking hands, Annette unzipped and pulled down Lance's trousers. She shrieked in fear and primal anticipation. "It's so big," Annette exclaimed.

Lance gently assured her she would be ready and enjoy the experience; after all, they had all night. Lance was amazed by how she was as blindingly white as fresh fallen snow. Annette had perfect proportionality, foot to foot, toe to toe, breast to breast, perfect pairing. No flaws, discoloration, dark spots, or birthmarks. He spent the whole evening kissing, tasting, and touching every part of her body. "*Elle était parfaite*" (perfect). Lance led her to the tub and guided her into the warm bubbling water. Lance opened a natural sea sponge and the scented soap. Now he proceeded to scrub, wash, and kiss every area of her body. The texture of the sponge acted as an additional stimulation. Starting at her neck, Lance washed and kissed her body above the water. After he washed her breasts gently tweaking her hard nipples, Lance had her stand. He now started moving from waist down, slowly washing, massaging, kissing. Admiring her altar of pleasure in its visual perfection, Lance pulled her to him and kissed her swollen clit. She had such a sweet yet tangy taste. Annette's muscles tightened, and she went into a spasm. Lance held her tightly until she reached her plateau. Annette's body slowly returned to its normal level of functioning. Lance dried her with a bath towel and put her in a white terrycloth robe.

"Lance, thank you. I felt wonderful and so comfortable with you." As she sat on the bed and came back around to her senses, she was sitting at eyeball level to his huge erection. "Lance, this is something my fiancé taught me." Annette took the tip of Lance's rock-hard cock in her mouth and began stroking it back and forth, her tongue dancing around the circumcised head. Lance took her right hand and placed it on his shaft and her left hand on his nuts. Moving in metronomic rhythm, it was not long before Lance exploded in climax. Lance grabbed Annette's hair holding her in place. Although she gagged a bit, Annette swallowed most of his semen. Lance sweetly kissed her. They both shared the sweet taste of his warm, salty fluid. Lance pulled her gently in his arms, and they laid back and cuddled. Annette was moaning again.

At this phase, both were feeling a general sense of well-being. She had the loveliest voice. Lance smiled and started kissing her, tongue buried In her mouth. "I am going to take you on sexual stimulation trip. Bringing up your excitement slowly but methodically, your body is my tempestuous instrument, and I will play it until you are satiated." Lance was looking to put her on fire by teasing her body's sensory receptors. She responded in kind. He ever so slowly ran his fingers over her ears and neck. He kissed and ran his tongue into each ear, gently kissing the earlobe, sucking on them. Surprising her, Lance worked his tongue into the center of her ears. Working his way down her neck, he held and kissed one hand and then the other placing each middle finger in his mouth and sucking on it. Lance's hands kept up a busy pace of touching, tweaking, massaging every area of her body, touching, kissing, sucking, or licking. The only area he avoided was her clit. All these nerve endings. Lance sought to build up her excitement. A quick tongue worked teasingly down the neck to her breasts. While massaging and tweaking the nipple on her left breast, he took her right wrist and kissed it ever so teasingly. He then again took her middle fingers into his mouth and sucked and moved them it in and out, continuous motion constantly moving up and down her body slowly moving his fingers, tonguing areas including her armpits. Lance was listening to her breathing, speeding up. Lying on her back, Annette's sexual excitement was escalating. Lance's fingers gently, teasingly brushed her over her entire body. Lance knew where and how to touch her for maximum affect. Lightly up and down, shifting to a brisk, circular motion. Heavy breathing allowed Lance to be aware it was seductive. He kissed her stomach around her belly button sliding down to her pelvic area, stimulating this area without touching the clitoris, promoting blood flow to other erogenous zones. She was releasing intoxicating pheromones quite noticeable in this area. Oh, so close but never touching.

Suddenly, Lance now shifted to massaging the arch of her foot. He was aware of the fifteen thousand nerve endings located there and began bringing them into play. This experience enhanced Annette, preparing her for exhilarating lovemaking. Lance kissed her feet deeply, moving his fingers and tongue over around and between the toes.

Annette was there, peaked. "Oh, Lance, please fuck me now. Stick that big cock in me and let me have all of it." Annette spread her legs opening paradise.

Lance took his rock-hard member and slid it up and down between her clit and her ass back and forth. Suddenly, Lance slowly entered her wet and dripping pussy, ready she was. It was still a tight fit.

Annette was now screaming in ecstasy. "Oh yes, oh yes, oh my god. That's it right there." Her eyes rolled back into her head, and she rocked, reached euphoria in orgasmic relief.

Lance, slowly moving in and out, short strokes, and then deep, still finding her G-spot, brought her around again as he exploded, filling her with what seemed gallons of his cum. This was one of nature's rewards for being alive. They had just shared souls, each taking a part of the other and now satiated and comfortable with each other. Sex shared between two individuals both reaching new plateaus was certainly a wonderful gift from nature. For the few that reach this nirvana, there are no descriptive words as wonderful as this shared memory.

They cuddled and drifted off to sleep. Annette surprised Lance. She got up, leaning on her elbow taking hold of his flaccid member. Kissing and sucking on it, she ran her tongue around the tip and began caressing and stroking his balls. Lance responded gently, taking hold of her head and guiding it up and down. "My turn," said Annette as she rose on her knees, straddled Lance like climbing onto a horse, sliding his big hard member deep into her vagina. Now she was the driver using Lance's prodigious erection to find her G-spot. On top with a grin of delight, she was pumping away like a pile driver. Lance assisted by fondling her clit and massaging her nipples. She was soaring to sensual paradise. Annette collapsed on Lance holding him tightly, a grin spreading from ear to ear. "Lance, that was wonderful, exceeded my dreams and expectations. Dinner was beyond special. Dancing and drinking, gorgeous. Showing me off tonight, sensational. Yes, of course I noticed all eyes were on us as a couple. Thank you for making this last moment as a single girl over the top. I appreciate the experience you brought and bringing me to thrilling new moments of pleasure. I will be married next week and move to Oregon. I will treasure this experience forever and deny it ever happened. It's 6:30 a.m., Lance, I have got to go to Stephanie's office, change, go home, and shower. My fiancée gets home from work at 9:00 a.m. Boy, I'm sore down there, what should I do?"

"Annette, the minute he gets home, take him to bed and have a quickie."

Lance had the valet bring the Caddie. He dropped Annette at Stephanie's casino. A quick kiss goodbye, he never saw her again. Once again in Lance's life, it all fell in place.

## 38

# Apartment Move

At work, a fellow firefighter asked Lance to share rent in a three-bedroom apartment. Why not? thought Lance. No lease, just month to month for Lance. Billy the firefighter and his girlfriend, Carla, had room one. Lance had bedroom number two. Leon and his girlfriend, Colleen, had room number three. With this assortment of strangers, what could go right?

One evening Lance brought home Cynthia, a freshly divorced young mother. Several glasses of wine and Lance, after much sweet-talking, took her into his bedroom. Overcoming her fear and objections, Lance became her second lover. Even though she was twenty, she still looked like a teenager and brought a memorable moment into Lance's life. Lying back on the bed, Lance slid down her panties. There, in front of his eyes, was the most sensuous mound of Venus Lance had ever seen. Her flawless white perfect hips and legs were the background for a perfect V-shaped black pubic hair. Perfectly symmetrical with every hair in place as though it had just been brushed a pretty vagina an artist would appreciate, Lance thought she would have been the perfect model. Lance prepared her, enjoying the sweet pleasure of his tongue finding her clit. She had a natural taste, sweet and enchanting. Lance, from his chemistry studies, knew that Saccharin, the oldest artificial sweetener created in 1878, was three hundred to five hundred times sweeter than sugar. In his mind, she topped that. She was hot and soon stiffened in orgasm. It was Lance's turn; burying himself in her, she put her legs around Lance's back matching him push for push, each slamming away until luscious relief. Cynthia dressed and kissed Lance. "Thanks, Lance, I will remember tonight. I am looking for a husband and future for my kids, and I do not think that is for you." Lance never saw her again but never forgot that night.

In the other bedroom, Colleen, Leon's girlfriend, heard every seductive word and listened to the entire performance. Two days later when Lance was off duty and the two of them were home alone, Coleen sat down and talked with him. Lance's sweet-talking had turned her on. That night Lance snuck into her bedroom. Colleen and Leon, although sharing a bedroom, had separate beds. Lance, at her pleading invitation, joined her. For two hours of just fun lovemaking in her bed, Lance went off to his room after. The room smelled of sex, an odor not describable but recognized instantly by the olfactory glands. To cover the smell of sex, Lance went to the kitchen and burned some popcorn in the microwave. Unfortunately, Leon was awake, pretending to be asleep. His girlfriend's getting into a passionate entanglement with Lance did not exactly make him happy. In fact, he was quite upset. He felt emasculated. Coleen said, "Too bad, Leon, I have decided to move out."

Billy and Carla were pissed at Lance. Leon was bowed up and angry. The three of them left for work. Coleen asked Lance to help her load her car. When her car was loaded, she gleefully gave Lance a blowjob while discussing about what a bad girl she was and left. Lance knew he was now persona non grata at the apartment. He left his keys and moved into a two-bedroom apartment. All he needed now was a roommate.

## 39

# Santa Monica

Lance really missed the ocean. He missed the days of living on the beach in San Diego. Sun, sand, and surfing were his third favorite way of passing time when he did not have duty. Sex, of course, was first and getting a high second. At the start of a four-day vacation, Lance got a call from a professional hooker girlfriend named Bridgette. She had just spent the night with a wealthy customer and had a pocket full of cash and chips from casinos up and down the strip. She told Lance, "Let's divide the chips. You cash in one side of the strip, and I will do the other. We will then jump in my car, go to California, and play on the beach for a couple of days."

Lance needed no arm-twisting. "I am in," he said, grinning.

Five thousand in cash later they were on the way to California. Bridgette was a fun person to be with. They joked, laughed, listened to music, and talked incessantly. She was smart and good enough looking to work the strip. While driving, she was wearing a miniskirt and no panties. These were the days when service stations filled your car, checked your oil, and washed the windshield. Imagine how clean the young boys got the windshield in front of the driver once they saw Bridgette's uncovered Grand Canyon, her money maker. One time the attendant had another attendant help. While they were all leering over the view, Bridgette and Lance had a good laugh.

First stop, the pier in Santa Monica. Bridgette parked her car, and the two of them went out on the pier to eat some burgers, fries, and a beer. Lance showed her the famous Route 66 end of the trail sign. They also found a poster of a beach party taking place that evening. Lance and Bridgette went to Santa Monica to go surfing and partying. At the beach party, they just blended in. Sand, beach, nighttime with hundreds of young bodies dancing, talking, drinking, and smoking dope. Even if you were not doing drugs, you certainly got a contact high. Some clowns started to lob empty beer bottles into the crowd, so Lance, Bridgette, and her new friend Roman Estevez left and went to the apartment Roman shared with his brother. Lance was hearing how out of the world sex under drugs was. He was not alone, so why not. They smoked some dope. Lance passed out and slept for twenty-four hours. Roman Estevez and Bridgette got stoned, fooled around, and had a great time. Roman was young, good-looking, and fell right in with Lance and Bridgette. She and Roman began with long-distance dating, and in three months, Roman moved to Vegas. The romance with Roman and Bridgette fell apart, but Lance had a new running mate. Roman moved into the apartment with Lance. One of the advantages of having a roommate from Santa Monica was all the California girls Roman knew came to Vegas.

Lance often had a difficult time waking up after a hard night of partying. As a single fireman, he needed some assistance to ensure being able to wake up on the mornings when he had duty. He knew he would usually get a good night's sleep while at the station, so he partied late. A simple solution, Lance placed five alarm clocks in his bedroom, two electric clocks and three wind-up alarm clocks with bells placed in empty pans for the noise multiplication. At 6:00 a.m., the whole apartment building was awakened. Rumors of seismograph readings were exaggerated. All of the clocks had to be silenced, and none were in reach of the bed. Once Lance was up, after silencing the alarms, he was functioning and got to the fire station early. Lance did not see something like not being unable to awaken as a problem at this point in life.

Two sisters a year apart, nineteen and twenty, showed up one weekend. Ellen and Tina, easy to see the family resemblance. Both blonds, tall, five foot six. Ellen was wearing Daisy Dukes, Tina striped bell bottom pants with light and dark stripes. They wore matching black Santa Monica T-shirts with pictures of the pier. Obviously, they were California girls as they filled the air with happy talk, wearing sandals and beads and braless, naturally tanned on the beach bodies, both with firm breasts with prominent nipples showing through their T-shirt tops.

At the apartment, eight o'clock in the morning, Tina asked, "What time is it?"

Lance responded in his announcer's voice, "I am the keeper of the time. Let me introduce you to the clock room."

As he led her into his multi-clock bedroom, she shut the door behind her. "I have seen your clocks. Now it's time to show me your cock."

Lance was pleased to pull out and show off his prize "Gewehr."

"Holy shit!" said Tina as she sat down on the edge of Lance's king-size bed, or as he referred to it, his workbench.

Lance removed her T-shirt, and as soon as it was off, she wasted no time putting the head of his penis in her mouth. Slowly at first, and then picking up the pace, she licked the head of Lance's penis. Tina now took all of Lance she could fit in her mouth. Moaning with pleasure, Lance gripped her lovely blond hair on each side. Now Lance was thrusting smoothly like a giant piston. Tina massaged his balls and then surprised Lance by slipping one of her fingers up his ass tickling his prostrate as he came shooting wads of cum into her mouth. She did not gag swallowing almost all the spurting flow. Swallowing and licking her lips, she said, "I can't do this at home." Lance removed the rest of his clothes; Tina removed her Daisy Dukes, no panties. Lying back, spreading her legs, she growled, "Turnabout is fair play." Lance gleefully went down on her sliding a finger up her ass as she came. A wonderful weekend of partying and Sunday, the sisters went back to Santa Monica.

# 40

# Lance's Routine

Lance had now developed a routine. He had three bars and two clubs he visited on a regular basis. If he was not at work, he was at the gym working out, at his apartment sleeping (rarely) or at one of his hangouts. Lance worked ten days a month. The balance of his time was spent drinking and making sexual conquests. Life was simple. He was at work, working out, looking to get laid, or out screwing around. He was well known in his social circles. Apparently, the girls talked. Being well-endowed brought many a curious lady to his bed.

In order to keep and enhance his persuasive skills, he took a part-time job selling cars at a lot his buddy Kirk, the attorney, was part owner. Having great social skills, bartending had taught him when to talk and when to listen. This job provided him with a free demo vehicle to drive and an entertaining method of meeting people from all walks of life. Selling cars was a wonderful way to improve one's personal skills, honing the ability to convince people of almost anything. Kirk, as an attorney, oversaw contracts, leases, depositions, finance laws, and bank flooring. Lance just loved people and was constantly working on using the final objection close whether he was using it to sell a car or to seduce a new sex partner. Lance became quite skilled at both. This was Las Vegas, and sex was for sale, whether legal or not. Many of Lance's car customers were working girls. They were good clients, paid in in cash and on time. The car lot's private back office was available when sex as a payment was credited.

Lance had lived in Las Vegas long enough not to be a gambler. He had friends that were now pit bosses and showgirls. One female twenty-one dealer Lance shared living quarters with for a month would sit down and deal from the bottom, middle, and top of the deck, hands faster than the eyes. He lived with and knew the people who worked in the casinos. Reading the bodies' tells worked whether selling cars, playing cards, or getting sex.

One evening, as a reward for a record month, the sales crew went out to a buffet dinner. While passing a slot machine, Lance put the change in his pocket in the slot machine at the casino entrance. The machine hit three bars, alarms went off; bells and whistles sounded. Lance had hit the jackpot and won a brand-new fully loaded 1969 Corvette. Lucky Lance? He was surrounded with casino management and staff inspecting the slot machine for tampering. He called over his attorney friend, Kirk, who was there for the dinner. They made sure the casino provided Lance a fully loaded model equipped as the demonstrated Corvette model in the casino. Lucky Lance? It took a ton of money to pay the taxes and registration. Lance sold his older Corvette and now owned the new one free and clear.

Lance was sitting on his favorite stool at Jack & Jill's Bar and Grill when she came in alone. He had met Gabriela and her husband previously. They had gotten divorced on Friday. Here she was on Monday afternoon sitting next to and hitting on Lance. She was a young Chicano woman with black eyes and shoulder-length black hair. At barely five feet and ninety-five pounds, she was almost childlike in her size. She climbed on a stool next to Lance making them the only two customers in the place at two in the afternoon.

"Do you mind if I sit next to you?" she asked in a sweet pleading voice.

Lance put a twenty on the bar and told Jack, the barkeep and owner, "Set the lady up, please."

They finished their drink, and she asked, "Could you please give me a ride home?"

Lance was glad to oblige, knowing she lived less than two blocks from the bar to her front door. Lance gladly took her hand, led her to his Vette, and opened the door for her. When she invited him in, Lance was not surprised. The two of them sat on the living room floor shag carpet. Two bottles of beer were on the coffee table. Gabriela laid back on the floor. Lance laid down next to her. Mutual hugging and kissing. Both of them knew where this was leading; they were two horny consenting adults. Lance unbuttoned the top button on her jeans, slid the zipper down, slipped the jeans and her panties below her knees, climbed on top, and slid into her wet and waiting womanhood. Lance ensured that she reached climax before letting himself go. A lovely moment for both. As they lay there wrapped in each other's arms, she thanked Lance. "I really needed that." She had married her high school sweet heart when she turned seventeen. He was eighteen. Five years later she had faithfully followed her Catholic vows. He divorced her. Lance was her first sex aside from her husband. Gabriella pulled up her jeans, excused herself, and went to the bedroom. She reappeared in her nightwear and handed Lance a robe, taking his hand and leading him to her bed.

For the next several hours, they discovered and became familiar with each other's bodies and needs. Reaching their bodies' sexual peaks, they fell asleep, exhausted in each other's arms. Lance slept well. He was awoken by the smell of coffee, homemade tortillas, eggs, and chorizo. Hot breakfast served by one hot little Hispanic woman. Dressed in a see-through nightgown, Lance snuck up behind her. A big hug and he rubbed his erection against her tiny, little ass. She turned around with a spatula in one hand and grabbed Mr. Wiggly with the other. "Breakfast first," she said. Lance, dressed only in his underwear, sat down, drank an orange juice and coffee, and ate wonderful breakfast tacos. Lance now walked up to Gabby and dropped her gown placing his right hand on her pussy fingering her vagina. He picked her up, put her on the table, and buried his face in that lovely black bush and had her for dessert. She was operating on overload.

The four days went quickly. Gabby had a five-year hunger, and Lance was there to fulfill it.

Ollie's Oasis was a country redneck beer bar Lance frequented. Walking through the front door placed you in the in the center of the bar. It was dark and smoky. It was always a shock to walk out the door into the bright Vegas day. Lance often thought Vegas was so bright and hot that it was only twenty-five feet from the sun. Inside was a long half rectangle-shaped bar, red vinyl cushioning, and matching barstools with metal legs. The only real lighting inside was back bar giving the barkeep enough light to mix drinks and count money. The owner, Ollie, was a retired military alcoholic. Many a night Lance covered for him and helped him close. There was a jukebox with all the right country drinking and cheating songs with a wooden dance floor surrounded by red vinyl booths, each with four seats. A great place to get drunk, get laid, or just feel good. The crowd was mostly local working class. Lance knew many by first name: Cooter, Tex, Bull, Rufus, Dallas, Mary-Jane, Cindy-May, and sweet Maria, the sexy Chicano chick that carried a straight razor. He knew all of the usual crowd, this being one of his hangouts.

Lance noticed them, a new couple. They drifted into town as most young couples did. Their dream, to live in Vegas. Darryl and Loretta Jane Smythe sat at the bar and ordered two draft beers. There was a shake of hands and an introduction. Learning they had just arrived, Lance welcomed them and paid for their beers. Darryl was unemployed and accompanied by Loretta, his wife and shadow. The three of them shared a few drinks and conversation. Having just moved to Vegas from Georgia, Lance made some suggestions where Darryl might find a job. Lance had been to Georgia numerous times and knew the two of them were in for major culture shock. The Vegas economy was good, and Lance ensured them that if they really wanted work, it was there. He said good night to Darryl and his little Georgia peach. He then went home to crash; Lance had duty in the morning.

The next several times he saw them Daryl was rowdy drunk, and Lance had to help Loretta get him to the car to take him home. Lance saw her several times drinking alone at the bar. Lance was sitting and yakking with the bartender, Tiny, who was four feet five inches in height and weighed three hundred plus pounds. It was going on three in the afternoon and the usual one-hundred-plus degree weather outside. The front of the club faced west and caught the brunt of the afternoon heat. The entry door swung open, and the sun lit up that portion of the dark bar like a giant spotlight at a grand opening. In walked Loretta, glowing in the light. She came into Ollie's moving slowly forward in a dumb beast-like manner with one saggy eye. Her husband had come home drunk and hit her. Darryl now spent his time continuing to get drunk and feeling sorry for himself. She walked over, sat down, and said a big howdy to Lance. Lance, of course, bought her a drink, put it on his tab. Lance knew the club's owner, Ollie, well. Loretta said, "Lance, let's sit in a booth. I need to talk to you." Lance ordered a pitcher of beer, and they took their glasses to the table to talk in private. "Lance, I came to Vegas with Daryl because I want to work as a hooker." Loretta sat next to Lance.

He poured her another drink and listened to her story. She had moved out away from her husband after he had beaten her, bruising her face and blackening her eye. As fresh arrivals in Vegas, they were both out of place. Las Vegas is a different world. One night while waiting on dinner at a strip casino and getting a little impatient, Lance announced, "I am hungry enough to eat the hostess."

Her response, "Can I get that in writing?"

In the small world surrounding this bar, Loretta had moved in with Lance's Chicano girlfriend, Gabriela. *I guess girls talk*, mused Lance as she asked him if he knew any hookers. "Lance, Gabriela said she believed you could make the connections for me, hook me up to get started."

Lance tried to talk her out of making such a move. Lance even thought Vegas did not turn women out. He offered to put her up and help her find a job and place to live. "Loretta, I know about a dozen or so professional women and have a good general knowledge of how the profession works in Vegas. I have lived here for years and have both friends and customers in the profession. I have sold cars to numerous working girls." Lance did his best to try to talk her out of making such a move. "Let me warn you this is not a glamorous life. You will be moving to the dark side of humanity and be required or forced to do many unpleasant things. I have to leave early today. I have duty in the morning. Think about our conversation, and if you still want to, I will get together with you on Wednesday afternoon. I will drop in at Ollie's at one o'clock." Lance went by the dry cleaner's to pick up his uniforms, headed home, took a shower, ate a piece of cold pizza, and crashed. Lance was thinking this could only happen in Vegas.

Wednesday morning Lance was off at 7:30 a.m. It was a slow twenty-four-hour shift, so he had gotten a good night's sleep. Lance went to the gym, worked out for an hour, and swam for another thirty minutes. At home he jumped in the shower, toweled off, and then read the paper. He had a quick bowl of oatmeal for breakfast. Donning a snap-button shirt, Levi's, and black cowboy boots; a quick trip to the car wash; then off he went to Ollie's. Loretta was waiting and greeted him with a big friendly smile and a genuine glad-to-see-you hug.

"Lance, I allowed Daryl to drag me to Vegas. He is of no consequence to me now, and I need to get a restraining order against him."

"I will call my attorney friend," said Lance. Climbing in the Corvette, Lance got hard when she grabbed his leg. "Do you like Chinese?" asked Lance.

"Love it," said Loretta.

They picked up a double order to go. Next stop, his apartment. After some wonderful food, silly fortune cookies, and several glasses of wine, she stripped. Her body was youthful, her tits and ass superb, with a nice flat tummy and long muscular legs. Not an ounce of extra fat.

"Loretta, I know you have a plan, and I will do this for you. I am going to introduce you to three girlfriends. One, two, or possibly all three are working or have worked as prostitutes in Vegas. I will not tell you which. I am putting you on display. They will look you over, talk to you, and test you. Vegas is not an open or free market. Freelancing here is not legal. One of the three ladies I still date on occasions. This is the first step. You are not committed to do anything at this time, nor are you accepted. This is stage one."

"Oh, great, Lance, when do we start?" Loretta blurted out.

"I must get to work early tomorrow. Thursday, when we go to Gabriella's, you need to pick up several dress-up outfits. I will take you to a different home of each of the three women on Friday, Saturday, and Sunday. Here is my card in case you need to call me. There is a white robe hanging in the bathroom. Go take a shower so we can get to bed."

Lance called Gabriela, told her the plan, and asked if she needed anything, thanking her for helping Loretta out.

There she stood wearing his terrycloth guest robe. It was open in front, and Lance got a good view of her excellent body. She had dirty blond hair, and that was a natural color, as was her blond pubic hair. Lance had long ago figured out; if you want to know what color a woman's hair is, look at her pubes. Lance sat on the bed and had Loretta pull off his cowboy boots. Without hesitating, she was unsnapping his shirt, tossing it aside. Both hands went to his zipper and then a scream of anticipation. She had only one love, her husband, Daryl. Lance's member was so huge in comparison she cried in anticipation. She had her lovely warm mouth around the head of his penis licking and stroking. Lance allowed this until he became overstimulated. He pulled her head back by grabbing her shoulder-length hair, threw her on the bed, and drove his large member home deeply penetrating her pussy.

"I want all of it. Ignore my screams, just give me all of it."

They fucked until exhausted. Alarms went off, and Lance was out of bed and in the shower. Loretta made coffee and French toast. They ate, and he dropped her off on the way to the fire station. Once again, his spider sense went off, tingling, but he chose to ignore it again. He was too close, so he chose to see where this thing was going as opposed to leaving and always wondering what might have happened.

# 41
# Three Twenty-Seven (327)

A typical firefighter duty day. Muster in and roll call at seven thirty. Lance was the assigned emergency medical service (EMS) driver. He and his partner did the truck inspection, inventory, and washed the emergency truck. It went on all EMS calls and multiple alarm fire calls. To say it another way, the EMS unit made the majority of runs.

First run of the day was an injured man down the six-hundred-block Tonopah highway. Donning combat gear and rolling code three, red lights and siren, they arrived at the scene in a Chevrolet Impala with the hood up. One man was down on the ground, another was jumping up and down waving his arms. They had been cranking the engine with the carburetor removed. The coil was still in place with the wire pulled. When the gas came out of the fuel line, the spark from the coil blew off the valve cover hitting the injured man in the head. A mark from the valve covers, 327, was impressed backward upon his forehead. The mechanic side of Lance knew exactly what had happened. With some difficulty, he put on his serious professional face. The man stood up dazed and asked what happened. Lance and his partner took his vital signs and called an ambulance to transport Mr. 327 to the hospital for further testing.

Back at the station during lunchtime, Lance called the three girlfriends he had known for years: Cindy, a school executive secretary; Sonia, currently working as a hooker on the strip; and Rita, a manicurist for the stars. Lance asked each to give him things they observed in Loretta and any suggestions. The plan, Lance would take Loretta to each one of their homes for dinner. Lance handed each a list of questions for them to fill out in their observation, impressions, and recommendations. Lance had all three them all ask Loretta the same questions. They were not to share that part with Loretta. At the end of each one of those three evenings, Loretta and Lance went to his apartment for sexual games. At the end of two weeks, Lance would tell her if she had made it and would be introduced to and able to join in the sisterhood of Vegas. Lance considered prostitution a simple fact. He neither condoned it nor condemned it. He did find the laws regarding it silly and obviously written by men. This was Vegas, and there were prostitutes. Lance had traveled the world, and in every port, there were prostitutes.

Roman called and asked Lance if he could accompany him on the next trip to Santa Monica. "Lance, you can stay at my brother's apartment for free. He will be out of town."

"Roman, I have a chick living with me at the moment trying to stay away from her husband. Can I bring her along?"

"Of course, Lance, she is welcome."

Another four days in California. Lance borrowed a red Ford convertible from the lot. They all packed their shit in the trunk and hit the road. They did a quick stop in Barstow for gas and food, and their next stop was Santa Monica. Good music, good company, the trip went fast. First stop, Roman's brother's apartment. Wow, it included a view of the beach at Santa Monica. Roman gave Lance the key, and he called Heather to come pick him up; she lived minutes away. Heather showed up with some righteous weed. They all shared a joint, and then Lance and Loretta were left alone. A shower, sex, and a nap in that order.

Lance was having a fabulous dream. He opened his eyes and found out it was real. Loretta was up on one elbow with Lance's member in her mouth, kissing and stroking it. They were still naked, so Lance grabbed her two legs, brought her up on top of his face, and they had a sensational shared experience. Sixty-nine, you don't get any closer than that. Loretta was having fun with her new boy toy. A quick shower, shave, and toothbrushing, and they were off for breakfast. They walked to the pier and ate bacon, eggs, and potatoes. Much coffee was consumed.

"Lance, as I told you, I am changing my life. Please take me to a drugstore so I can get some hair dye."

Lance had lived with his sister and mother, so dying hair was not a new experience. "Loretta, men will be aware you are not a natural redhead once they see your blond pubes."

"Lance, I am dying them too."

"You can do that? Won't it burn your female parts?"

There went a lifetime of confidence in hair color starting at the age of sixteen with Amanda with the corn silk pubes. The whole hair-color situation now seemed absurd. Suddenly, Lance had a female friend that he knows is blond who has red hair and red pubic hair. This reminded Lance of debate class and one of his favorite logical fallacies. Post hoc ergo propter hoc—when the rooster crows immediately before sunrise, the rooster causes the sun to rise. Thus, if a woman has blond hair and black pubes, she is not a natural blond. Not always so.

Roman came by with Heather. They smoked a joint and walked the pier and the beach enjoying the high, tripping, laughing, and just being silly. Heather had three days off and decided to accompany them back to Vegas. Loretta told her girlfriend after the trip the if she had a chance, she should have sex with Lance; it was really good. Upon returning to Vegas, all three women who had met and tested Loretta came to the same conclusion. She was too sweet and innocent and did not need to be spoiled by the professional life. Lance took her to dinner and informed her; she cried like a three-year-old whose ice cream had fallen on the ground. She said, "But, Lance, what am I going to do?"

The girls had found her a job as a cocktail waitress. Not a lot of money but good tips. She followed up the restraining order with a Las Vegas divorce with Lance as her witness. Six months later, she married an electrician, had a couple of kids and a fairly normal life.

## 42
# Stocking the Lake

At this moment in time, Lance was in his sexual prime. He was acutely aware of the need to find a willing supply of woman looking for sex, not husbands. Having died, Lance knew life was short. He knew how to live in the moment taking your pleasures while you can. Sometimes opportunity shows up at just the right moment in your life. Lance again, not by accident, was in the right place at the right time riding the sexual revolution wave.

The state of Nevada tried to make getting divorce as painless as possible with minimum requirements, a six-week residency and a witness to verify that. Divorce for almost any reason and no proof required from 1931 through 1970, hundreds of thousands of people took advantage of liberal Nevada divorce laws. This constant migratory flow led to six-week room rentals with a free witness included. The witness testified in court that they had seen this person every day for six weeks. Divorce granted—next.

Dude ranches were popular. Divorcees, mostly women, spent six weeks riding horses, relaxing in the sun, and making the rounds also riding the help. Many a young man got worn-out working as a cowboy at divorce dude ranches. Hundreds of thousands of marriages came to an end in Nevada. A steady six-week rotating supply of women getting divorced, getting even, and looking for the fun they thought they were missing, Lance was resourceful enough to seize upon this opportunity. He was in the right place, Las Vegas, at the right time. He rented a house. Lance now had a house with five bedrooms and two baths. With his construction skills, he built a wall separating four bedrooms and one bath from the main side of the house. He now had four private bedrooms with front and rear entrances and shared bath to rent. The five acres it sat on provided plenty of parking. With this mass migratory movement of women seeking quickie divorces, Lance placed an advertisement: Bedroom for rent, free witness included. The phone began ringing. Lance began scheduling his life around wonderful six-week increments.

One of his divorce tenants was Sharon. She paid Lance in cash for her six-week divorce stay. Lance went to her car to get her bags. As he opened the door to her room, she was standing there naked. "Lance," she said with a Cheshire grin, "you are the first man to see me naked except for my soon-to-be-divorced husband. Like what you see?" She dropped to her knees as she saw Lance's rapidly hardening cock. "Wow, you should have put the size of that beautiful love muscle in your rooms-for-rent ad."

"Sharon, I am at your service at this moment. Between my job and other engagements, I may not be readily available for all your needs during your six-week period here. The price of the room includes a witness as advertised. I love sex. You are an exceptionally attractive woman." Lance now removed his clothing slowly, seductively. Now he also stood naked with a huge erection and queried, "Sharon, do you like what you see?"

She took her first chance to explore sexuality outside marriage. Hot and ready with her squinty eyes, she started out by taking the head of Lance's cock in her mouth. "Oh yes, come do me whatever way you want."

Three hours later they both retired for the night.

Sharon was so hot and adventurous; Lance took her to join in some nude swimming at Lake Mead with Roman Estevez and his girlfriend, Heather, from Santa Monica. Out to Lake Mead in the morning, the four of them hiked back to an area away from public view. Out came the beer, and off came the clothes. Lance and Heather were impressed by each other's naked bodies. He never hit on a friend's girlfriend. A fun couple of hours drinking, diving from cliffs, and goofing made for an enjoyable day. Lance and Sharon went home to his place to cool from the swimming and were sexily, hotly stimulated. The next six hours was spent playing with and enjoying each other's bodies. Just another tenant at Lance's rooms to rent Vegas. Six weeks later they went to divorce court, and he swore he saw her each and every day. Lance thought he had died and went to heaven or *Nirvana. Four rooms filled with divorcing horny women constantly changing with new prospects. What could go wrong?*

*The well went dry, and Lance could not get it re-drilled due to new water rules and regulations. More rules. Lance had to give up the house, move, and then find other fertile fields.*

# 43

# Fire Department

For ten days a month, Lance was a serious, hardworking professional firefighter. Through his hard work and studies, he got promoted to driving the rescue unit. The fire department was divided into three platoons working twenty-four-hour shifts. Each platoon had a locker to keep its food in the kitchen for their shift days. Each firefighter contributed money to the chow fund for their meals while working. The quickest way to get cooking duties was to complain about the food. Some shifts had great cooks. Sadly, at other times, they could not prepare a hot dog. Lance's shift at every month ending would take the balance left in the chow fund, and his engine company went down to the local casino. There they bet on the horses. If you are ever in Vegas, do not be surprised to see a fire truck parked in front of a casino. Not an emergency, fire, or routine inspection, just the captain placing a bet.

There was a two-bell call for downtown Glitter Gulch. A gray-haired grandmother in her eighties was having trouble breathing. First response firefighters placed an oxygen mask over her face. She responded immediately, got her color back. Her daughter said, "Mom, let's go home."

Rather than follow up with medical treatment, she said, "Hell no, I'm winning," got back on her stool, and began pulling the handles on two slot machines.

*La vie est belle.*

Call completed, while riding back to the station, Lucky Jerry told Lance he was flying the next day, working on his commercial pilot's license, his dream. "Want to come along and fly with me?"

Lance of course said yes; he loved flying in small planes.

Jerry picked him up in the morning, and the two went out to the airport. Jerry checked in at the flying school, and they jumped into a little Citabria airplane. This is a plane designed for stunt flying. "Lance, I have to practice loops and rolls." Climbing into the two-tandem seating, front and rear, Jerry, as part of his checklist, ensured Lance was properly restrained in the back seat with the military style five-point seat harness. "You are going to need this, pal." The Citabria, a light single-engine, two-seat, fixed conventional gear airplane, was made to manage aerobatic stresses. In two hours of flying, they put the plane through its paces. Lance, with his stainless-steel stomach, did not get sick from the acrobatics. They landed, and Lance bought lunch at the airport.

Lance had duty the next day. Listening to the dispatch radio, Lance heard the engine company from a different station responding to a call. A small plane had a violent collision with the ground. This turned out to be the same Citabria Lance had been flying in just the day before. The cloth covering on the plane peeled away, burying itself nose first forcing a fifty-foot-deep hole into the desert, pilot and passenger killed. Same plane, the Citabria, next day. Once again Lance had narrowly averted death. Moving in life from a submarine sailor to a firefighter, he understood he was constantly flirting with death. His small plane fascination was just icing on the cake. Lance did for a moment think about his flirting with married woman, death, and the grand scheme of his existence. The thought quickly passed.

# 44

# Gina the Receptionist

Off shift, Gina, the receptionist at the car lot, had taken a liking to Lance. Several times she remained after closing having Lance drive her home, claiming her car was in the shop. One Wednesday evening Lance worked late. She gave him the sly-eye look coupled with a smile. He had sold a car for cash. While completing the paperwork and logging in the trade, Lance thought he was alone. Gina surprised him stepping into his office, saying she had something to show him. She led him by the hand to the owner's office. Up on the second floor, it had a glass window on the front side overlooking the sales floor. Usually, it was covered with remote-controlled curtains. A soundproof room for making deals? At the back wall stood the owner's desk. It was custom-made stained solid walnut in a renaissance style. It was intimidating, six feet long by four feet wide. Lance sat down in the boss's leather chair, put on his come-on-to-me grin, and asked Gina, "Show me what you do for Harold when you come up here and he closes the curtains." She had earlier removed her slip and panties, and as she walked in front of the desk lamp, Lance could see her prominent black pubic hairs through her skirt. Lance was in an extremely playful mood. He had already closed and locked the front door. He surreptitiously opened his fly on the way to the owner's office. While sitting, he pulled out his erection. "Gina, do you know what to do with this?"

She dropped to her knees and took his Murasaki katana into her mouth, vigorously licking and stroking while massaging his balls. Lance exploded filling her mouth with cum. She successfully swallowed most with a little sweet, salty fluid dripping down her chin. Gina now laid back on the desk pulling up her miniskirt. She had removed her panties previously. "Now, Lance, do you know what to do with this?"

Lance slid up to her and went to town on her, face first into her black hairy breach. How he loved to eat pussy, and hers was wonderful and responsive. Lance was gifted with a long and very agile tongue. He could touch the end of his nose with it easily and practiced movements with it every day after brushing his teeth. Clean healthy breath, strong teeth and well trained and exercised tongue muscles. Was Lance becoming preoccupied with sex? Gina crossed her legs over Lance's head and almost crushed him while screaming in ecstasy. "Lance, I knew you were a player." She now removed the rest of her clothes. Lance followed suit completely disrobing himself. Gina brought out a bottle of wine in one hand, two glasses in the other. "I know you see a lot of women." Gina stood up and turned around. "How do I compare?"

"I would give you an A plus," Lance responded. "You must be asking for a reason."

"Lance, Harold pays me a cash bonus for sex. That is why I know this room and where everything in here is. I am considering for the money going into the trade full-time. We both know you have numerous hookers that buy cars from you. How about introducing me to the right people?" Gina now stood and laid forward over the desk patting her behind and begging Lance to fuck her as hard as he could. He slid his cock up and down her dripping wet pussy lips and then slowly at first penetrated her about an inch. Slowly with each stroke, he went in a little deeper. Sliding his right hand down, he started to finger her clit. Then he did four strokes slowly and four rapidly varying the process until she screamed, her pussy tightened up, and she came again. She totally relaxed and fell asleep. Lance grabbed some Kleenex, dried himself off, and dressed. Here was a girl that was just as much fun with your clothes off or on. Gina woke up; it was 3:00 a.m. She smiled, quickly dressed, and they walked out holding hands.

The next day at work Lance asked Gina to join him for a drink after the car lot closed. He met her at the Silver Saddle Saloon. He felt this was a safe place to hold a what-if conversation about selling sex. At his request, Bridgette, Lance's hooker friend, dropped in and joined them in the booth. The trio went to Gina's two-bedroom apartment a couple of blocks off the strip. Bridgette was wearing a yellow and flowery top, a short skirt with hemline just below her butt. She had excellent legs and enjoyed being a sexual tease. She guided them to the living room. Bridgette put out a bottle of red wine and a wood cheese board with an ensemble of little squares of cheese, an adorable set of miniature swords from Toledo, Spain, laid out to stab and eat the various cheeses. Wine and cheese or wine and sex. *Life does not get any better*, thought Lance. Now Lance and Bridgette sat down on a brown leather couch. She told Gina about a dozen real, brutal, and scary moments in her professional life. "Gina, don't do it. One day you will thank me for this conversation."

Monday, at the car lot, Gina put in two weeks' notice. She moved back in with her parents in Salt Lake City to finish her degree.

# 45

# The Spa

Roman Estevez from Santa Monica called at that moment. He was interested in renting an apartment at a spa and wanted Lance as a roommate. Both were committed to working out to keep in shape. The spa had a weight and workout room, heated and unheated Olympic pools, and three different temperature spas. Like Vegas, the spa facilities were open twenty-four hours a day. Lance loved it. Daily Lance did one hour in the weight room, two laps in the unheated Olympic pool, one lap in the unheated pool, and then each of the three hot spas until totally relaxed. The apartment contained a large living room, small but adequate kitchen with a bar and stools for eating. There were two bedrooms on opposite sides. Each was large and had its own private bathroom and walk-in shower. Perfect place to live and work out. It had plenty of parking which Lance now needed as he occasionally brought a demo vehicle home. Timing is everything, and opportunities were Lance's to pick and choose as he saw fit. Lance returned the pickup he used to move at the car lot and swapped it for a 1966 Austin-Healey 3000 Mark III sports convertible. Actually Lance was test-driving for himself. Lance was not a gambler and rarely entered a casino. Lance already owned a Corvette and would not sell it. The Healey was being considered as a possible second car for racing. It was smaller than the Vette and lighter.

The first week living at the spa, Lance went to a bar he knew was usually full of female prospects. Lance was horny and needed to break in the new pad. The Jackpot Bar, where a fellow firefighter worked part-time, was one of Lance's favorite playgrounds. It was spring, the weather perfect. The weather in Las Vegas was usually hot, cold, or windy. Most evenings were pleasant and good convertible weather. Lance went racing down the strip in the Healey with the top down, four speed with overdrive—what a fun car to drive. As Lance walked in the door, Kevin sat up his drink Jack and water back. "Put it on my tab, Kevin, what's up here?" Nothing exciting. The bar was dimly lit, U-shaped with twenty barstools on chrome legs with oversize red Naugahyde seats. Another twenty tables, each with four chairs, surrounded the wooden dance floor. No band on stage at this hour early in the evening, around 6:00 p.m. An organized group of divorcees had taken up about half the tables and were keeping the cocktail waitress Helen jumping. She was a typical Vegas gin jockey, five feet plus, bleached blond hair. She was wearing a push-up bra, half of her titties popping out. She was wearing a red miniskirt with the same color as the barstools, black fishnet stockings, and red high heels. She would not have looked out of place in any bar, lounge, or casino in Vegas. She was busy hustling tips trying to get by. Living in Las Vegas, Lance knew how critical tips were to workers in the entertainment industry. Hell, many jobs did not pay a salary; the person's total income depended on tips. Lance was drinking his Jack and trading bullshit with Kevin who was double-shooting Lance's drinks. A very thin, pale woman, five foot four, maybe one hundred ten pounds, wearing a white blouse, no bra, had perky nipples sticking out. She had closely cropped black hair, black bell-bottom slacks, and tennis shoes. There were five empty barstools on either side of Lance, but she slid into the one next to Lance on his right-hand side.

"Kevin, give this lovely woman whatever she wants."

"My name is Sheri, and the reason I sat here is because I want you. I just arrived from LA, and I need a place to rest my head."

"Sheri," replied Lance, "follow me out to the spa." Lance fired up the Healey and drove slow enough not to lose her. How excited was Lance? This certainly was not Lance's first rodeo. There was something about this Sheri and her open "I am in charge" sex drive. He had an erection in the car driving home. He parked, and Sheri pulled up next to him. She brought in a small suitcase and followed Lance to his bedroom. Sheri now took control, closed and locked the door. She pulled Lance up close enough to feel her heartbeat and stuck her tongue into his mouth, kissing and teasing. As Lance grabbed her breast, she grabbed his Mr. Excalibur, expressing happy surprise.

"Lance, I think we are going to have a good time together."

They shed their clothes in seconds. Lance kissed her neck as she collapsed on the bed. Lance laid down, and Sheri climbed on top. Straddling Lance, she slowly lowered herself onto his cock taking in all of it. He gripped her tightly as she moved up and down in a rhythmic motion. Lance took his right hand and began massaging her swollen clit. Lance and Sheri were on a sexual experimentation honeymoon, each learning what the other one liked and sharing in each other's fun.

The next night she astonished Lance when he parked the Austin-Healey. As small as the car was, she still found a way to give him a blow job. At the spa, they took a bottle of wine and two glasses. With hot bubbles surrounding and blowing up and tickling both of their bodies, Lance had Sheri open the flap on her one-piece swimsuit. A lesson not forgotten about women's swimsuits from his young days with Amanda and her corn silk. Lance dropped his suit and penetrated her, kissing, playing around, having wonderful sex. It was around midnight, and they assumed no one was around. The security guard showed up. He had one of those pencil mustaches that made him look evil like some TV villain. He was either following the rules and making his rounds or a pervert. He lectured them on bringing glasses to the spa area. Lance never moved. The entire time he remained with his dick buried deep in Sheri, never losing his hard-on. As soon as the guard was out of sight, Lance began pumping again and Sheri pushing back stroke for stroke. Lance got the feeling she had gotten extremely aroused by getting caught having sex out in the open. She shuddered and quivered as she had multiple orgasms. Once again Lance proved, just like on the Greyhound bus, sex in public with an audience was not a problem. She had some thyroid problems with cold hands, almost all fingers turning blue. That night when she grabbed Lance's nut sack with her icy cold right hand, he woke up screaming like a little girl.

The next day Lance had duty. When he was called to the phone at the Fire Department, his roommate, Roman, attempted to explain how Sheri had moved in with a neighbor. Apparently, Sheri got tired of Roman walking around the apartment in his underwear hoping to get a blow job. "The neighbor hoped you weren't angry or upset about her moving in with him."

Lance, without hesitation, told Roman, "Thank him for me." She and Lance had great sex but no real future together. After hanging up, Lance wondered if he had a future. At what point may his successfully seducing another man's wife bring the cuckold's revenge?

Lance was driving to work one morning and noticed an attractive young lady wearing a skirt. A magic gust of wind blew it up over her eyes showing some sexy legs and bright international green-colored panties. She recovered, pushed her skirt down, looked at Lance, and smiled. A wonderful start to an enjoyable day. The next day after working, Lance had a two-day off. Go to the apartment or have a beer at his favorite watering hole? Lance flipped a coin, and the bar won. Lance parked and ambled inside. It was ten o'clock in the morning, a bright, hot sunshiny day in Vegas. Not a cloud in the sky. From 112 degrees Fahrenheit to seventy-two in the bar. The dimly lit bar took some adjusting by the eyes. Sitting down on his favorite barstool, his buddy, the bartender, had his draft beer ready. They were pleased to see each other, no one else in the place. They were shooting the breeze, killing time, when suddenly the front door slowly eased open. Against the bright sunlight outdoors and the dimly lit bar was the appearance of a woman that could have been described as a delightfully attractive woman. Yes, an angel in Las Vegas. She walked into the bar, carrying a reflective purse that caught everyone's eye. He immediately wondered what goodies she might have inside.

The bar had about twenty stools and six faux leather wraps around booths seating four each. She strolled down the bar body moving, swaying, while mesmerizing Lance and the barkeep. She wore a white short-sleeved blouse and a black leather miniskirt barely covering her long sexy legs. Empty bar yet she slid onto the stool next to Lance. She smiled, ordered a Michelob and another round for Lance. Names exchanged during a handshake, Inga got right to the point. "I am so lonely. I just can't stand another day being alone in my apartment watching TV."

Lance was quick to pick up on her vibes and offered to follow her home. She smiled, finished her drink, and led the way. Lance followed Inga's car and parked next to her at her apartment. Inga in the lead, Lance right behind her, walked into her apartment. It was a cookie-cutter two-bedroom. There was a wall, closet, then next, the hall entryway. On the right side were the kitchen, the living room with a couch, glass coffee table, and recliner facing the console TV on the other side of the room. Master bedroom with bath, one guest bedroom and guest bath were in the hallway. The walls were off-white, no pictures or paintings hanging. She set her shiny purse on the breakfast counter. Inga poured two glasses of red wine as she indicated to Lance with her hand to sit on the couch. The air was thick with pheromones, his and hers mingling. Lance could tell by her voice how tense and nervous she was. By this point, Lance had dated and had given massages on numerous dates. Putting his skills to work, Lance pulled Inga to him; starting with her neck, he began massaging her tightened muscles. Inga began loosening up, moaning on how good it felt. She melted in his hands.

Lance commanded, "Inga, lie down on your stomach and I will work on your back."

She complied, and Lance unzipped the back of her blouse and began working the neck and shoulder area. Skillfully as he had been trained, he worked this area down to her bra. Lance casually unsnapped her bra. She hollered, "Don't do that."

In his most soft and comforting voice, he said, "Inga, it's okay. I will re do it when your massage is over." Having access to her entire back, Lance worked from her buttocks to her neck. his hands slowly moving to both sides including the part of her breasts that were now exposed.

She was purring. She suddenly sat up and asked, "Do you have any venereal diseases?"

Lance answered truthfully, "No."

Inga now took charge and told Lance, "Take a shower."

When Lance stepped out of the shower, he found her lying on the couch naked flat on her back, now showing off her ample breasts and prominent nipples. Inga took off the towel Lance had wrapped around him, and after a careful look at Lance's schwanz, she smiled. "Good-looking and well-endowed. My husband is stationed in Germany for six months. I need sex now." She grabbed Lance's cock and took the end of it into her large mouth with the reddest of lips. She moaned as Lance reached down and kneaded her nipples. Lance pushed her head back, got on his knees, and buried his face into her dripping pussy. She wrapped her legs around his neck in a headlock moving in a frantic rhythm. Lance chewed on her clit until she came in no time. Now she was ready for Lance. He pulled her to the floor, spun her around. With her knees on the floor and her body bent over the couch, Lance hit her from behind. Slowly he worked her, with his big penis inside her stroking and his nut sack bouncing against her clit. "Oh god," she moaned. His hands massaging her breasts, Lance waited till she came. He was large enough to find her G-spot, and she loved that. Lance had a new lover. They both wanted to see more of each other and did whenever their schedule allowed. Lance spent many a day and night with her. When her husband returned from Germany, she introduced him to Lance. Lance shook hands and left for the evening. Never did he figure out her game, but Lance was never comfortable around a husband he had cuckolded.

Two young ladies, a pair of confidantes, often hit the bars together. Lance had noticed them and occasionally shared a toast and conversation. Kathy was five feet one inch and a classic beauty. She had been an airline stewardess. Her girlfriend, Debra, was six feet tall. Athletic, she was with a perfectly sculptured body. Alas, when it came to looks, Debra was less than attractive. She was a tall and sultry woman probably 60–70 percent in the appearance lottery. Lance pondered how different might her life have might have been had she gotten a face to match her body. One night she cornered Lance and told him flat out she wanted to take him home and seduce him. "I am super horny, and I need you," pleaded Debbi.

Lance smiled, jumped into his Corvette, and followed her home. Debbi shared a two-bedroom duplex with Kathy. Lance parked on the street and followed. "Kathy is gone for the weekend," whispered Debbi as she unlocked the door. "Lance, please remove your shoes and leave them in the tile hallway to protect our white carpet."

Lance took a glance at the interior. Nice black leather couch and recliner, a glass coffee and matching end tables, two blue matching lamps with flower print shades, a separate dining area, and a breakfast bar with four stools. Behind the couch was a print of *The Starry Night* by Vincent van Gogh. Lance liked the layout. There were two master bedrooms each with their own baths, common in Vegas upscale apartments. Debbi took Lance by the hand leading him to her bedroom. The bedroom had Spanish tile flooring with matching throw rugs on each side of the four-poster California king bed. Four king-size pillows with satin cases matched the sheets. There were matching end tables with lamps and each one with scented candles teasing Lance's olfactory receptors.

"Lance, there is soap on a rope in the shower, shampoo, a hanger to put your clothes on, and a white terrycloth robe. It should fit you. It was my ex's."

Lance, following Debbi's orders, neatly hung his clothes on the hanger. Shower time over, Lance stepped out, dried himself, and put on the robe.

In a deep and sexy voice, Debbi pleaded, "Lance, I am waiting for you." Debbi was ready, wearing a matching robe. She undid the belt, and her robe fell open revealing a stunningly beautiful body. She gently removed her robe as Lance hypnotically watched. She was moist and ready, and when Lance pulled his robe off, she screamed. She pulled Lance onto her while falling back on the bed. She was a screamer. "Fuck me, do me." Her rapid breathing filled the room as her body flushed with heat.

Lance hollered, "Tell me, Debbi, you want this, how much do you want it?"

Suddenly her body stiffened. She rolled her eyes into the back of her head and had an earthshaking orgasm. Lance joined in with this excitement and filled her with his seed. They both collapsed in exhilarating ecstasy. After resting up and catching their breath, Lance noticed the flickering light of the candles on the ceiling. New orders from Debbi. She had Lance lay flat on the bed with his head on one of the pillows. They now went sixty-nine as she climbed on top. She had Lance stick a large black vibrating dildo she had covered with KY jelly up her ass. More moaning and screaming and another overwhelming orgasm. Cuddled up, they both fell asleep.

At six in the morning, Lance awoke to the smell of coffee and bacon. The morning started out slowly, coffee brewing, caffeine smell filling the air. His eyes started to adjust to the dawn's sunshine as it slowly rose above the barren brown mountains. This woman could cook eggs, bacon, pancakes, coffee, and orange juice. Still adorned in their terrycloth robes, they ate breakfast at the kitchen bar. She thanked Lance for the evening, but Lance interjected, saying, "Debbi, it was an absolute pleasure being with you."

"Lance," she stated with a serious look upon her face, "I am getting married and moving to Los Angeles next weekend. I know this night will remain our secret."

He pulled her close with a big hug and promised as he explained his philosophy. This was their sexual secret. Wonderful moments between two people were not to be shared. Honestly, Lance was sorry to see her slip away. Another sexually great one slipping away to get married. A shame that happened all too often lately.

Visiting Tommy at his apartment, it was a chamber-of-commerce-perfect kind of day. Lance threw on his swimsuit and grabbed a lounge chair at the pool. One of the benefits of this apartment was the Olympic-sized pool. There were chairs and tables with umbrellas and about a dozen lounge chairs. Lance sat in a lounge chair hoping to work on his tan. At the deep end was a standard low diving board with all the appropriate safety signs. At noon, the Vegas sun was directly overhead. A gorgeous young lady in a bright yellow polka-dot bikini the size of a postage stamp walked to the board, jumped on the end, and flipped into the pool. She came out of the pool dripping and sat down on the recliner next to Lance, breathtakingly good-looking with wavy wet black shoulder-length hair clinging to her. The second thing he noticed were her lime-green eyes flashing the tell.

"Hi, my name is Rhonda. My friends call me Ronny."

"Well, hi, Ronny, my name is Lancelot, but my friends call me Lance. Ronny, there are a dozen lounge chairs here, yet you sat down next to me. What exactly can I do for you today?"

"Lance, my husband constantly comes home and accuses me of cheating."

"Ronny, are you cheating on your husband?"

"No, Lance, I'm not."

Lance, without hesitation, said, "Would you like to?"

Ronny stood up, grabbed Lance's hand, and led him to her apartment on the third floor. As they walked through her apartment's front door, before she could close it, her neighbor caught her and begged her to babysit her kids. A medical emergency. Lance, ever the gentleman, quietly left the two of them talking. They never crossed paths again.

One night while out wilding led to an accidental discovery. Miha lived in a house in a middle-class subdivision in Vegas. Yes, all the houses looked the same. Out drinking with friends, someone piped up, "Hey, we can all go crash at Miha's house." Lance crashed on the couch. Around

3:00 a.m., he woke up to Miha having his dick in her mouth and hands around his granite-hard cock. No, it was not a wet dream. He and Miha became friends. She was about twenty-eight. When she laughed, which was seldom, it sounded like a dryer full of marbles. She was tall, had a flat stomach, small but very erect breasts, and was a full-blooded Cherokee. She just loved to suck cock, any cock. She was also a great fuck and had multiple orgasms easily and often. She and Lance hit it off sexually. Whenever her husband was out of town, which was quite often due to his job, she touched base with Lance. She never hesitated starting out by giving Lance head. Miha also loved different positions and getting fucked in the ass. One New Year's evening they timed their lovemaking to come at the stroke of midnight. Others kissed; they came. She loved to have sex in public places, elevators, sneaking behind buildings, in the car, in a busy shopping center. She, like Lance, was constantly horny. She loved sucking his huge cock, and Lance loved eating her wet black hairy pussy.

Lance was making the rounds at his usual watering holes. He observed a couple of his female friends and joined them at their table. Lance was introduced to a new young lady, Sara. All three of the group worked together at the phone company. The new girl, Sara, had just recently got divorced and needed some company. Lance came recommended (it was great to be well-endowed and sexually gifted). It was not long before Sara followed him home and they were in bed making love. Lance just loved recently divorced women. They suddenly had sexual freedom and wanted to experiment and find out what they felt they were missing. Sara was no exception. She was hungry for loving and responded with ferocity. She got up dressed and went home surprising Lance on the way out after exchanging phone numbers and promising to get together tomorrow. The surprise? She had to get home to relieve the babysitter watching her two kids. Sara had so impressed Lance that he spent the next day sharing a smile for all to see. Something special had occurred in his daily life bringing about a change neither he nor Sara had contemplated. How was it possible that a woman so average and plain could have given rise to such strong emotions? She weighed 110 pounds, had black wavy hair and dark as coal eyes. Sara was fun to be with before, during, and after sex. They seemed to be on the same frequency and finely tuned to each other in all areas. Sara had married her high school sweetheart. Married at seventeen, she had a daughter that was nine and a son that was five. Like the water falling over Niagara Falls, Lance was quickly being drawn into her world and life. Within a week, Lance had moved into her three-bedroom house in a nice subdivision. Amazingly, Lance and her nine-year-old daughter hit it off and became buds immediately. Suddenly these were happy days in the kingdom. Sara was happy to have a man to share her life with her. After nine of years of so-so sex that became more of a required duty as opposed to satisfaction, Sara now shared in mutual orgasms. Sara and Lance went out clubbing, dancing, and to other social obligations. One Saturday Lance's firefighting had him assigned for first aid duty at a city park. He called Sara and had her come visit. Within minutes, Lance had Sara locked in the restroom, pulled down her jeans and panties, and was administering first aid with his face buried in her crotch. After Sara came, Lance, still in his firefighter's uniform, bent her over the sink and buried his member deep inside. They both achieved orgasm. Sara drove home, and Lance finished his shift and returned to the station.

While living with Sara, the recently divorced phone operator, Little Sara, who had occasionally babysat, moved in. Her mother had her legally declared an adult and then threw her out. She still had six months left to graduate from high school. Little Sara agreed to working as a live-in babysitter in exchange for having a home until she finished high school. Big Sara, Lance's girlfriend, worked for the phone company and had odd hours. Split shifts most evenings she worked. This left Lance and Little Sara home alone. Once the kids were asleep, they watched TV. They talked. She told Lance about losing her virginity and how unrewarding she felt as it took place. She had barely allowed the football star to have her, and he came after two or three strokes. "Is that all it is?" she asked. The kids were down for the night. It was February, and Lance had a nice fire warming the dimly lit living room. Little Sara got out of the shower and sat down next to Lance wearing a red terry cloth robe. As she spoke, she slid closer to Lance. "My mom took me to the doctor's for birth control pills. She took me to the sheriff's office and had me declared an adult. I sleep in the bedroom right next to Big Sara and you. I have heard Big Sara moaning in pleasure and wondered what is it you do that brings on her moaning." She was, of course, a novice in the art of seduction. "Lance, I want to learn from you."

"What about Big Sara?" asked Lance.

"This will be our secret, between us, not the rest of the world," she replied with an irresistibly alluring look.

Lance was overwhelmed by her presence, her fresh sexual enticing smell. Lance thought back to his fourteenth birthday and how Mrs. Jenkins began teaching him about the ways of the world. One of his most rewarding life experiences. Now he had a sixteen-year-old, not a virgin on the beach but inexperienced and wanting to learn. It was his turn to be the teacher, to pay forward. After all, not everyone can be Mother Teresa. Lance had more than enough experience to become the teacher. Her gorgeous youthful curiosity stimulated Lance. He raised his arm, pulled her deep into the couch, and buried his tongue sliding between her lips dueling with her seeking tongue. Little Sara felt every nerve vibrating. Lance looked straight into her eyes and stated, "This is ours and no one else's. You are correct. We have the right to share and enjoy each other."

Little Sara fell back into the couch as Lance dropped down on his knees, touching her tenderly over her entire body. Lance insinuated his tongue between her teeth again while his hands softly parted the robe exposing her young nubile body dreamily tempting Lance's entire being. Kissing, he dropped from her hot lips to her firm young breasts. Sara was pushing them up for Lance and her pleasure. Her nipples were as hard as a brass nozzle but extremely sensitive to his every kiss and touch. His warm hands touched and fondled both breasts.

In his most seductive voice, Lance announced, "I want you, Sara, all of you."

Little Sara managed to slip out of the white robe entirely. What Lance could not touch and kiss, he readily feasted upon her naked entirety with his eyes. As Lance pulled her up to him wrapping an arm around her and fondling one breast, his other hand traveled up her leg. As his hand slowly crept up her leg, Sara started crooning and moaning, his compelling, well-practiced hands fondling her here, massaging her there gently stroking her skin. Skillfully his hands raised her desires to a tsunami level. When Lance reached her bud, softly caressing and driving her crazy with his slow circular caressing, she felt hot flashes emanating from her surrendered body. She felt his breath and his hot lips pressing against her bud and suddenly the tongue forcing itself into her passage. She was ready. Lance dropped his skivvies and put her left hand on his member. "Oh god, it's big," she exclaimed and laid back with her knees open, awaiting penetration. Sara was not disappointed as Lance suddenly penetrated her inner body. Now Little Sara gasped; the babysitter was now moaning like Big Sara. She moaned so loud that Lance put his hand over her mouth, afraid she would wake up the kids. For the next three months, Lance was busy with both Saras. What a joy to have a succulent sixteen-year-old senior make herself available while Sara worked and then to have Big Sara come home ready for romance. Little Sara graduated from high school, moved in with a boyfriend, and won several local beauty contests. She still kept in touch with Lance and occasionally joined him for an evening of sex.

Big Sara had innumerable troubles with her ex and decided to move back to Oregon. Lance had a cousin Albert that lived in Portland and agreed to take her there so her parents could come and get her. A U-Haul trailer attached to the back of Lance's Cadillac Coupe DeVille, and off they went. Kid's furniture and clothes and the great trip began. Lance knew it was a long drive and took some uppers to keep awake. He had a distance of over a thousand miles and fifteen plus hours of driving. He loved to take long trips and was intent on driving start to finish. His cousin Albert lived in an old five-bedroom house with some hippie friends. At the Oregon-California border, Sara and the kids wanted to stop and eat. An all-you-can-eat place fit the needs of the moment. Sara was paying for the trip including gas and food. Lance accompanied them but was wired and not hungry. Sara insisted he eat something, so he took a child-size bowl of spaghetti. When Lance found out the owner had charged her full price for his little plate, he got angry. He picked up a plate and started eating. When he was getting his fifth plate of food, the owner offered his money back if he would quit eating. Lance successfully delivered the trailer and kids to her parents' house.

Arriving at Cousin Albert's house in Portland, Sara and Lance were shown their bedroom. Time to rest and party. Rest first. Crash city, they slept for about twelve hours. They then took a shower, wore clean clothes, and ate breakfast: bacon, eggs over easy or snotty, as Lance called them. The day was spent at the house. What a fun place. The old house was two stories with a basement and attic. The stairs that noisily creaked and groaned led up to three of the five bedrooms. A red brick facade on the outside and antique plaster covered the interior walls. An odd picture here and there, none by artists Lance recognized. A gas furnace in the basement provided hot water to the radiators in each room. The furnace at times growled giving the impression the old place was haunted. At least that was what Lance believed. The only one home at noon when Lance and Sue woke up was Melinda. She was sweet and shy and did not fit in comfortably with any group. She was twenty years old and had married her high school sweetheart. One night while making love, her twenty-one-year-old husband had a heart attack and died while lying on top of her. She had not mentally fully recovered. Lance wondered if she ever would. What a tragedy she had to bear at such an early age. Often, she would just break out in tears and cry like a baby.

Around five thirty, the rest of the house tenants arrived. Cousin Albert arrived with his girlfriend, Julia, and two large hot pepperoni pizzas. Excellent choice, who does not love pizza? His roommate, Marvin, and his girlfriend drifted in each carrying a gallon jug of a local Portland wine they were so proud of. All the windows were open, and the rain brought in the pleasant smell of the trees. This was so refreshing and invigorating, not hot dusty desert air. The group sat around the living room and shared pizza. Red wine and pizza got all feeling mellow. The stories began as they were apt to. Albert brought out a package of Nestle chocolate. Soon a dose of mescaline was prepared for everyone.

Sara had never taken drugs and was hesitant but convinced by all it was okay. Soon all were tripping. They had the TV on with no sound. Each one of them picked a character and filled in their own voice. Great fun, lots of giggles and laughter. Sara took Lance by the hand almost dragging him to their bedroom. Clothes were shed. Lance and Sara were well familiar with each other's bodies, wants, and needs. This was different. Sara pulled Lance onto her naked body, both enjoying the mescaline moment, the riot of colors, the flashes, the sheer multiplication of the body's senses beyond normal. A state-bound moment of sheer pleasure. Lance was so stoned he thought he could hear her heartbeat. "Wow, Lance, your body is hot, a glowing inferno." Sara sighed and cooed, "That was the greatest sex I have ever had." The next morning, she had dragged Lance to Keller Fountain downtown Portland trying to score some more mescaline. No luck, he took her to the bus station to head on out to her parents' house in Medford, Oregon. Lance and Sara were sad. They had crossed paths, hit it off, and really liked each other. Once again life got in the way. Driving home alone, Lance was brought to tears while reminiscing. It was enough to take the smile off the Mona Lisa. Lance really missed Sara and her kids. He often wondered what his life would have been like had she stayed. *Where am I really going with my life again?* wondered Lance.

# 46
# Charlie

Arriving back in Vegas from the Oregon trip and a quick shower done, Lance hit the bars and clubs. Amazingly, a woman with one of the hottest bodies Lance had run across was hitting on Lance. Her girlfriend tried to intercede, but Charlene, or Charlie as she called herself, was in the mood and followed Lance home. She was wearing a one-piece bright-red leather minidress with the hem just below her butt, matching go-go boots, and a smile that would light up a room. When she bent over, you could see her panties. No bra, perky breasts, more than a mouthful. Italian family, wonderful olive complexion, dark black hair, and eyes the color of black coffee. Lance guided her to the master bedroom. He went to the master bath to take a leak, and when he came out, she was lying down on the bed wearing only her thong, her clothes lying pooled on the floor. Lance removed his shirt, dropped his pants. Not wearing undies, he now stood naked with a swaggering hard-on.

"Oh yes, I was right," she moaned. Charlie ripped off her thong. "Now fuck me with that big donkey dick. Ignore my screams, just give me all of it."

Lance was thrilled to see her in bed and ready, this hot, sexy woman. He went down on that bushy black hair pie and brought her to her first mini orgasm. They fucked four more times that night. When Charlie woke in the morning, she said, "My girlfriend was afraid you would take me home and fuck the shit out of me. She was right. Life is good."

Lance remained living in Sara's house another three months until it was repossessed. Charlie was a twenty-one dealer and a professional poker player for five years. Off-the-charts brilliant and due to her profession, she was adept at reading body language. She knew Lance was hot for her body. At a friend's house, she broke out a deck of cards and said, "Watch close. Pay absolute attention." Charlie dealt from the top, middle, and bottom of the deck, and she was so good no one could tell. Lance knew she could perform the same kind of magic in the bedroom. Three weeks of hot steamy loving. Sex with her was like eating ice cream and having a brain freeze. You can't wait to get over it, but you go right back for more ice cream. The two of them hit it off. Together they were as comfortable as an old broken in pair of shoes.

Lance got a phone call from a fellow firefighter who was also a realtor. A lease on a two-bedroom house was coming up on the market. Charlie was all hot and excited about moving in with Lance. The same day Roman called him and told him there would be an apartment available at Players Apartments where he had just moved in. This was the most popular singles apartments in Vegas at the time, and a vacancy occurred very rarely. Lance was faced with another what-should-I-do decision. Lance went with Charlie and looked at the house. He then went to Roman's apartment at Players and was shown around. The Players' apartment complex consisted of single-story, one-bedroom apartments surrounded by a six-foot wooden privacy fence. A tenant was issued three keys. The first one opened the gates to get through the fence into the apartment complex, second the key to the apartment, and third key for the gate to the nude swimming pool. The complex had two pools, one a regular swimming pool and the second the nude pool. They were all one-bedroom apartments. The apartments' entry was a sliding glass door with privacy curtains. Stepping into the living room on the right was a breakfast bar, and behind that the kitchen to the left a couch, recliner, and coffee table. Walking straight forward was the bedroom door. Each had a king-size bed and a master bath. Tile floors in the kitchen and bath area, nice soft carpeting on the floors, good enough to walk on barefoot or have sex on. Lance had to decide. Move in with Charlie or move to Players with this rare apartment opening. Once again, he was guided by his penis, not his heart. Lance paid the deposit and first month's rent at Players Apartments. Lance, without hesitation, moved into the Players Apartments.

His first step was sticking his divorce certificate to the toilet seat with tape. Once again, every time he took a leak, it was there to remind him,

"Marriage, no way." This was his talisman. The document was a charm to avert evil marriage and instead bring good fortune. Yes, Lucky Lance. In his mind, at this time in his life, Lance was only in it for the sex. Get high, get drunk, get laid, not necessarily in that order. Once again, he was at the right place at the right time. The hottest singles apartments blocks from the strip. Following Maslow's pyramid of needs in Lance's mind, he had reached the top of the pyramid, self-actualization.

# 47
## Players

Lance and Roman now found a new sandbox to play in. Just a mile away stood a big and popular venue, Let's Dance. In the evening, it was filled with locals and tourists. It was a converted warehouse no-frills venue. It had a big dance floor and a powerful sound system. The band played a mix of long single records popular at that time to keep people dancing. It had plenty of parking and a small cover charge to keep out the deadbeats. This venue was hot and attracted college students, young men, and girls. The drinks were reasonable, and it was just a fun club to visit. Lance and Roman went there often. On Friday and Saturday nights, it was crowded. Fortune again shone on Lance. Both of the bouncers were fellow firemen. He and Roman were able to sneak in no matter how crowded. Did he have this town wired or what? As you walked through the front door, a left turn took you to the tables along the dance floor. A right turn took you to the bar and tables on that side of the dance floor. A hall led to the restrooms. A confluence of young attractive people was packed wall to wall. Lance was there often enough to be a regular. The bartender and cocktail waitresses knew his drink, called a suicide. This was a tall glass filled with seven different kinds of rum. Many a young maiden and divorcing hot little darlings found and seduced poor lucky Lance.

Heather came to Vegas to visit Roman for several days. Lance, back at his apartment, heard a knock at his front door. Lance was bewildered. Roman's girlfriend, Heather from Santa Monica, was telling Lance, "Roman locked me out."

*Now what?* thought Lance. *I don't want to piss off my friend, but I can't let Heather remain in a strange town locked out.* "Heather, let's go try one more time," said Lance. Roman was not answering the phone. Lance and Heather walked back to Roman's apartment. He refused to let her in or even answer the door. Suddenly Lance had a new girlfriend. Now when she came to Vegas, it was to see and stay with him. When Lance went to Santa Monica, he stayed with her, even if he was traveling with a girlfriend. Sweet!

Roman's brother was moving in with a new girlfriend in Santa Monica. Roman only had a little two-seat sports car. He rented an open trailer, and Lance borrowed a Ford LTD wagon from the lot. Off to Santa Monica to get Roman's stereo. While loading the trailer, the Clock sisters Tina and Dawn showed up and said, "Vegas, oh, wow, we're coming." Stereo loaded in the trailer, they swung by and got the sisters. They sat on the back seat and lit up a joint. Some good dope. The four of them were laughing, giggling, and tripping. On the freeway in Pasadena, red lights and siren could be seen and heard. California highway patrol pulled them over. The good news, Lance carried his firefighter badge in his wallet. There was a quick inspection of the trailer hookup, then "have a safe trip," and then again on the way to Vegas.

Once they arrived, they unloaded the trailer at Roman's apartment. Dawn and Tina crashed at Lance's. After returning the trailer, Lance and Roman came home and crashed for about three hours. Lance awoke to the smell of pizza. Everyone ate, and the sisters said, "Let's all go to the nude pool." Roman and Lance were ahead of that parade. Lance opened the nude pool door with his key, and the four shed their clothes. Lance had seen Tina on their first meeting and knew her body well. A pleasant surprise, both had shaved their pubic hairs. Standing next to each other, they could have passed for twins; the only noticeable difference: Tina's sister, Dawn, had a birthmark the shape of a butterfly on her left thigh. From behind, they both looked the same. *C'est si bon.*

There was a waterbed lying there, warm from the Vegas sun. King-size, it was perfect for the four of them to play sex games, swapping and just enjoying life as it surely was meant to be.

# 48

# Vernon

Vernon attended college and worked at the car lot part-time. He called Lance aside to tell him a story. Vernon had known Lance for around a year. Vernon had an adjunct professor whose husband could not satisfy her sexually. He got off watching her screw other men. He really loved watching her sucking and fucking a Black man. Vernon had filled that role often. "Lance, I told him I would bring you along tonight to participate. Buddy, I told him you were a player willing, able, and discreet. Are you interested?"

"Step into my office, Vern," said Lance, pulling out two cold cans of Coors, handing one to Vern. They were buds and occasionally went out barhopping. "What are you not telling me? Who is this guy?" Lance asked.

"He is her husband. I met him at the college."

"What is in it for her?"

"She digs it performing sex while he watches."

"Where does this action take place?"

"They rent a room at the Paradise Motel," Vernon added.

"When?"

"Tonight, at seven."

"Why?" Lance asked.

"She is hot and loves sex in all manners. She requested adding you."

"Does her husband ever get into the mix?" inquired Lance.

"No, he just watches Jody get laid. Room 114, see you there tonight."

At seven, Lance knocked at the door. Herbert, her husband, opened the door. His wife, Jody, was stripped down to her bra and panties, standing at the edge of the king-size bed. Here was a well-built woman of thirty, short blond hair.

Vern said, "Herb, do you want me to fuck your wife? If you do, you must take off her bra and panties."

Herb meekly obeyed, removing her bra and sliding her panties to the floor. Vern removed his shirt and pants with his big black cock standing at attention. Lance walked up to her, and Jody grabbed his crotch. Lance was excited as she removed his pants while he slipped out of his shirt. Herbert's wife stood at six feet tall, with large fleshy boobs with giant nipples, a flat stomach, and bouncy ass with long black pubic hair. She sat on the bed taking Lance's huge member into her mouth. Lance told her to spread her legs and started to finger her pussy and ass. Vernon dropped his cock into her hand; she was blowing Lance and jerking off Vern. Now she got to switching her mouth between Lance's and then Vern's hard members. Her husband was sitting on a chair watching. Lance blew his load, and she immediately took Vern's member into her mouth. Now Herbert and Lance were watching his lovely wife finishing giving Vern a blowjob. She was white as a China doll, and that big black dick sliding into her mouth was stimulating. She just laid back now and said, "Please, one of you fuck me."

Vern put a pillow under her ass raising her wet hairy vagina and penetrating her. Now with Vern banging away long hard strokes, she gasped at every drive. Lance now straddled her treasure chest placing his dick between her boobs. She held them together, and Lance did her upper deck. Every long stroke she licked the head of his cock. When Lance came this time, he covered her hair and face with cum. Vern was not far behind as she moaned, shuddered, and came. Her husband brought a warm washcloth and wiped her hair, face, and the cum dripping from her pussy. He hugged her, gave her a big kiss, and poured a glass of wine for all four.

Lance said, "It's getting late. Shall we call it a night?"

"Oh, no," she said, "I need one of you to do me in my ass." Grabbing Lance and Vern, she took their dicks in her mouth again swapping from one to the other. When they were both hard and ready, she had Vern lie on the bed. On her knees, she started giving him head. "Lance, please do my ass. I want all of it, every inch pounded into me."

Lance knew she had as many sex nerves in her ass as her clit and deep-stroking found them all. Lance was deep-fucking Herb's wife in the ass, his balls loudly slapping against her clit. She was moaning louder, hollering, "Guys, fuck me in the ass and face harder till you come."

Vern filled her mouth with cum a little dripping down her chin. Lance blew his load up her ass. Everyone was happy. Lance left and jumped in his Corvette and headed for home.

The night was bright as it always was in Las Vegas, the city of lights. Top down, Lance took a pleasant ride along the strip, a mega-million plastic facade, with the constant changes, blowing up casinos and building a bigger, more pretentious one like a Potemkin village. Tourists just getting out of shows, all dressed up looking like a Hollywood movie set or a cheesy Elvis movie. The air smelled of losers. Gamblers from all over the world were looking for that one big lucky score. There was always a crowd twenty-four-seven at the Western Union office, people waiting on cash to get more chips or just to get home. Lance went home, showered, and slept.

One day a gambler from New York came by the car lot. He offered a signed title to a brand-new Oldsmobile convertible. The caveat, someone had to take him to the airport and take him and his ticket and make sure he boarded the plane for New York. He knew if he was given the cash, he would have lost it at the tables. Las Vegas, people were drawn to casinos like sailors to the red-light district. Top down in the Olds, Lance drove him to the airport, delivered him, making sure he got on the plane. The trip back to the car lot in the new Olds convertible was superb.

## 49
# Jump the Grenade

Lisa, how did she and Lance get hooked up? He and Roman were out clubbing and met the two of them. One redheaded beauty and one not so attractive. Lance jumped the grenade. What are friends for? Lisa, five feet eight inches, skinny Olive Oil body, boobs like lemons, with not enough ass to sit on a Harley, big oversize owl glasses covering brown eyes; she had the kind of eyes that crazy people have, scary. Her hair was natural-looking, brown hair. Her eyebrows had to be penciled in to see. Her nose was thin and bony, not large but hawklike. Her eyes were so close together Lance wondered how she could see. Blue jeans, probably girl size, rolled up at the cuffs. She wore black tennis shoes. His friend Roman was hitting on her friend, Nancy. She could be a playboy centerfold model. Roman and Nancy left for his apartment. Lance drove Lisa to her place. Lance escorted her into her apartment. Ever the gentleman, he agreed to a glass of wine. Lisa came out dressed in a nightgown with a bottle of body oil. "Lance, please rub my back." Lance was highly skilled at back rubs by this point in life. Lisa put a towel on the couch, dropped her robe, and lay on her stomach completely naked. Lance intuitively warmed the scented oil in his hands. Beginning at the shoulders, he applied the oil in long strokes downward. Now her entire body, backside, was covered with oil. Lance now used long sensual strokes making sure he got everywhere. Using gentle but firm strokes, he followed her body's contours. Teasingly he occasionally blew on or kissed areas as he worked from shoulders to the soles of her feet. Lance played every square inch of her body as a sensual playground. Lisa was now hot and ready. "Lance, please take me from behind." Lance had found a woman who used a backrub as foreplay to get her ready. And ready she was. As Lance slid in from behind, she got up on her knees, and they did a modified doggie style. She loved it; Lance loved it. About once a week she called, and Lance joined her at her apartment for massage and sex. On the last meeting, her request was, "Lance, I am tired tonight. Could we just do the backrub?" Lance warmed up the lotion, gave her a backrub, and she nodded off and fell asleep.

Her girlfriend, Nancy, came out and covered her with a blanket. Now she took Lance by the hand and led the way into her bedroom. She had a large beach towel on her bed and two scented candles burning on each nightstand. She handed Lance the body lotion, removed her clothes, and lay on her stomach. Lance thought, girls talk. A back rub and a pleasant surprise. She rolled over on her back and had Lance go down on her. Wow, a natural redhead, beautiful red pubic hair. A perfect figured beauty. How pretty. She could have been a centerfold that needed no airbrushing or an artist's model ready for his brush and canvas. When she was ready, she told Lance, "Drop your pants and let me see that monster prick I have heard about."

Lance now was hard and hot; this redheaded pussy did that. The minute Lance had his large full length inside her, she tightened up quivering as she experienced her first orgasm. Lance let her relax, pulled out, and they both lay back catching their breath. Lance now sat up and said, "How about a glass of wine?"

"Sounds good," she responded, putting on a nightgown and heading to the kitchen. Back with two glasses of wine, she sat on the bed.

Lance got up and told Nancy, "I am going to enjoy this glass of wine while you are sucking my dick."

"What?"

Lance now put his rock-hard member at her face level, telling her, "You know you want to."

Nancy smiled as she started licking the end of his penis slowly taking more and more into her lovely wet mouth. As he moved back in forth in motion, she took one hand and started to massage his nuts. Now taking her A game, she started to lick Lance's balls and slid her tongue up and down his shaft.

Speeding up, she eyeballed Lance, and he told her, "Don't stop. Go all the way."

She grunted and took him deep. As Lance blew his load, he held her head in place with his hands. She swallowed all his load without gagging or missing a drop. Lance finished his wine while she sipped hers. They laid down hugging and giggling like old lovers. Nancy now again took Lance's member into her mouth and brought him around again. She slid herself over Lance's face, and they began licking, sucking, and bringing each other to the edge one more time. Nancy laid back, spread her legs, and Lance started sliding his hard-on up and down from her clit to her butthole, slowly sliding it in then pulling his member back out, teasing, each time going a little deeper, the sliding it up and down her crack rubbing her clit and butthole before next insertion. Finally, she was screaming, "Lance, just fuck me!" He did, she did, and the both collapsed in total exhaustion. She woke Lance in two hours, had him get dressed and sneak out before Lisa woke up. The next time Lance stopped by the apartment, it was vacant. Not unusual in Vegas; people moved out of homes faster than apartments in other cities. Just one more here today, gone tomorrow.

# *50*
# Heldorado/Cindy

One of the many things Lance had grown to love in Vegas was Helldorado, the annual parade and celebration of Las Vegas's history as a frontier town. While at a Helldorado concert, he met Cindy. They talked, danced, and enjoyed each other's company. They got stoned and had a fun day. Lance was there with Roman, and she was with a boyfriend. Cindy was a typical Vegas divorcee: married when she was twenty, divorced at twenty-three. She was cute, not beautiful. She was dressed in a country outfit with hat, tight jeans, and cowboy boots. She was hot. From behind with the tight jeans, teasingly sexy. Great ass. Still a small town, Lance knew they would cross paths again. Exactamundo.

At the Silver Saddle Club, Cindy, like Lance, was out prowling. They saw each other, and out to their cars and were back at Lance's apartment in minutes. Roman was along. They split a bottle of wine. Cindy then told Roman, "Go home. I am here to fuck Lance, and you're not staying to watch." This night she was wearing tight leather slacks that looked like she was poured into them. Divorced for three years, she had a good job with benefits and pretty much did what she wanted, when she wanted. Roman left and went to his pad. Cindy closed and locked the apartment door. She led Lance by the hand into the bedroom. After some major effort, they got her out of the leather pants. She was wet; her panties were dripping. Lance was happy. Once again, he had met another woman who was ready to have sex any place, any time. At 3:00 a.m., she got dressed and went home to shower and get to work. Lance went back to sleep. Cindy would often call Lance for a nooner. With her work in close proximity, she had an hour for lunch. Time enough for a snack and some great quick sex. The snack was irrelevant. Cindy was so excited about sex Lance thought she must have had electricity running through her nervous system. One night Lance turned off the light to see if she glowed in the dark. Cindy, like Lance, did not discuss past or current lovers. On one rare occasion while she did have Lance on his back while riding his love muscle—this was one of her favorite positions—while climbing the mountain to sexual satisfaction, she blurted out how she had often screwed her ex that way. Cindy became one of Lance's comfort gals. They shared many sexual adventures. If she needed an escort, Lance was there. If her ex-sister-in-law came to town and wanted to get laid, Lance was there. If Lance had out-of-town guests, Cindy was there. They really liked each other with no strings attached.

Lance's new neighbor, Dan, was a regular at titty bars. Lance never saw the attraction of watching stripteases and paying way too much for watered-down whiskey. Working as a bartender at a topless bar in San Diego had jaded Lance to its draw or interest. One night Dan came home about half loaded with two of the dancers from a North Las Vegas club. Dan announced in his slurry drunken voice, "I brought one for you, Lance. Meet Lucy-Mae." A quick howdy and Dan left taking one girl to his apartment. Lance sat down visiting with Lucy, and they got to know a little about each other. Lance offered her a ride home or to sleep on the couch if she preferred. Lucy instead closed and locked the entry door and began her dance routine. A one-man show. Lucy was a professional club dancer and worked the circuit. She was a native Texan and slowly, teasingly, she danced and removed her clothes until down to her cowboy boots.

"Hi, I'm Lucy-Mae from Dallas Texas," she announced during her one-man show routine.

Lance found her strutting around naked quite pleasing. She was a natural blond with wispy but well-trimmed pubic hair. Being a welcoming host, Lance put on some music and began dancing as he slowly and teasingly removed his clothes. Even though Lucy was only twenty, she took Lance's cock in her hand, knelt down, and took a mouthful. This was not her first rodeo; she was good at oral sex. A good-looking total package, Lance now had found a cowgirl who became sexually aroused from the exposure of her genitals to strangers. Enough of a show, Lance raised up and led her, all five foot ten of succulent blond, to the bedroom. Both hands everywhere, Lance's clothes were removed. Lance fell backward onto the bed. Holding both of Lucy's hands, she fell on top of him. Kneeling as she took Lance's huge member in her mouth, Lance turned her around. Now he had access to her lady parts. This sixty-nine was so fine. His talented tongue went to work. That sweet blond pussy tasted like heaven. Grunting and groaning, a mutual orgasm was achieved.

"Lucy, remove your boots and let's cuddle."

They fell asleep in each other's arms. For a very brief period, Lance dated this exotic dancer. This sweet but needy young girl still on occasion reminded him of what he had supposedly learned while being a bartender at a titty bar in San Diego. Lucy-Mae from Dallas, Texas, was—in a word—flaky. Only twenty, she had a three-year-old daughter. Lance agreed to accompany her and her daughter trick-or-treating that Halloween. Parking in a residential neighborhood, they began to knock on doors. Her daughter, Janie, was so cute dressed as an angel. She went up to the first house with Lance and Lucy side by side. She knocked on the door, but her tapping was so light they did not hear her. Lance knocked; they answered and put candy in her little basket. During the walk to the next house, he explained to her she had to knock really hard so the people inside would answer the door. Walking onto the next porch, Janie leaned back and swung mightily. In life, timing is everything. At that exact moment, the door opened from the inside. Janie's fist led her flying into the house. She did a somersault and was lying on the floor faceup, basket of candy spilled and adults she did not know all looking down on her. Only her mother allowed to help her up. She gave Lance the evil eye. In her mind, she felt that he had planned the entire incident and set her up.

Tuesday as usual was a slow day at the car lot. Lance and Bill were both working. An adorable girl-child who looked to be between fourteen and sixteen wandered onto the lot. She looked as if she had just got out of junior high. Not still a girl but not quite a woman. She wore a tight blue jean miniskirt and a white gingham sleeveless blouse. She had shoulder-length blond hair, white tennis shoes, stunning variegated eyes with patches or spots of unusual colors for eyes. Lance could never be sure what color they were. She was short at four feet plus, ninety-five pounds. Her small firm budding breasts without bra stood out pointing forward with pride. Lance opened the front door and said, "How can I help you?"

She smiled. "Hi, I'm Penny."

Lance read her sexual interest immediately being no stranger to the tell.

"I just got here from Utah. I ran away from my boyfriend, and I need a place to stay. Can you help me?"

Lance brought her into the office, sat her down, and gave her a glass of water. "Tell me more," said Lance, as Bill sat and joined in.

"I need a place to stay for a couple of days to get my shit together."

"How old are you, Penny?"

"I am eighteen."

"Can you prove it?" asked Bill.

"No, my boyfriend stole my wallet with all of my money and gambled it away. I do not know anyone in this town."

Bill and Lance offered to contact the authorities and get her help, but she said, "No, please don't do that. I just need a place to sleep for a day or two."

Bill was married and said, "Lance, you're single and have an apartment. Take her home and give her a chance."

Penny, in her little girl voice, said, "Lance, I will make it worth your while." She insisted, "Lance, I want to come home with you if that's okay."

"Bill, can you cover the lot? It's slow."

"Go, Lance, and get her out of here. I will see you tomorrow."

Penny grabbed her purse. "Let's go."

They jumped into Lance's Corvette. Lance burned rubber on the way out and went through the gear's power shifting like he did at the drag races in Henderson. As Penny caught her breath, she said, "Lance, I am so excited I can feel the world spinning, or maybe it's just my heart racing."

For just the enjoyment of it, Lance took the scenic route down the strip. This ride was awesome both day and night. Off the strip he parked in front of his apartment. Lance opened the six-foot-high wooden door that let you into the complex and then the door into his apartment. Penny ran off to the bathroom while Lance sat on the couch.

As Penny was peeing, Lucy-Mae, the dancer, showed up. As she was standing at the sliding glass door, Penny, this nubile young lady-girl, came into the room wearing only her top and panties. "I came over to spend the night with you, Lance. Who is she?"

"Lucy-Mae, meet Penny. She just arrived in Vegas and needed a place to stay for a night or two."

The two of them eyeballed each other, and Lance stepped in between. "Lucy, she is my guest, needs help, and I want you to treat her with respect. Now she and I are going to bed. You can stay and sleep on the couch, leave, or join us." Lance could hear her tires squealing as she left.

Penny took Lance by the hand, led him to the bed dropping her top. She sat on the edge of the bed and told Lance, "I have only had sex one time with my boyfriend last night. I liked it, but not him."

Lance looked down at this tender little nubile girl-woman, and he was as hard as a stainless-steel flagpole.

Penny unzipped his pants, pulled his giant member out, and gasped. "I did not know they came that large. Please don't hurt me."

Lance smiled, pulled off her tiny, little panties, and admired a true blond woman. Her pubic hair was short but so blond it was almost invisible. Lance went down on her, and she quickly loved it. Now Lance had her set up on the edge of the bed and instructed her on how to suck his dick. She was a quick study and was soon overwhelmed with his load of cum squirting down her throat. They both laid back, satiated for the moment sharing each other's body warmth. For occasions like this, Lance kept a tube of KY jelly in the nightstand. He lubricated her while sliding his fingers in and out from the clit to her butthole, two fingers in her tight little pussy and a thumb in her ass. Now Lance snapped his fingers.

"Oh, let's do it," she screamed. "I am ready for that giant penis."

Lance climbed on top and slowly inserted himself. She admirably took it all, and they matched each other stride for stride. Wonderful sexual relief. They fell asleep in each other's arms.

Morning, it always shows up. Lance got a call at the lot asking about Penny. Two of his favorite working girls had decided to adopt her and help her get on her feet. Once they promised Lance they were doing it for humanitarian reasons and not turning her out, he agreed. They picked her up at Lance's apartment. Lance never saw her again. A week later, Lance's hairbrush, a gift from his mother she had borrowed, was returned.

At Let's Dance, one of his usual watering holes, Lance noticed a woman sitting alone. Sandra was in her mid-twenties and rather plain-looking. She still had the attractiveness of youth but kept it hidden. She just was not presenting herself well. Natural brown hair the color of mahogany, shoulder-length, shiny with curls. She was sitting by herself, and Lance started out dancing with her. When the song ended, he joined her at her table and ordered another round. Sandy was another recently divorced woman. Tonight was her first venturing out on her own. Very bashful and not easily forthcoming, she needed a friend, someone to just listen. She dressed very conservatively: a plain brown top and a cotton skirt below knee level. Lance offered her uncritical company. He was empathetic, having been there himself. She had married her college sweetheart, given him three years of her life, yet he was an unfaithful gay narcissist. Lance was always amazed at how such a lovely attractive young woman could have so little self-confidence. She wore little or no makeup. Her marriage had taken a toll on her mental state. She was slowly trying to get things straight in her head. She had come home from work and caught her husband in bed with his boyfriend. Shy and sweet, she could not understand how he could do this to her. She felt they had good sex, yet it was not enough for him. Lance sat and talked with her for hours. Lance had never really gotten over his marriage and divorce even though he never felt he had any choice but to get clear of Delilah. "Sandy, you are beautiful, sexy, smart, and good company. I have enjoyed meeting you, and I am open to talk with you at any time. You need to quit blaming yourself and get on with your life." Lance walked Sandra to her car. Lance handed her his card. "Feel free to call me anytime you would like to talk, no obligation." One of Lance's pluses—empathy.

# 51

## Lucky Jerry

Lucky Jerry, cohort fellow fireman and party bud, had a house on an acre in North Vegas. He had a sensational man cave—wet bar with eight stools, surround sound stereo, TV, a fully stocked wet bar, a swimming pool and spa, and a really cute wife, who, as a stewardess, was seldom home. A fellow partier and good friend, Lance often went by his place. Lance had a bedroom to use there. He needed it for times when he had gotten carried away with drinking and drugs. Sitting, drinking, smoking dope, dancing, partying, and generally having a good time took place. Jerry loved to cook, and good food was shared. Lance often showed up with friends, often one to three girls. On one exceptional evening, a top-down, outdoor temperature of seventy-five degrees and humidity around 40 percent, a person could get high driving around in a Corvette enjoying the wind blowing over them. Life was good so far. Lance brought himself Little Sue, and her girlfriend Robin followed. Robin was eighteen and glowingly beautiful. For some reason, Lance and Robin hit it off. She was seven months pregnant, lonely, and did not get out much. Lance and Jerry dropped some acid. Hallucinogens rapidly reshaped his vision of reality. Increased libido and sexual arousal soon had Lance tripping, and he and Robin were alone in the guest bedroom. They tore each other's clothes off, both with passions out of control. Lance went down on her giving her a new experience. Robin laid back and said, "Fuck me, oh, please fuck me!" Lance was doing everything he could to be good and gentle with her. He laid sideways to enter her due to her swollen condition. "No, Lance, get on top and fuck me. I need it so bad." Lance was glad to oblige, now fully in the moment with the acid running his brain, all senses peaking at overload level. Lance could have heard a mouse fart in a tornado. When she came, she screamed. Lance, meanwhile, while coming, had a vision of the horn of plenty spewing forth fruit and other wild multicolored visions. Lying back in each other's arms, both were happy to have shared this experience. It was Lance's first time to have sex with a pregnant girl. Tripping on acid just accentuated and made it way beyond a normal physical orgasm. Not much was remembered after that. They clung to each other as though they were the only two people in the universe and barely hanging on to touch with reality. Bang, bang, bang on the door.

Jerry said, "My wife is home with my three-year-old daughter." Robin and Lance were creating a large volumes of noise and using several words you won't find in the Bible. Lance and Robin had had just shared wonderfully satisfying sex. Little Sue drove everyone home. Around a year later, Lance ran into Robin and her new husband. She was thrilled to see him and wanted to talk about good old times. Her new husband, not so much.

Lance had no desire or interest in plus-size women. One of his running mates was in a relationship with a girl whose roommate was in that category. Sofia certainly was attractive. Long curly black hair, icy blue-green catlike eyes with dark thick bushy brows. Lance got to wondering about her pubes and, oh yes, playing with her fifty-inch plus-size breasts. One evening the four of them shared a joint. It was the beginning of a wonderful relationship. Once he had tasted the fruits of her body, he wanted more. She was superbly funny, warm, and relaxingly comfortable to be around. One Saturday evening she called Lance. "I'm horny, got some mescaline to share, how soon can you be here?"

Lance took some mescaline at his apartment and took a shower. He was really tripping on the colors. On the drive over, he loved the way the lines in the road moved in beat with the music. Music was a huge part of the trip. When Lance arrived, she was wearing a thin nightgown, and Lance was admiring those lovely large breasts and the loveliest black pubes, her hair pie. The drugs greatly enhanced the feelings and made being alive, touching, tasting, seeing, smelling all more sensitive if not mind-boggling.

Moving to the bedroom, she began messing around. "Lance, tonight I am in charge. I will begin by removing your clothes. Your body is mine tonight, and you will follow my orders."

Lance grinned in stoned anticipation, lying back on the on the bed. She began by massaging his feet and sucking on his toes. At this point, the mescaline was kicking in, and all sensations were hypersensitive and constantly changing. Lance, on the bed naked, grinned as she dropped her negligee to the floor. Sofia licked and kissed Lance from his toes to his lips and everywhere in between, dragging those wonderful boobs along his sensually heightened body. Mescaline made feelings during foreplay mutually incredible. Lance was thinking that if you had never seen a woman of this stature naked, you certainly had missed something. She started at his feet. Slowly licking her way up his leg, the higher she got, the longer, wetter her tongue. Lance was in sensual paradise. Now she was licking his scrotum, one ball and then the other, climbing from there to the base of Lance's rock-hard cock. With senses multiplied by the mescaline, he was delirious with pleasure. At that moment, she owned him. With their heightened state of consciousness, the sex was, for both, almost mythical. During sex, visual distortions began. Lance, at some point, felt as if his body had melted, and Sofia's tongue was flamingly hot. Wonderful experience, Lance was glad she was in charge.

# 52

# Many Wives

One of the bonuses of working at the car lot was exposure to the constant stream of customers from all walks of life. Every interface helped Lance develop his soft or people skills. In sales you learn how people think and work. Even though he was a part-timer, Lance had made many trips to the Los Angeles Dealers Auto Auction. The car lot bought and sold cars at the auction. Sometimes they used a car transport, an eleven-car-capacity truck. At other times, it involved driving cars to LA or bringing a bunch home with tow bars. Often they hired drivers in Vegas to transport the vehicles back from the auction. Lance was usually in charge of the drivers. He made sure they got to where they were supposed to be on time, well-fed, and rested. He was also responsible for the accounting and providing the receipts for expenses and paying the drivers. They were approaching San Bernardino when one of the new drivers, Ralph, began talking about his new wife. Ralph braggingly felt that marrying wife number six, he had finally found the perfect one. He was forty-five, and this was his first driving trip. The three-hundred-plus-mile trip could become boring depending on the company. Ralph was one of those people who went through life with no gravitas; whether a victim of life or poor decisions was unknown. Lance was again, just like in his bartending a girlie bar days, having to manage a group of people with disparate skills. Silence went on as the carload of drivers moved on for about fifteen minutes. At that point, Ralph blurted out, "Gee, I have bought a lot of furniture." Great observation.

A rather successful auction, they brought back seven cars. Good stock for the car lot. Ralph mentioned he had a Chevrolet pickup he would like to sell parked at his house in Kingman, Arizona. Lance rode home with him the next weekend. It took Ralph two six-packs to drive home. Lance nervously rode along as he blew through the desert roads at speeds way above his ability to react, especially considering the number of beers consumed. Ralph introduced Lance to his new, perfect number six wife. While she and Lance were talking, Ralph's dog bit him in the hand. His new bride, the perfect one, was so angry Lance thought she might also bite drunken Ralph. Early on Lance had learned women do not like drunks. Lance was given a pillow and blanket; as usual, he slept peacefully. He awoke to the smell of bacon and eggs. With the keys and title to the Chevy pickup, he drove back to Vegas stopping once for gas and coffee.

Lance sold a Mustang fastback to a buyer who had moved to Vegas from New York. Vinnie paid cash, and Lance never inquired into what he did to survive or get by. He always had a pocket full of hundreds. He was married, had brought his wife from New York. Vinnie brought several car buyers to Lance at the lot. They always paid cash and were not too interested in negotiating a cheap price. A finder's fee was paid to Vinnie of course. One day Vinnie called Lance and asked to borrow the apartment at Players. He had a hot young lady and needed a place to take and romance her. Lance met him at the gate and gave him the key. They were hanging all over each other and panting. She had brown doe-like eyes. Looks? Like one of those sculpted Roman goddesses Lance had seen in Italy. Lance and Vinnie's relationship was based on "do not ask." If you need to know, I will tell you. Their next meeting at the lot Vinnie explained. She had caught her husband cheating, and that was her revenge sex.

Two weeks later Vinnie showed up with Clarice, eighteen years old and wanting to experiment with her sexuality. Vinnie took her into the bedroom and spent two hours playing sex games. When he was spent, he told her to just lie in bed. "Lance, it's your turn," Vinnie said with a smile.

She said, "Something is going to happen," as Lance stripped and joined Clarice in bed. Admiring her eighteen-year-old flawless body, she rapidly became a willing sexual toy for Lance to have his way with her as soon as she saw his large stiff cock. She had spasms of lust like she had been hit with an electric cattle prod. She grabbed Lance by his member, pulled him into bed, and inserted him into her hot, moist pussy. Her hunger, sexual needs were amazingly strong. Lance blew a large load of cum as she wrapped her legs around his back and tightened like a vice. As Lance was regaining himself, she called out, "Hey, Vinnie, come join us." She got on her knees and took Lance's cock into her mouth while the now recovered Vinnie fucked her from behind. "Not enough," she said and had Lance fuck her in her virgin ass. The two of them screwed her, ate her, and she gave everyone head. After about six hours, Lance and Vinnie were all fucked out. Not Clarice. Vinnie found Lance's neighbor at home and invited him to the party. Now it was his turn. After an hour, he went home and got his camera. Now he got pictures of all four sucking and fucking. At four in the morning, Vinnie took the girl by the name of Clarice home; she lived with her parents. Lance showered, changed his sheets, and slept for twelve hours.

A week later his neighbor gave him copies of the pictures. Lance looked at them and then burned them. He figured no good could come from them. He heard Clarice had taken on three or four men one night again. Never confirmed and they never crossed paths again. Lance assumed that Clarice was not her real name. He had known nine girls in Vegas claiming the name Bridgette. This was Vegas, and it was common to make up a name rather than giving up your real identification.

# 53

# **Druggie**

Lance went to a free concert at UNLV (University of Nevada Las Vegas). Lance loved concerts; he often met new people. He was like a bee at the Rose Bowl. Smoked some weed and took a bota bag of red wine. People's eyes were moving. Lance wondered, *Do they also have voices in their heads?* Wandering around enjoying the crowd and the music, good weed enhances that. Bumped into Sheri, the girl from LA who had lived with him for a week at the spa. Sheri was at the concert with her live-in boyfriend, a cabdriver. He went overboard, bugging her, "Sheri, do not get lost in the crowd. Stay with me."

Totally ignoring him, Sheri quickly led Lance by the hand through the concert crowd, dancing around and over people on blankets and towels instantly melding into the crowd. Moving as nimble as a rabbit, she got to the parking lot. Sheri paused and caught her breath. "Lance, I have wanted to talk to you. Please drive me home."

Lance was driving a Pontiac Grand Prix from the car lot. It ran like new, and the air blew ice-cold. As Lance was driving her home, she put her head on his lap, unzipped his jeans, and grabbed hold of Lance who was hard as usual. "Hello again, Mr. Excalibur," she moaned as Lance was apt to call his member after King Arthur's magical sword. Sheri went down on Lance and kept giving him oral sex. He blew his load as they pulled up to her apartment. Sheri, as usual, swallowed the evidence.

Lance walked arm and arm with her through the front door. Just as Lance sat on the couch, Sheri's boyfriend came through the front door. "I am glad you made it home safe," and then gave Sheri a big tongue and spit-swapping kiss. Lance just grinned, as did she while looking over Fred's back. Lance was stoned and perhaps a little drunk. Too much grass, wine, and sunshine. Crashing on the couch, Lance slept for about two hours. Sheri and Fred slipped off to the bedroom.

Lance awoke to seeing Sheri sitting at the breakfast bar wearing a blue robe. She dropped the robe, standing there naked, hollering, "Lance, fuck me, please fuck me. Do me again with that big dick. Penetrate me with Excalibur. You are so large you always find my G-spot."

"What about Fred?" asked Lance.

"He took a sleeping pill and won't wake for eight hours."

Lance, sitting on the couch, grabbed her by the thighs. As she got closer, he moved to her pussy sliding his tongue in. She cried in excitement. She buried her pussy in his face. He slid his hand down her wet pussy and slid his index finger up her ass. Lance was operating on enough of her sex nerves to bring her to orgasm. Now Sheri pushed Lance down on the couch. She straddled him slowly lowering herself on his cock. They were both so wet and well lubricated. As she was pumping, Lance now began playing with her boobs, caressing and tweaking her nipples. She slammed into him, her ass smacking, then she began to quiver as her orgasm took over. Sheri proceeded to have one of the most intense orgasms of her life. Timing perfect, Lance exploded inside her at the same moment.

Lance was telling her, "Be quiet and quit screaming. You will wake Fred."

"Just as wonderful as I remembered. Thank you. You are one of the few men I have met that looks better with his clothes off. A fabulous fuck, you are always ready and hard, and you release gallons of cum for the money shot. Do not tell Fred. I just started a company making porn films. You are tall, good-looking, well-endowed, and always ready to get a blow job, eat pussy, or fuck for hours. You have no problem performing in front of others. I need a male stud to star in my movies. This is what I wanted to discuss with you."

Lance pulled Sheri close and gave her a great big hug. "Sheri, that is one of the nicest handful of compliments I have received. I love having sex, as you know. Anytime, anywhere, with or without witnesses." *His medulla oblongata was attached to his dick. He almost always had a hard-on.* His medulla, an important part of the brain, without thought, it transferred neural messages to the penis. Lance's penis had muscle memory. "The offer is tempting, but I am a professional fireman, and not if but when this gets out, it would ruin my career." Lance remembered how quickly he had burned the pictures of him and Clarice.

The singles apartments had a nearly even split between single men and single women renters. One of the first to draw both Lance and Roman's attention was Kim. She and the woman who lived across the way from her would lie on lounge chairs at the normal pool. Kim was hot and lay there with her bathing suit top undone. She was a big tease and would rise up to say hi just enough to show off her boobs but not expose her nipples. Of course, she was on Lance's "want to spend some quality sexual time with" list. He placed her on his mental list. Just seeing her sent little dopamines running thorough his body high-fiving each other.

Lance seldom went grocery shopping. He either ate out or at the fire station. Hell, there is no shortage of places to eat in Vegas. At one weed-smoking party at his apartment, everyone was too stoned to drive yet had the munchies. The only thing in Lance's fridge was cheese and prunes. Four people too stoned to drive had eaten three boxes of prunes. Everyone spent the next day remaining close to the restroom as the results of consuming all the prunes.

Today Lance headed for the market; he needed shaving cream, toothpaste, and soap. A lady checking out in front of Lance had in her cart two wineglasses, wearing a tight black revealing one-piece body dress, looking good and hot. Wondering who she was sharing her wine with, Lance got a boner. Waiting his turn to check out, he heard someone holler, "Lance, Lance." Around the corner came Sandra. She was wearing white shorts, a crop top tied just below her boobs, and white tennis shoes. He did not recognize her at first; she had bleached her hair blond. She had done a complete makeover: eyelashes, bright red lipstick. And she smelled wonderful. They walked to the parking lot, and Sandra said, "Lance, are you busy?"

"Sandra, I am off for the next two days. What did you have in mind?"

"Lance, I am ready to be a woman again. Are you interested?"

"Sandra, of course. Follow me home."

Lance pulled into his parking slot at Players Apartments. Sandra was right behind and pulled in next to him. She grabbed Lance by the arm as he opened the outer entrance. His apartment was first on the left. Lance opened and closed the door. She drew the privacy curtain closed, pulled Lance up to her. They held each other's hands and kissed. Her hungry tongue moved around his. Now they were glued together, each one ripping clothes off. Her blouse hit the floor, and Lance was tweaking her nipples. Her tits were stunning. Her nips were almost as hard as his cock. Lance pulled her with him while walking backward to the bed. Sitting on the bed, Lance ran his tongue over her nipples one and then the other. Grabbing her by the waist, Lance removed her shorts. Surprise, she was not wearing panties. Lance hopped up, pushed her onto the bed.

Removing his pants, Sandy gasped. "I had no idea you were so big." She took Lance's hard penis into her mouth, slowly licking and sucking on it while moving her head back and forth in a steady rhythm. Lance was so stimulated he stopped her. He took several deep breaths to regain his composure. He did not want to screw up or disappoint this young woman. Sandra now lay back seductively and started rubbing her clit. Lance took over and started licking and sucking on her clit. She now placed both hands on the back of his head pulling him in to her womanhood. Pulling his face away, "Lance, I am so ready. Fuck me." Her wet pussy enveloped his cock. She slowed, her body quivered, and she came. Lance exploded seconds later. "It has never been that good," she gasped. They took a quick shower, and Lance brought two glasses of wine and some cheese. As they shared a bottle of wine, she told him how she was so surprised at how well-endowed he was.

"I know you are excited. Just breathe, Sandra, and slow down. We have all day."

Six hours of sharing mutual sex and both were happy. When Sandy left Players Apartments, she backed into the dumpster. Being empty, the ear-splitting noise of her bumper hitting the dumpster reverberated like a large drum. Lance was sure everyone in Vegas heard it. No physical damage. Now Sandy had a new name—Dumpster Dolly.

# 54
## Cindy's Dad

Cindy, the school executive secretary, wanted to visit her dad in Los Angeles and asked Lance to accompany her. She and Lance were pals. Aside from wonderful sex, Cindy was delightful company. Lance readily agreed provided they spent the next day at the beach in Santa Monica. He called Heather, and she was looking forward to their visit. The used car lot Lance worked at part-time bought and sold many vehicles at the Los Angeles Dealer Auction. Lance could drive the three hundred miles to LA with his eyes closed. He picked up Cindy at 5:00 a.m. on Tuesday. The three-hour drive was fantastic. Stopping for gas and lunch in Barstow onward, they rolled. Cindy loved to tease Lance and slid her miniskirt up and masturbated entertaining the truckers they passed. As she moaned and reached orgasm, it turned Lance on watching out of the corner of his eye while keeping the car on the road. Now she took her wet fingers from her pussy and passed them under Lances nose. He took them in his mouth and licked them clean. Lance's cock was now as hard as a baseball bat and dripping pre-cum. Cindy wasted no time unzipping Lance's member, setting it free. Good thing the car had a tilt wheel giving Cindy all the room she needed to suck Lance off. He gently held his right hand on her head bobbing up and down sucking and licking. Even though the air in the car was on max, tiny beads of sweat broke out on Lance's face. He loved the way Cindy gave him head, holding and stroking his cock with one hand and massaging his nuts with the other. These two had history. They shared sexual needs and wants. It was great having numerous women friends like Cindy. Often she would call Lance for a nooner as her office was close by. Quick sex and a sandwich addressing two appetites. Lance was feeling relieved and stress-free. Getting a good blowjob will do that.

Rolling through down town LA, they found her dad's hotel. He was dressed and ready, and Lance took the three of them to lunch. Her father was, in Lance's eyes, old. Worn-out casual shirt faded red, blue jeans that had lost most of their color. As he stood to welcome them, Cindy jumped into his arms, and a long "I love you" ensued. When they let go of each other, she said, "Papa, this is Lance, a good friend of mine."

Lance reached out and took his hand. He was surprised by the strength of his grip.

"My name is Anthony, but my friends call me Tony." Nice guy for an old alcoholic. He lived in a cheap hotel leaving enough retirement money to keep him in food and booze.

They all enjoyed a cheeseburger and fries at a local walk-in restaurant. Cindy and her dad were really lovingly close. Lance was proud to share this family moment with them. After dinner and a night of sipping cheap wine, Cindy and her dad were reminiscing. Before long, her Papa was falling asleep in his chair. He was so kind; he had rented a room a floor above for Cindy and Lance. Cindy tucked him in and took the key, and Lance to the elevator. The hotel was clean and well maintained. Nothing brash and gaudy like the Vegas hotels. Due to the building's age, it showed signs of wear. Lance was sure the carpet and paint were older than him. Lance noted the different areas of escape, a habit his firefighting had taught him. After all, the place had old people who were heavy drinkers and smokers. Lance had been dispatched to fight many a fire started by a passed-out smoker. There was a slight but not obnoxious odor that permeated the hallways. The red patterned carpet was traffic-worn and fading. Cindy turned the key, opened the door. Lance flicked on the light. The room after an evening of drinking wine was welcome relief. A quick shower and they cuddled and went to sleep nude.

Lance was having a sensational dream. He opened his eyes and found Cindy with her lips wrapped around his cock. There was no better dream than you getting a blow job, waking up, and it was happening. Turnabout was fair play, and Lance had her kneel as he slid underneath and had pussy for breakfast. Mutual satisfaction, they dressed and packed. Lance took the luggage to the car. Cindy rounded up her dad, and they went to the same restaurant for breakfast: bacon, eggs, toast, and lots of hot black coffee. Cindy hugged her dad with a tearful goodbye. All were saying their goodbyes. This was the last time Cindy saw her dad alive. It was 9:00 a.m. and on the road again, taking the short drive to Santa Monica. Lance had called Heather; she was waiting. The morning clouds had not burned off. Lance thought they looked like fast-moving cotton balls, more like an artist's version on canvass than the real thing.

Good girl Heather, she had gotten up early and had breakfast ready when Lance and Cindy arrived. Cindy and Lance were still hungry. The three ate breakfast: French toast, coffee, and orange juice. Heather was off to work. "I have a date after work, so I will be home late," she shouted as she waltzed out the door. Lance could only think of the Beach Boys song "California Girls." She was all of that. Tall, natural blond, lived on the beach in Santa Monica, tanned head to toe, deep baby blue eyes and large perky breasts, hourglass figure, thin waste, and perfect ass and the legs of a goddess. She was an overwhelming beauty. She and Lance had a paradoxical relationship. He would visit her for two to three days. At first wonderful, and by the end of the three days, not so much. She came to Vegas to visit, and two to three days, time to go home. They had a strong sexual attraction to each other. She was so sweet to all, and Lance appreciated that. Lance washed, and Cindy dried the dishes. Knowing they had the entire day, Cindy said, "What now?"

"Sex and shower, or shower and sex?" responded Lance.

Cindy was already naked and ready. After the wonderful relief of shower sex, they dressed and walked the beach and pier. The two of them had a lot of fun beginning where Route 66 ended, at the landmark Santa Monica Pier. Its neon gateway sign was one of Southern California's most recognizable icons. Walking out on the pier put them out over the surf. Spectacular views up and down the coast. Next a fun ride on the carousel. Lance loved the carousel, which was built in 1922 with forty-four hand-carved horses, and the calliopes musical accompaniment. The smell of the ocean at the end of Route 66 was always enjoyable. A walk to Muscle Beach, dodging the roller skaters, street performers. Sex, sun, sand, and perfect California weather. After a wonderful day at the beach, Lance and Cindy bought a pizza and a couple of bottles of Merlot. They sat on the couch, ate until full, and drank enough wine to get silly. Cuddling up like lovers do, Cindy was worn-out and fell asleep. Lance was mentally reminiscing about what a wonderful day at the beach and a memorable trip this was.

The front door clicked, and in walked Heather. She quietly got a blanket from the hall closet and covered Cindy. "Lance, pour us a glass of that wine. I need to talk to you."

Washing two glasses and topping them off, Lance turned around to see Heather. Wearing a blue nightgown and matching panties, she approached with her melt-any-man smile. Lance asked, "Heather, how was your date?"

With her sugary, half-whispering voice, she told Lance, "I won't go into details, but we had sex. Lance, I knew you were here, and I am glad Cindy is asleep." Heather, with her adorable come-to-me wrinkle in her nose, now dragged Lance into her bedroom. Off came her robe and panties. "Oh, Lance, you know how much I need you."

Lance, without hesitation, went down on her luscious blond pussy working her until she came. Now Lance mounted her driving hard. They were well tuned to bring each other to peak performance, and they did. Lance kissed Heather good night and quietly crawled onto the couch with Cindy.

Morning came early for Lance and Cindy. Suitcase in the car, they said goodbye to Heather and hit the road for the three-hour trip back to Vegas.

# 55

# Sunrise Mountain Bar

At the base of Sunrise Mountain stood a bar, one of three in that part of town just outside city limits. The owners were a great couple, Mark and Pat. She cooked, and he tended bar. They were living the dream owning a successful bar and restaurant in Las Vegas. Lance was a regular and knew the crowd that frequented the place well. A perfect dichotomy. Lance was as comfortable in a *honky-tonk* bar that played country music as in a rock and roll venue easily using his chameleonlike qualities to adapt. An assortment of working-class people and a confluence of the population in Vegas visited these three joints. Close to the Air Force base and the strip, it was frequented by the people that make Vegas work, carpenters, plumbers, dealers, showgirls, schoolteachers, fireman, electricians, pit bosses, etcetera. Having lived close by before moving out to the strip area, Lance was part of the social fabric here. His romantic prowess had led to numerous liaisons at these locations. Yes, happy hunting grounds.

Donna, the owner's oldest daughter, would spell her dad at Sunrise Mountain Bar as a bartender. She was good and knew many of the same crowd of people. She had introduced him to Ralph, her brother, when he was home from college. Her younger sister, Kathy, was a rebel and rarely discussed by the family, and if she was, usually in not so pleasant of terms. One night Lance was out drinking and carousing at another neighborhood bar, the Nellis Pub. Here he found Donna being harassed by a half-drunk guy hitting on her and generally pestering her and insisting she dance with him. Lance, all six foot three of him, walked up to Donna and said, "Honey, it's time to go home." They left the bar, together arms draped around each other. Donna gave him a big hug, climbed into her car, and went home.

The next day rumors were flying that Lance and Donna were dating. They both decided to play it up for several days and had great fun with it, especially with teasing her parents. Donna and Lance were more like brother and sister, so much alike. They were friends and chose to keep this as a platonic relationship. This silly rumored relationship blew over. Imagine Lance's surprise when he got a phone call from Donna with a request. Her wild and crazy rebel sister had left her boyfriend in California and desperately needed a place to stay and hide out from him. She of course included hiding from her parents. "Lance, would you please help her out?" pleaded Donna. Being a friend was a two-way street, so Lance of course said yes. Wow, Donna dropped off her younger sister at Lance's apartment. Conveniently Lance had two lives: one near his apartment just off the strip with casinos, clubs, and rock and roll venues; the other life at local honky-tonk bars, a short drive-in mile but a different culture away. Donna told Lance, "No one must know she is back in town, especially my parents."

Of course, Lance was a little bit leery. Having a houseguest cramped his style. Lance, the big softie, however, easily coalesced. Donna stood five foot two, was blond and good-looking. Attractive, yes, but *Comme ci, comme ça*. When Kathy showed up, Lance was truly taken aback. *Could she have been adopted?* he wondered. He certainly was puzzled how the two could be sisters. She was tall with a vivacious body, six feet, with stunning curly bright red hair. She had the build and attractiveness of a Vegas showgirl. She started out apologizing about her intrusion. Lance welcomed her with simple kindness. Once again Lance, ever the gentleman, told her she could sleep in the bed, and he would take the couch during her visit.

Kathy just smiled, dragged her suitcase into the bedroom, stating, "Lance, I need a shower. Will you join me and wash my back?"

Ever since corn silk, Lance could not say no to a redhead. This naked redhead had Lance momentarily paralyzed by her beauty.

"Lance, if you are as good a fuck with that great big penis as I hope, I will sleep in the bed with you."

Once again Lance's reputation had preceded him. In a rare moment for Lance, he needed to find his voice as she stood there, bright red curly hair, her face was aflame with desire. She was so excited he could almost feel the universe expanding. Lance told himself, *Breathe, Lance, breathe.* For five weeks he had this magnificent houseguest. Then seemingly at the speed of light, she was gone. Back to Hollywood and its party life. Lance began wondering again. Sex, drugs, and rock and roll—Lance was getting all he wanted, perhaps more than he needed. Some days, however, he was tired of being the boy toy.

## 56
# Rachel's Handcuffs

A friend of Lance and his attorneys buddy, Cliff, a major player in the entertainment industry, had a son named Ronald. One day Ronald's wife came by the car lot and asked Lance to drive her car; it was making funny noises. She drove Lance's Corvette, and he followed Rachel to her house. "Lance, Ronnie is out of town for the week. I know my car is okay. It's my sex life that is lacking. You come highly recommended by a friend as the right person to 'satisfy my urges.'" Rachel flipped the garage door opener; Lance pulled her car in as the door rumbled closed. "Lance, I don't want to share this with the neighbors."

Lance of course was wondering why the neighbors would not notice her driving his bright red Corvette. Taking Lance by the hand, she led him straight to a bedroom. Intrigued was Lance with her amber wolflike eyes. The room was painted black, with mirrors on the ceiling, scented candles burning on each nightstand. The smell of strawberry, one of Lance's favorite essences, was permeating the air. A small go-go reflector globe spinning with little one-inch mirrors flashed as a strobe light hit it. As Lance followed Rachel in, she latched the door behind her. There were leather straps, sexual lubricant, and a leather whip in plain view in the room. Inexplicably she was suddenly naked. Hot, for a thirty-eight-year-old woman. She had a pixie hairdo as black as Batman's cape with matching bearded mound of Venus. First naked impression, Lance was pleased, some deep primal need. His eyes looked her over imagining licking every inch of her six-foot body.

Her velvet voice said, "Lance, get naked. We are going to have some unconventional sex." She was coming on to Lance like a horny teenager. This dark and quiet room was cave-like without the bats. Many times, Lance had dealt with teenage women with raging hormones. This thirty-eight-year-old was surprisingly sexually aggressive. Some super drive combined with years of experience. She knew what she wanted and had set up the room, stocking it with the appropriate toys. "Don't be nervous, Lance."

He thought about a shark. First you see the fin and then the wide-open jaw full of teeth as it closes in on you. She had the kind of eyes that were mesmerizing while stealing your soul.

"Relax, Lance, this room is soundproof," Rachel announced. "No matter how loud the scream, it won't be heard. I will teach you to perform what I need." She sauntered up to Lance, started by licking his right hand, placed it on her clit, and started a grinding motion. Dropping his pants, Rachel took hold of Lance's hard-on, with her hand stroking it smoothly with delicate strokes. Now both dripping with pre-cum, Rachel dragged Lance to the bed by his huge cock. Smiling she sat on the edge of the bed on the black satin sheets. "Lance, you really are amazingly gifted," she moaned. She then slipped it into her ready and talented mouth sucking, kissing, "uhm-mmm" moaning, and stroking teasingly then stopping.

This was when he noticed the handcuffs attached to the headboard. This woman is not packing a full seabag, thought Lance. Some kind of alarm went off in Lance's head. He did not want to open a Pandora's box he could not close. "Rachel, I apologize, but I can't do this." Believing this could not end well, Lance quickly pulled up his pants, slipped in his man parts, zipped up, and headed out the door. Quickly firing up his Vette, he backed out of the garage into the street. Heading down the road, he quickly covered his face with his hands as he saw Rachel's husband, Conner, pulling in to the driveway Lance had just left. Way too close to be caught playing with another man's wife. Just three days before, a fellow firefighter had been shot dead in bed while fooling around with another fireman's wife. Being a boy toy on call for frustrated housewives certainly was not without risk.

# 57
# Metamorphosis

Lance had spent his life surrounded by attractive people like himself. With the exception of the accident's temporary bruising when he died, he belonged in that group. Age wears the mountains, deepens canyons, melts icebergs, shifts tectonic plates, volcanoes erupt, and continents move. His generation had coined the phrase "Don't trust anyone over thirty." Lance knew his biological clock was pulling the strings outside of his control. Lance was now in his twenty-eighth year and was acutely aware his time would arrive when he was no longer attractive to girls. He stopped by a convenience market to get a beer. A girl, probably sixteen, came up to him and said, "Mister, you left the lights on in your car."

Lance curiously queried, "How do you know it is my car?"

Her response, "You are the only one here that looks old enough to have a new car."

Obviously, this aging process was already happening. At this point in life, he was now running with married, divorced, established, and postgraduate students. He had led a life of serendipitous sex. Here he was living in the perfect singles apartments including a nude pool two blocks from the Las Vegas Strip. A great career making good money in a respected profession. Perfect job for a single man in Vegas having twenty days a month off. He worked ten full twenty-four-hours-a-day shifts, but it was needed time to recuperate. Known as a player, he was getting sex, drugs, and rock and roll in humungous amounts. His hobby, *adultery.* He had successfully aligned the pieces of the puzzle for the good life as he saw it. Lance noticed how the little fluffy parachutes of nature, the dandelion went flying wherever the wind carried them. His sperm enjoyed the same proliferation. Lance had slowly evolved from a bright but rowdy child morphing into an adult playboy. The best thing about being attractive with a large penis was that he did not have insecurity. A time and a season with testosterone level peaking. Lance, at the age of twenty-eight, was aware of sooner or later becoming an adult. Old, fat with thin gray hair? Lance thought, like Icarus, *he had dared getting too close to the sun, especially living in Las Vegas.* No one in his family got bald. At this time in his life, he had run out of virgins, or more likely virgins did not seek him. There was no shortage of women looking for sex and finding it with Lance. Many a day there were two or more when he had sexual liaisons with ladies having strong needs. *La vie est belle.* Life really was good. And yet there was the dream.

Lance awoke in his room at Lucky Jerry's house after an afternoon and evening of sex, drugs, and rock and roll music. The memory of the night before was a little hazy. Lance remembered partying and three girls stopping by. Between alcohol, drugs, and loud music, all had danced and screwed until exhausted. Lance awoke alone and wondering if perhaps he had been put on earth for some other purpose. He suddenly was not happy about letting his mind and actions being controlled by drugs, drinks, and his penis. Somehow, he needed to regain control of his life.

# 58

# **A Good Run**

Lance was born into the lucky top 25 percent of the appearance lottery. He was not movie star perfect but close enough. Think Clint Eastwood–Brad Pitt combo. A lifetime of lifting weights and working out, when Lance walked into a room, all the young girls' heads turned. Is it possible to achieve success and happiness just by looking good? Lance did not know for sure, but he maximized the hand he was dealt, hoping when it was his final time to die, death would come during an orgasm. Why not go in the moment of maximum pleasure? Lance did not expect to be a millionaire by thirty—hell, he did not expect to live until thirty.

At this juncture in life, Lance believed in his mind he had the world where he wanted it. An exciting and rewarding career in Las Vegas or sin city. Twenty-four hours a day, seven days a week action year-round. His version of homeostasis. Minor adjustments occasionally to keep the party train on the rails. He was as adept at picking up women as a UPS driver is at handling a dolly full of packages. Great singles apartment, a seemingly unending supply of female sexual partners. No one owned him; he was happily divorced. His reminder of course not a silly little note on the fridge, but again his laminated copy of his divorce taped to the toilet seat. Every time he peed, this reminder was right there in plain sight. Any female guest observed this statement, a warning if you would. An abundant supply of booze, drugs, and women. Handsome with a big dick that kept them coming back and referring their friends. Yes, girls talk, some married, some divorced, some hookers, and some just coming to grips with their sexuality. A fun and challenging part-time job selling new, used, and abused cars. This was an entertaining and mentally challenging second job, an open window to the Las Vegas population. Sex, drugs, and rock and roll. Lance was proud of the fact he had risen from recruit to private and finally to five-star general in the sexual revolution. The best thing was his having a large penis that they kept them coming back. At this point in life, Lance felt like he was an internal combustion engine moving through constantly controlled small explosions. "Lance is now full-grown. I like him." What could go wrong?

The phone rang. It was Sandy (Dumpster Dolly) calling. She was ready for another round of sex with Lance. He showered, shaved, and took a hit of mescaline. If you have never had sex while on hallucinogenic drugs, you have not lived. At least that was how Lance and millions of others saw life at that time. Sex on mescaline was infinitely better, more memorable and enjoyable. Lance thus was quite happily stoned when he arrived at the Let's Dance club. Sandra, his dumpster dolly, was meeting him there for drinking, dancing, and then home to his Players apartment for sexual intercourse. Sex du jour. Ah, life in the fast lane.

## 59

# The Shelly Mensa Surprise

Lance was standing on the left side of the dance floor, holding his suicide drink, and looking over the sea of people. Concentrating as best as he could with the effects of the meth toying with his brain, he was hoping to find Sandy amongst the crowd. An alluringly hot young redhead mistakenly thought Lance was unable to get through the crowd. Yeah, right. First, she smiled, opened her eyes wide to gaze at him, tilted her head, and said, "Follow me." She set off all his alarms, some he was completely unaware of that had remained dormant for years. Forget Dumpster Dolly. Lance loved the way she walked and swayed through the crowd. She had an interesting aura about her. There was something magical and beguiling about the way she moved, taking control. She giggled nervously as Lance followed her to her table. Her big brown eyes became the size of hockey pucks when Lance, returning the smile, uninvited, sat down at her table. By pure serendipitous chance, Lance had stumbled upon a twenty-two-year-old college student. She was shy yet Mensa-level brilliant. All at once she, the quiet, meek individual, had taken charge. "Follow me," and Lance, the confident, take-charge guy, just followed her like a little puppy dog. Role reversal? Beautiful but wonderfully naïve, she made conversation easy. Lance felt warm and secure just sitting and talking with Shelly. It was like they had known each other in a different life. These two total opposites, upon meeting momentarily, switched roles, personalities. Maybe Jung was right about totally opposite personalities shadowing each other by the attraction of looking upon the unlived half of ourselves. Little did Lance know fate had stepped in letting him just stumble upon the missing piece of the puzzle. Lance got her phone number and left her and her girlfriend. He was pumped up about his new female acquaintance. Lance went home and crashed; sweet dreams were to follow. Was it the mescaline or the girl?

# 60
# Shelly's Mom

Lance, as soon as it was prudent, called Shelly and arranged for a date. He was as excited as a teenager on his first date. Lance went by the car lot and picked up a loaner vehicle, a cherry Cadillac hearse. This was fun to drive, had ice-cold air, and always drew reactions. In Vegas, if the air doesn't work, the car is no good. Lance still was operating on living day to day by taking life as it presents itself. Lance had not shifted his thinking at this moment. Little did he know or was aware of catastrophic changes coming his way.

As Shelly was to learn, Lance being in the car business would often show up in different types of vehicles. Perhaps a hearse was not the best choice for a first date. Here these two independent souls that collided on that night strictly by chance were going on their first date. Both were smart and independent. Shelly was an only child; he had been on his own for many years. She was a college student working on her dream; he was living his. This evening was to be Lance's first meeting of Shelly's mother. Little did he know how protective she was of her only daughter. She began almost immediately attempting to give Lance a third degree. She immediately set off his bullshit meter. She came across so tough mosquitoes couldn't bite her. How was it possible that her sweet, innocent young college student daughter got hooked up with a divorced player? Lance and Shelly's mom certainly did not start off as instant buddies.

Lance, by this period in his life, was a successful adult. He had read Machiavelli. Lance had dealt with naval officers, Fire Department chain of command, a hand full of attorneys, bankers, credit agencies, an ex-wife, numerous bosses, and hundreds of customers both buying, selling, and having their cars repossessed. Five years carrying a firefighter's badge and dealing with the public in emergency situations. On one occasion he had a security guard, whose car was repossessed, pulled his gun on Lance demanding the return of his car. After multiple near-death situations, Shelly's mother did not intimidate Lance. Lance handled her mother with professional kindness. This was, comparatively speaking, to Lance, a cakewalk. Little did Lance know his current lifestyle was beginning to fall out of control.

It was spring and a gorgeous Sunday. The owner of the car lot put dealer plates on a six-wheel-drive ammo carrier, and they went tearing around the desert, the lot's owner and his wife and the two top salesman, Lance number one and Willy number two. Willy brought his wife, and Lance brought Shelly. A large cooler was full of iced beer and two bottles of red wine. A fun day, they were able to put the six-wheel-drive ammo carrier in low range and let it run on its own through the desert. They stopped to eat picnic lunch at a remote location. Lance and Shelly took a blanket, shared lunch and some kisses. The two old married couples harassed them. Lance and Shelly overnight became inseparable. If they were not at school or work, they were together clubbing, visiting friends, or just hanging together. One day at the apartment—yes, she was now living with Lance over her mother's loud and strenuous objections—Lance cooked lunch: steak and potatoes au gratin. Lance invited his sister, Stephanie, and her husband, Norman. Having a French mother, both Lance and Stephanie learned to cook and enjoy the proper wine with a meal. Now Shelly was surprised by Lance's cooking skills. Lance loved Shelly, but her culinary skills were lacking. Stephanie's husband was an accountant at the casino, and he dressed professionally bland like a mortician.

After dinner and copious amounts of wine, Sister Steph said, "You two are perfect for each other. Why don't you get married?"

Was it the wine, the love bug, or Stephanie's persuasive voice? She and her husband drove Lance and Shelly to the Clark County Courthouse. Clark County, Nevada, was home to Las Vegas and called the marriage capital of the world. Even though they were third in line, they both signed the license and got married. At that time, it was easier to get married in Las Vegas than to hit the hard eight at the dice table.

"I do," they dreamily stated, "to have and to hold from this day forward, for better, for worse, for richer, for poorer, in sickness and in health, to love and to cherish, till death us do part. This is my solemn vow." Now for better or worse? Both of those situations followed of course. Lance was mesmerized by her looks, brilliant personality, and as an awesome sexual partner. Her first move after marriage, when they arrived back at the apartment, Shelly went to the bathroom and removed the divorce certificate from the toilet seat and left the seat down. She was already marking her territory. Lance was thinking of the song "The Times They Are a-Changin'" by Bob Dylan. These newlyweds started out spending most of their time in bed getting to know each other. A pattern began that followed them on into the future. Where she went, Lance went. They became a true couple. Were there days of wine and roses? Yes, and some of them in the beginning were quite thorny. Vegas was a gambling town, and Lance's droogs, knowing Lance well, were betting big money it would not last six months.

The morning after they got married Lance woke up and saw his new wife, Shelly, sleeping next to him. He was overwhelmed with love for her. She arose and called to inform her mother. "Mom, Lance and I got married yesterday."

The new mother-in-law then had a panic attack. Her naive daughter Jill had been swept off her feet by a married man. She could get it annulled. "Just come home, honey, we can fix this." Her mother, Priscilla, then called in her sister Paula from Los Angeles for reinforcements. Her sister Paula arrived. She had a face too round, jutting jaw, birdlike nose large enough to require tacking on a windy day with a serious expression, an affront to happy thoughts. Lance and Shelly met with both. Lance was unimpressed. Shelly was unmoved by their petty concerns and stood by her man and vows.

More first storm clouds. Her mom, aunt, and grandmother incessantly clawed at her. "Girl, you screwed up, but it is not too late to fix it."

Young and confused, Shelly decided to listen to her mother and leave Lance. She called and told him so. Lance calmly told Shelly, "I will pack all of your things. Come and pick them up."

Shelly arrived at Lance's apartment. He had gathered her belongings, boxes of them, and put them in her car. A force much greater than them took hold, and they spent the next two hours in bed, makeup sex. It was good. When they finally opened the privacy curtains to the front sliding glass door, the neighbor across the way had taken all of the boxes of Shelly's stuff out of her car and stacked it in front of Lance's door. This marriage, a rite of passage, was not to be taken lightly. Not by Lance, not by Shelly, and with time and understanding, it glued these two together. As time passed as it invariably does, they realized how much they had in common. They were friends and really liked each other. This friendship, like fine wine, just improved and mellowed over the years. No way for them to see into the future at this time.

# 61
# Transformation

Lance, at the time Shelly arrived, was a lost soul but unaware of it. Years of drinking, drugs, and multiple sex partners, had he spent all these years acting out Darwinian impulses. Ever since he died, he blamed life for his disappointments; perhaps sex, drugs, and rock and roll were really not worthy goals. Lance recognized that by getting married, he had crossed the Rubicon. He certainly remembered his painful past marriage. Fear of the future? Shelly alleviated that. This was a new start in a new direction. Internally, Lance knew this was his second chance at life. Realizing at times his own culpability, he was now making plans for the future, knowing he had one. Perhaps he had been looking at all the wrong goals and only selfish achievements. He was tired of being a boy toy; he wanted to live a better life from this time forward. Lance stood up for her against her mother, and she for him. They became a team, a separate autonomous unit.

# 62
# Career–Ending Crash

Timing is everything. The engine company Lance was assigned to was called out on a two-bell. The fire engine had an Opticom. This changed the traffic light to all red, both directions. When the engine reached the intersection, it had to maneuver around the dual four lanes of traffic. Just as they pulled into the intersection, a lady gunned her car and ran the red light. Her car hit ripping out the diesel engine. It then turned upside down, landing on its roof on one of the three cars in the left-hand turn lane. They had to use the jaws of life tool to extricate her from her car. The crew gently loaded into an ambulance. There were two people hurt, the lady and Lance. Lance was thrown forward and ripped his elbow tendon, a permanent injury, tennis elbow. Tennis, his new wife's favorite sport.

Decision time. Lance had numerous adult decisions to make, looking at the facts:

1) Firefighters and policemen traded spots for the most to die in the line of duty annually.
2) Firemen were allowed to retire ten years early because they did not live as long.
3) Getting to engineer and driving a truck was almost impossible, thus the possibility of promotion was slim to none at all.
4) There were very few old (over thirty firefighters).
5) Lance was a newlywed that had just taken oath, "till death do us part." He should not rush into that.
6) A wedding vow, to be faithful, and he meant it.

Step number one: Lance resigned from the fire department. For the first time in many years, he was open to listening and guidance from another. Shelly was incredibly smart, very observant, combined with great communication skills. She had Lance's attention and ear. The old Lance, the sex, drug, and rock and roll guy, had to die. Delilah was an example of what the wrong woman could do to a man. Shelly was the absolute opposite. She offered Lance nothing but support and backing both in public and private. Shelly had the ability to find the hidden and buried treasures, skills, and dormant talents, many he had kept tucked away for all these years. After all, everyone's life is a lie if someone else is telling the story. Events that took place in Lance's life were not all random and arbitrary. A sudden vortex, very deep and rapid change, took place in Lance. Yes, Lance was twenty-eight years old now; he was finally grown up and no longer addicted to sex. Single friends, both his and hers, faded into the background. Lance's apartment was no longer a gathering place for stray women. If Lance went to the beach in California or to the local convenience market, it was with Shelly. He listened to her and moved from Players Apartments, as he was no longer a player, stopped going to clubs, and took her with him wherever he went. She became his lifetime companion and best friend.

Did they live in a Hollywood happy-ever-after life? Of course not. There were peaks and valleys. They both had to undergo many changes. Now when Lance went to the restroom, he had to make sure the seat was up. Lance did not pee on the seat. Shelly was smart enough to look before she sat. Under Shelly's tutelage, Lance quit drinking and drugs. Lance had finally learned to say no. More often than not ,she was right. If her first impression of someone was avoid them, do not get involved, Lance eventually learned she was intuitively correct and listened. She became his Polaris, his guiding Northern Star. Under her leadership, he bloomed. Shelly finished her first of three degrees. Lance returned to college and graduated magna cum laude. Lance no longer went to bars or clubs or even the grocery store without her. They had two children and took on the role of parents and became stand-up community members. Lance spent the remaining years of his life being thankful for that chance meeting that brought her into his life. He became a faithful, loyal husband and model citizen. This, by no means, diminished the innumerable experiences he had growing up during the sexual revolution. He was thankful to every girl and woman that shared the experience. Now the rules have changed. Now Lance himself had to change.

Seeking peace from family on both sides, they smartly moved out of Las Vegas. Lance's skills in sales and dealing with people allowed him to find immediate employment anywhere. Shelly continued her education. New town, new home, and new college. It was not easy, but Shelly kept on working on Lance until she had him housebroken. He loved her and loved it. Shelly had become not only his wife but mother of his children. Best friend, lover, and confidant, they tackled life and the world together. She, in turn, gave him the most precious gift—her youth.

# About the Author

Garret D. Onderdonk III is still telling stories. Garret's family moved to Las Vegas, Nevada, in the middle of his senior year in high school. Before that year ended, he died. A resuscitated Garret graduated with a diploma in the mail and a new attitude. He enlisted and became a qualified submarine sailor. He saw a large part of the world. After discharge, he went on to bartending. Next a professional firefighter. A couple of friends gave him a wrecker, so Garret opened a wrecking yard. He then parlayed into numerous businesses employing 183 people. He moved on as an entrepreneur opening and selling numerous businesses. Garret married the most perfect woman in the world. Wanting to raise a family and live in a normal town, they sold the business and moved to Austin, Texas. Garret retired from the state of Texas as a project manager. The little voices in his head told him keep writing.

Garret
- graduated magna cum laude from Texas State University;
- earned the title of Distinguished Toastmaster, writing and delivering over one hundred speeches;
- spent five years as a professional firefighter; and
- held a Texas State master's license in air-conditioning and refrigeration.

Garret is a member of
- United States Submarine Veterans,
- Leander Writers Guild, and
- San Gabriel Writers League.